LAP DANCE LUST

LAP DANCE LUST
A COLLECTION OF
EROTICA STORIES

BY
RACHEL KRAMER BUSSEL

Published in the United States by Cleis Press, an imprint of Start Midnight, LLC, 221 River Street, Ninth Floor, Hoboken, New Jersey 07030.

Printed in the United States
Cover design: Jennifer Do
Cover Art: Adobe Stock / LIGHTFIELD STUDIOS
Text design: Frank Wiedemann

First Edition.
10 9 8 7 6 5 4 3 2 1

Trade paper ISBN: 978-1-62778-335-4
E-book ISBN: 978-1-62778-548-8

Contents

INTRODUCTION: PUSHING MY EROTIC BOUNDARIES

It's hard for me to believe it's been twenty-five years since I first started writing erotica. My earliest forays into erotic writing were largely either autobiographical or based deeply on my own fantasies and proclivities. But the more I wrote, the more I wanted to explore other characters, other people, and other sex acts outside of my own lived experience. I wanted to push my own erotic boundaries, to dance on the page with sex that I was curious about, sex that turned me on personally as well as let me live vicariously through my characters. I wanted to give myself permission to be brazen and filthy, to experiment, to feel a range of emotions around sex, and bring them into the erotic realm.

The stories I've collected here are some of my favorites and ones that readers have told me they've found especially moving. I've tried to include a range of types of stories, from the humor of the dishwashing fetishist in "Doing the Dishes" and professional exhibitionist eater in "I'll Have What She's Having" to the playfulness of gay sex competition "Sexathon" to the raw desire in tales like "Belted" and "A Slap in the Face."

Within these pages, you'll enjoy everything from showing off on camera to getting a very sexy lap dance to sex on the job, a trans boxer in the ring, a bittersweet breakup, and a shoplifter's comeuppance (pun intended). There's spanking, public and private bondage, open relationships, fetishes, and feelings. I couldn't include all my dirtiest stories, but I've tried to offer up a sampler platter that covers a little bit of all the aspects of sexuality I've most liked exploring within the erotica genre.

While I'm a very different person than I was twenty-five years ago, in many ways, I'm still the same: curious about sex in all its forms, eager to go to the edge with my characters, and see where being their most wild, unashamed, and daring selves takes them. These characters toy with public sex, sex on the job, and get turned on by everything from dirty talk to dirty dishes to being spanked, slapped, pinched, and beaten. They cry and laugh and smile. They fall in love and lust and are wet and hard and horny.

I hope these stories turn you on and inspire you to explore the kinds of sex you desire—and perhaps pen some smut of your own.

Rachel Kramer Bussel
August 2023

LAP DANCE
LUST

We pull into the shadowy parking lot in some corner of Los Angeles. I look around the deserted area, wondering where exactly we are, only half caring. Most strip clubs in LA are located in tucked-away corners like this one.

I'm a little apprehensive as we walk around to the entrance and part the strings of beads to enter Cheetah's—a strip club, a real live strip club! I've been dreaming of just such a place for years, but have never worked up the courage to actually go, until now.

I'd heard that Cheetah's was "women friendly," and from the crowd I can immediately tell it's true. There are plenty of guys but also a decent number of female customers who look like they're having a good time.

My three friends and I take ringside seats along the surprisingly empty stage and animatedly set about checking out each new dancer. Many of them are what I expected—peroxide blonde, fake boobs, very LA, and very boring. Some have a spark of creativity, and feign a glimmer of interest to tease out one of the dollars we hold in our hands, but many pass right by us or stare back with vacant eyes.

We watch as one girl after the other maneuvers around the stage, shimmying up and then down the shiny silver pole, twisting and writhing in ways I can't imagine my body doing. It feels surreal, this world of glamour and money and lights and ultrafemininity. I look and stare and whisper to my friends.

Though I'm having fun, the place starts to lose its charm when I have to get more change and still no girl has really grabbed my eye. I settle in with a new drink and a fresh stack of bills and hope that I won't be disappointed by the next round of dancers.

When the next girl walks out, I'm transfixed. She's the hottest girl I've ever seen. She's wearing cave-girl attire: a leopard print bandeau top and hot pants—all tan skin, natural curves, and gleaming black hair. She looks shiny, like she's just put on suntan lotion.

She slithers along, making eye contact when she passes us, crawling back across the stage, putting her whole body into the performance. She toys with her shorts, thumbs hooked into the waist, before sliding them down her long legs to reveal black panties. I know that she's the one for me, that I really like her and am not just an indiscriminate ogler, when I realize that I preferred her with her shorts on.

After her performance, I offer her a wad of dollars. "Thanks," she says. "I'm Gabrielle."

"Hi," I say shyly. "I really like your outfit."

"Me too," she giggles, then she smiles before waving her fingers and gliding off the stage.

"Oooooh, you like her. You should get a lap dance."

"Yeah, get a lap dance! Get a lap dance!"

My friends are practically jumping up and down in their excitement, making me blush.

"Maybe."

"No, no, you should get one. She's totally hot."

"I know, I know, but let me think about it, okay?" They're so eager for me to lose my lap dance virginity, I'm afraid they may drag me over to her.

I need to get away for a minute, so I go to the bathroom. To my shock, I find her sitting inside, casually chatting with a friend. "Oh, hi," I stammer. "Is this your dressing room?"

She laughs. "No, but it's almost the same quality."

I smile at her and then go into the stall, nervous at having spoken to her. When I emerge and begin to wash my hands, she admires my purse. I tell her about it and then take out my sparkly lip gloss. She asks to try some, and I hold it out to her, watching as her finger dips into the red goo. We talk a bit more about makeup and then she says, casually, "Did you want to get a lap dance?"

Did I? Of course!

"Yes, I'd like that," I say.

"Great, just give me a few more minutes and I'll come get you."

I practically float out the door and back to my friends. *I'm going to get a lap dance, and I arranged it all by myself! Ha!* I feel like gloating. I wait patiently, trying not to let my excitement show in a big stupid grin.

After a few minutes, she emerges and summons me, leading me to the other side of the stage, against a wall where I've seen other girls pressed up against mostly older men. She seats me on a plastic-covered couch, then takes a chair and places it a few feet in front of me.

"So people can't look up your skirt," she tells me.

I smile to thank her for her kindness; it never would've occurred to me. I give her some larger bills, and we talk for a minute or two before a song she likes comes on.

And then, quite suddenly, it starts. She pushes me so my head is tilted back against the wall, the rest of me pressed against the sticky plastic, my legs slightly spread. She stands between my legs, then leans forward, pressing her entire body along the length of mine. She smells like sweat and lotion and some undefinable sweetness, and I breathe deeply. Even her sweat smells good, like baby powder.

Her soft hair brushes against my face and shoulders; her breasts are pressed up against mine. Then I feel her thigh against my hand; she's climbed up on the couch with me.

This is definitely not what I expected. I've never been to a strip club before, but I thought I knew the deal—I'd seen *Go*, right? You can't touch the dancers or you'll get kicked out.

But what if they're touching you?

What about her hand gliding along mine, the outside of her smooth thigh touching my arm, her slightly damp skin setting mine on fire?

The look she gives me is priceless: as her body moves downward and she's crouched near my stomach, I look down and her hooded eyes are on me, her face a vision of pure lust, her mouth slightly open. I'm sure it's a practiced look, but it feels as real as any look I've ever received, and it enters and warms me.

I think I know what I'm getting into; I've read all the feminist arguments, the sex worker manifestos. This is just a job and I'm a paying customer: one song, one lap, one transaction. But all of that background disappears, likewise my friends, my family, LA, everyone else in the club. It's just me and her, never mind the music; it's that look as she slides between my open legs.

I swallow heavily. I can't move, and I don't want to, ever

again. I just want to sit here and let her brush herself against me again and again as I keep getting wetter. And then her hand reaches up, delicately turning around my necklace, a Jewish star. It's the sweetest gesture, and something only another femme would notice or care about. She gives me a little smile as she does it, and I give her one back.

The song is almost over, and she gives it her all. Her body pushes hard against mine, pressing my chest, stomach, thighs. She's working me so good this huge bouncer walks over and glances at us suspiciously, but she turns around and gives him a look that tells him to move along. I like knowing that whatever she's doing with me is enough out of the norm to warrant the bouncer's attention. I feel ravished in a way I've never felt before; it's pure sexual desire, concentrated into whatever messages her skin and her eyes can send me in the course of a five-minute song.

When the song ends, I give her a generous tip, and she sits with me for a little while. She takes my hand in hers, which is delicate and soft, and I revel in her touch. It's tender and sensitive, and I need this, need to hear her sweet voice tell me about her career as a singer, her friendship with a famous musician, her upcoming trip to New York.

I need to hear whatever it is she wants to tell me, true or not. My head knows certain things; this is a strip club, that was a lap dance, this is her job. But inside, inside, I know something else. I know that we just exchanged something special. It wasn't sex or passion or lust per se; it was more than, and less than, each of those things. It was contact, attention, and adoration. Call me crazy, but I think it went both ways.

After we talk, I go back to my friends, but I feel a bit odd. I know they were watching, but did they see what really happened?

"That was some lap dance."

"Yeah, that was really amazing for your first time."

"She gave you her real name? That's a big stripper no-no."

"I think she liked you."

I nod and respond minimally, still in my own world. For the rest of the trip, whatever I'm doing, wherever I am, part of me is still sitting on that plastic-covered couch, looking down at her, breathing her scent, reveling in her look.

I haven't gone to any more strip clubs since, or gotten any more dances. How could they ever live up to her? I don't know if I want to find out.

SHARING THE PERFECT COCK

My boyfriend, Kyle, has the perfect cock. Really—if there were cock models, the way there are hand and feet models, I bet he'd be making a fortune off his pecker. It's tall and poised and beautiful, sleek and strong, with light-brown hairs curling at the base, as if a proud statue were rising from a vineyard. The first time I saw it I almost wept, but I resisted—and quickly got down on my knees. I've worshipped his dick, literally, since day (or rather, night) one and am just as smitten with the member as the man even ten years down the road. Don't worry, he's equally as enthralled with my pussy, and together we've had countless sexual adventures. But lately, I've come to the conclusion that his package really is too perfect not to share. I mean, what kind of selfish, spoiled brat would I be if I kept such a gorgeous cock all to myself?

Okay, you've got me. I'm the consummate selfish, spoiled brat, and I want to share his dick because I want to watch. I've been going wild picturing another girl's lips wrapped around that luscious fat head, her saliva dripping down his dick as she opens wide and takes him inside while he looks on proudly, brushing her hair from her face. I want to see everything I don't get to see when I'm lying on my stomach, ass in the air, taking a pounding from him as his cock smoothly dives inside me, my G-spot rushing toward him, my hips undulating beneath him, my body his for the taking; everything I don't get to see when his cock's all the way down my throat and I'm in blowjob heaven. Just thinking about his cock makes me horny, but usually I have it buried inside me, somewhere, swelling to fit my entire mouth, cunt, or ass, his hard length leaving me little room to think or look, I must simply feel him grinding against my sensitive flesh until he wrings me dry—or, wet.

I haven't told him yet, but I've been on a mission, a hunt. Every hot girl who passes my way, whether it's the waitress at our local vegetarian joint, with her long, braided pigtails and ripped denim skirt and camouflage shirt that just hints at the curves underneath. Or my boss's slamming secretary who I swear could make a killing as a stripper. She has flaming red hair, perfectly pink lips that she keeps natural or just hinting of gloss, and she wears these business suits that manage to be sexier than a bikini, her tits and ass practically popping out of their pinstripes. She gets away with her wild collection of stockings, in various hues with patterns and designs that could make even this confirmed straight girl lean down and worship my way from her feet on up. One time she even came back from a trip to England with black tights emblazoned with the Fab Four on them. Thankfully, our ad agency is pretty open to experimental dressers. She's never been anything but efficient and friendly, yet sometimes I detect a glimmer of something deeper, a womanly, sensual swirl to her hips; a gleam in her eyes that tells me she'd be perfect splayed across our bed with Kyle's cock spearing her over and over. But I know how badly that could go, so I move on.

In the end, Carrie, the girl who will grant me a front-row seat at my very own private sex show starring my boyfriend's dick and a beautiful babe, finds me. We meet at the gym, where she beckons me over so I can help her lift those last five pounds of a monstrous weight that I'm shocked her tiny body can handle. When she gets up, panting and exerted, instead of sticking out her hand for me to shake, she flexes her bicep, showing me just how strong—and sexy—she really is. Then she grants me a dazzling grin, showing off not just perfect even white teeth, but that the feeling is genuine, lighting up her whole face. I'd follow her anywhere if she'd give me another smile like that, and I know Kyle would too. We spend the rest of our workout time in close proximity, and I grunt extra hard as I push the weights with my legs, in part because my pussy is throbbing from my thinking about her sliding all over my boyfriend, brushing her breasts against his chest, her pussy hovering over his cock or his mouth, teasing him until he begs for mercy.

I know it might sound weird to you, but I don't want a threesome. While fun for other people, they've always seemed to me like too much work without enough reward—exciting, but not nearly as much so as watching this gorgeous woman devour every inch of Kyle. I want to watch him as I've never gotten to see him, his cock standing tall, his body at its most vulnerable as he strains toward her. I don't waste much time before bringing up the topic—unlike the rest of the gym-goers, who huddle around the juice bar for a dark green kale-filled smoothie, we head to a real bar, and over massive margaritas, I start to gush about my sexy man. I even whip out my favorite photo of him wearing just shorts on the beach in Hawaii, his skin tan and gleaming, his erection faintly visible, if you're looking. She licks the salt around the rim of her glass, then brings her tiny tongue back into her mouth and sucks. "He's quite the hunk—you're a lucky girl, Sarah," she says.

"You know, you could be lucky too," I say, taking a big sip from the light-green slush.

"I don't seem to meet guys like that, no matter how hard I try," she replies, her voice slightly wistful as her eyes focus on something far away, or far behind.

"No, I mean . . ." I trail off, putting one hand on her leg, lightly, as the words come to me. "You can share his cock with me." I look away for a minute, my cheeks burning even as I'm determined to share my fantasy with her. "I have this thing where I want to watch him with another girl. He's the hottest guy I've ever been with, and I just feel like his dick is too perfect to keep all to myself. We've been together, and faithful, for ten years. Believe me, he doesn't even know about this naughty little fantasy of mine, though I'm pretty sure he'll agree to it in a snap—especially if you're involved. What's not to like? He'll get to fuck a beautiful girl, you'll get to enjoy what truly is the finest cock I've ever seen, and I'll get . . . well, I'll get to watch." I say *watch* like I'm winning the lottery or diving into an ocean of chocolate, like watching her and him together will be the pinnacle of my life thus far—and I mean it.

She drains her glass, her eyes seeking mine, making sure I'm for real. "But . . . why?" she asks, more confused than disdainful.

"I don't even really know. It's not like it just occurred to me today. I've been having dreams where I'm lying in bed and he's on his back and some beautiful girl is moving all around him, exactly the same way I do. I start telling her how he likes his dick sucked, but then I realize she's got it under control." I pause, searching her face. "I know, most women would die of jealousy if their guy so much as kissed another girl, but I'm freaky like that. You can't have him, but I'd love it if you borrowed him for a night," I finish, not sure what she'll say.

"Can I see it?" she asks finally, after a silence during which I try to look anywhere but at her. The bartender refreshes our glasses, and I fill my mouth with the icy drink before replying.

"His cock? Sure—I'll email you a photo when I get home." I lean in close, pushing her hair back as I let my lips brush lightly against her ear, getting a bit of a shock as I do so. "Your mouth's going to water when you see it, I promise."

Carrie looks like she's trying to figure out what to say as she licks the newly salted rim of her glass. "Girl, I have to tell you, I think you're a little bit crazy. But so am I, and he looks so fine, I feel like I'd be kicking myself if I refused. He really doesn't know a thing about this yet?" she asks, her voice lilting upward.

"Not yet, but he will," I say, slipping her my card as she scrawls her information on a napkin.

We finish our drinks, but every time her tongue pokes out to lick the glass, I can't help picturing it winding its way along his cock. I'm ready to race home, and I do—right after she leaves, right after I sneak off to the bar's bathroom and bring myself to a quick, rousing orgasm as my fingers flick at my wet clit while my other hand muffles my moans.

When I get home, I find Kyle on the couch in front of a football game. I smile and say, "Hey, baby," but when he puts his arms out to welcome me, I instead reach down and grab his cock, sinking to my knees. I pull down the layers of his shorts and boxers to unveil a dick that's already half-hard and getting harder by the minute as I hold it. I lean forward and ever so lightly suck the head into my mouth, then sit back and let my tongue toy with the veins traveling up and down his shaft before pulling back to look up at him. I'm gratified to see his eyes glued on my face.

"To what do I owe this honor?" he asks, his face lined with sexy stubble, his light-brown eyes glinting as he tries not to break out into a grin.

"To a girl—Carrie," I say, then go right back for another lick. He moans as I inch my lips downward, taking half of his length into my mouth, but knowing he's not done growing. "I'm going to show her how to do this," I tell him, breaking my mouth's grip momentarily before plunging back down in one smooth movement, my lips wrapped around my teeth as I feel his cock travel all the way down my throat. I keep his full length inside me for as long as I can, breathing in his manly scent, feeling every bit of him pressing against my lips, my cheeks, surrounded by cock, cock, and more cock. Finally, I slide slowly, reluctantly upward, my cheeks already aching with that glorious effort my blow jobs entail.

"What?" he asks, his voice husky, his eyes slightly cloudy as I stand and then straddle him, his naked cock bouncing back against him, then getting flattened between us as I rub my pussy along his hardness.

"I'm going to give her a little show and tell, and then she's gonna fuck you and suck your cock while I watch. I'm gonna make sure she does it perfectly," I say, then quickly plant my mouth back on his pole, tasting my own heady juices. The whole scenario, from the feel of his hot penis in my mouth to picturing Carrie doing the very same thing, to his strangled moans has me soaking wet. When he pulls me up toward him, turning me around so my hips are hovering over his face, then starts to devour me as I swallow him, I relent, even though normally I prefer to do one thing at a time, fully savoring each sensation. As his tongue parts my lower lips—diving into my swollen, dripping sex—I shudder all over, my hard nipples mashed against his torso, my mouth slackening involuntarily as he pushes deeper inside. His hot tongue swirls in mesmerizing circles as I sink my lips down, down, down, until they meet the base of his cock, the head easing around the bend in my throat. His fingers ply my clit, parting the hood and massaging the hard button beneath as his tongue probes me, his lips and teeth and fingers making me rumble. I ease up on his cock, barely able to breathe, barely wanting to. When he adds a finger inside me alongside his tongue, I'm a goner, my entire lower half tightening and then sparking, my legs clamped around his head as I suck the crown of his dick for all I'm worth, rewarded by the hot spurts of come that erupt from him.

He kisses me between my legs a few more times and then we finally turn around, and I taste myself, this time on his lips. Kyle looks into my eyes, smoothing my hair off my sweaty forehead, his fingers tracing my brows. "I'll give you anything you want, but I have to tell you, I don't think any girl out there can suck my cock the way you do," he finally says.

"Just wait," I tease, my previously sated body already perking up again at the thought of Carrie grinding herself against my man. I move aside, looking up and down at the man I consider my personal male model, my own private piece of eye candy others may sometimes get to borrow as their eyes drink their fill while we walk down the street, but who I get to take home every night. Feeling him against me is still a thrill, a prize, a treasure, but sharing him is going to take things to a whole new level.

I just hope Carrie is as excited as I am. When I call her the next day, she tells me she had a dream about him, about us. "I was lying on my back, my hands above my head, and his dick was coming at me, so big and hard and powerful. I spread my legs at the same time I opened my lips and he entered me in one fast motion. I gripped the headboard, and pulled against it, and then you shackled me to it so I really couldn't move, and while he fucked my face, I watched his cock as it moved in and out. Then I saw you, naked, with your fingers between your legs, and I tried to focus on sucking his dick while memorizing the way you were touching yourself so I could do it later." Her words spill out in one big outpouring, racing ahead of one another, tripping over themselves in her eagerness to share her fantasy with me. The more she talks, the wetter I get, picturing exactly what she's described.

"I guess that means you're in," I tease her, knowing that I'd have a fight on my hands if I tried to refuse her at this point.

After that, everything else moves at warp speed. For the next few days, all I can think about is watching Kyle and Carrie, directing them in my own little play, and the very idea of her naked along with him, in a scene that I'd created but ultimately would only be a bit player in, has the part of my stomach closest to my pussy doing somersaults, dropping as far as it does when I ride a roller coaster. My body literally aches, and the night before we're to meet, when Kyle slides a simple finger inside me, I pitch forward, burying my face in his shoulder as I clutch him, my eyes tight as I squirm. "You're thinking about me with her, aren't you, Sarah? I know you are, and damn it, now I am too. You've made me want to fuck another woman, and even though I'm doing it for you," he says, his voice rough, almost growling, as his finger surrenders to my cunt's entreaties, pushing as far as it can go while the flat of his hand mashes my clit. "I'm gonna enjoy it. I'm gonna shove my tongue so deep inside her cunt that she'll scream." I reach for his cock through the haze, each of us alternating a fantasy web with our dream girl.

But as many scenarios as we've played out the night before, none of them could have prepared us for how hungry Carrie

is for him. Any reservations she may have had have clearly
vanished, because she pounces on my man immediately, as if
they've been the ones conducting the secret affair, negotiating
this night under cover of darkness, not her and me. I'm wearing
a silky sheer black camisole and the tiniest scrap of black lace
panties, which are soaked practically from the moment I put
them on. I've kept them on me, though, letting my scent per-
meate the room, dipping my fingers inside to offer Kyle a taste
of my juices as we wait. Then, all too soon, she's here, looking
even hotter than she did when we met, au naturel in a slinky red
dress that seems molded to her body. We converge in the living
room where she greets me with a full body hug, her hands traveling from my shoulders on down, and then I hear her say, "And
you must be Kyle." Unconsciously, I slip away, letting them get
to know each other. I head to the kitchen to make cocktails,
eavesdropping the whole while.

"Hi Carrie," he says, his voice deep and husky. "I've heard
all about what a naughty girl you are," and that's the last thing I
hear as I fumble with the ice cubes. I pour us all sodas, nixing the
alcohol, and quickly hurry back. I almost drop the glasses when
I see them kissing, his denim-clad leg thrust between her thighs,
pressing upward as she pushes downward. He suckles her lower
lip, tugging it between his teeth. I set the glasses down on coast-
ers, and he looks over and gives me a little smile. "You have good
eyes, my dear, very good eyes," he says, and pulls back enough
so we can both see how swollen his cock is. There's no need
for small talk, awkward or otherwise, and things are moving
along even faster than I'd anticipated. I follow them up the stairs,
watch his hand on her back pushing her up, and I have a feeling he's going to spank her from that slight show of dominance.
When she starts to go right instead of left, his other hand lashes
out, pulling her close, while the hand that was guiding her back

slides easily into her blonde tresses, tugging her head backward to expose her neck. "I'll show you where to go," he says, and she moans in response, giving me a glimpse of hard nipples pressed against the fabric of her dress. I realize she must not be wearing a bra and I feel a gush of moisture fall against my panties.

We reach the bedroom, his hand still tangled in her hair while his other hand immediately goes to his zipper. I step back, giving them a little room to explore but keeping them in my sight. I can see the tendons in her neck straining, her silent swallows as she looks up at him adoringly. She's caught the magic, the fever; that special ability he has to make powerful, sexy women quiver before him, eager to do his bidding. He lets go of her hair so he can push down his pants to reveal his hard, strong cock. He lets the jeans drop to the ground, then sits on the edge of the bed. "Down," he says, pointing, the single word enough to have her instantly on her knees.

This is the moment I've been waiting for, the one I can hardly believe is actually happening. She reaches for his cock with her hand, but he pushes it back and then leans over her, shoving his cock against her cheek as he fixes her wrists behind her back, her hands dangling down just above the end of her spine, right above her ass. "Keep them there. I just want your sweet little mouth," he says, the naughty words making me plunge my fingers into my wet panties for some much-needed relief. I try my best to stay silent, biting my lip as she kisses his cock reverently then licks her way in one long motion from his balls on up to the crown before taking him between her lips. I don't get to see the glory of his cock anymore, but watching her strain to wrap her lips around him more than compensates, maybe because I've been there countless times; maybe because I can hear her heavy breathing in the otherwise silent room, her snorts and gurgles as she swallows him. I peek around and see her rocking slightly, her ass bobbing along with her head, and know she's getting as wet as I always do. I give myself a mental pat on the back for having chosen such a perfect slut as Carrie, as my fingers dive inside my slit. It's hard to tell who'll be offended and who'll be turned on by the chance to bang your boyfriend, you know.

She's got his entire cock shoved down her throat, and her eyes gaze up at him, waiting for his next instruction. She keeps her mouth there, nudging the base, her lower lip flush with his ball sac, until she needs air, and then she slowly rises upward, unveiling his glistening cock for me. I add another finger, and feel my own breath shoot harshly out of my nose, my nostrils surely flared like a horse's, my noises of arousal joining hers.

Carrie starts writhing up and down, faster and faster; and Kyle, who's been trying to maintain a stoic expression, can't help but part his lips, his eyes starting to glaze. She's moaning now, her fingers twitching at their imposed exile from her pussy, when he pulls her up again. "You're a fabulous cocksucker, Carrie. I hope you get lots of practice because clearly you just need cock as often as you can get it," he says, his voice husky, not giving away any sense of just how much he's enjoyed her skills. "I think that made you very wet, didn't it?" he asks. He's not talking to me, and yet it feels like he is. I've orchestrated this little game, but they've run with it. They're not putting on a show for me; I just happen to be their audience, I realize as he sits up on the bed, propping his back against the headboard and lifting her dress off to reveal her smooth, naked backside. He hasn't looked at me once, his eyes fixed on her perfect ass curving across his lap. It doesn't matter though, whether they're trying to show off or not. Watching him do all the things he usually does to me, and seeing her react, has my eyes tearing with arousal, the way they do when I give him a really brilliant blow job. I wouldn't call them tears of joy, exactly; more like tears of overwhelming desire, my body's natural reaction to feeling like I might shatter, exploding in a fiery orgasm right there on the carpet. I dare to step closer and perch on a corner of the bed, so I feel it bounce as he lifts his hand and brings it down with a resounding smack on her ass. Her hands have automatically settled above her head, perfectly subservient, and now I see her bring her arm toward her mouth, so she can muffle her own cries as he does the same thing to her other cheek.

Handprints, large and pink, immediately flower on her pale skin, but he just keeps on going until her ass is totally his, marked by the power of his blows. I note the way her body moves slightly, her legs widening, her ass arching higher to make the most of his smacks. Soon even her arm can't muffle her sounds. He's had his hand pressed against her lower back, keeping her still so she can fully absorb his smacks, but at her cries, he moves to shove four fat fingers into her mouth. She immediately starts suckling them, as if starved, her face rocking against his invading fingers. This is all way too much for me, and I get up and grab my favorite vibrator. I briefly wish it were one of those small, silent ones, but those have never really done the trick for me. This is a dual-action powerhouse, and I lay it in front of me and hump it, sliding it inside me so I'm pretty much sitting on it before I let it start buzzing. As Carrie sucks and gets spanked, I let the toy whir against my clit and tumble inside my pussy, bringing me to a powerful climax in moments. Carrie turns her head and watches me, her eyes glossed over as he keeps on spanking her. Finally, he pauses, and the lack of noise suffuses the air. I'm spent, and I turn the vibe off. He slides his fingers out of her mouth, but when she whimpers, Kyle offers her his thumb, and she sucks it like a child.

He rubs his hand along her hot skin, then looks up at me, beckoning me forward. I inch closer, so I'm sitting on my knees, which are just grazing her hip. He reaches for my hand and lets me feel just how warm he's made her ass. I rest my hand there, gently curving my fingers into her sore flesh, while he dips lower, bringing two fingers into her hole. I stare blatantly, so close up, as they emerge covered in her juices, and I hear her sucking on his thumb, almost gurgling as his fingers torment her pussy. He adds a third finger and she cries out. "I think Carrie's ready for my cock, don't you, Sarah?" he asks me, though it's largely rhetorical—if he wants to fuck her right now, he will, and all three of us know it. When he says this, she buckles against him, and he pushes deeper, twisting his fingers around, making her come while I feel her body tremble below me.

Usually, he likes to be on top, doggie-style being his favorite, so I assume it's as a favor to me that he lies back against the pillows, sinking down so he's flat on the bed, and turns her around so she's on top of him. He pushes her up so she's straddling him, her hips near his, then nods toward me. I scurry to get a condom, then hand it to her, watching as he holds the base of his cock and she rolls the latex sheath along his bulging length. Her face is serious, full of concentration as she unrolls it. I'm back in the corner of the bed, my body heating up again as she completes her mission and climbs on top of him. I watch from behind, see her reddened ass as it rises up and down along his cock. I let my fingers drift to my cunt, but the urgency isn't there anymore. My fingers lazily part my lips, simply feeling the blood gently swirling below as he keeps his hands on her hips and guides her.

They're not too loud, so all I hear is the slapping as their bodies rub together. I'm suddenly wiped out, exhausted in a way only orgasm can make me, and I lie down next to Kyle, my head on an adjacent pillow, as Carrie smiles at me, her perfect breasts bobbing along with the rest of her. When his hands move around to cup her ass, squeezing it firmly and then pulling her cheeks apart, she pitches forward, tumbling on top of him and smothering my boyfriend with her blonde hair. A few strands land on me, tickling until she lifts her head and shakes them behind her. They kiss; a slow, passionate meeting of the lips as they grind together. I shut my eyes for a moment and find the image of them seared into my mind, captured indelibly. I purr without meaning to, open my eyes to find him sitting up, pushing her onto her back, and sliding out. He takes off the condom, tossing it to the ground as he now climbs on top of her. I don't know what he's doing at first until I see her hold her breasts together, and he slides between them. He spits into his hand to lube up his cock, then puts it back into her titty tunnel, and she pushes them tightly together. "Come on my tits," she says, her gaze fixed on his swollen head riding ever closer to her mouth as he thrusts in and out of her. She doesn't have to do much to get him to spurt, and when he does, I watch his hot lava arc over her body, then land all along her chest, leaving her covered in his white mess. He grunts, then jerks the last few droplets out of his dick before getting up to wash off.

Kyle's never much of a talker right after he's come. I'm still absorbing all of what's happened, my mind adrift as Carrie stares back at me lazily. I'm about to ask what she thought when she says, simply, "You were right. It's perfect," then smears his cream all over her.

I guess if there's any lesson to be learned it's that you shouldn't gloat over your prized possessions, be they a mansion in Malibu, a sleek sports car, or your boyfriend's killer cock. The best things in life, the ones that truly matter, aren't meant to be hoarded, they're meant to be shared. I'll probably lease out Kyle's cock again, maybe for our anniversary, but for now, I'm gonna spend some time savoring his perfect cock all by myself.

DOING
THE DISHES

The first time I did it, I did it for love.

The second time I did it, I did it to seduce.

The third time, I was ordered to do it.

And I loved every minute of it.

No, it's not something filthy at all. In fact, it's the opposite of filthy. I'm talking about doing dishes. I know, you're thinking, *how crazy is that?* But please understand. I get off on doing dishes. I cannot pass by a sink filled to the brim, or anything but empty, and just keep going. I'm lured to it by some force that draws my hands under the water, into the depths of suds and spoons and discards. Sometimes I even do it with my eyes closed.

Just as with people, all dishes and sinks are not created equal. While I'm an equal opportunity dishwasher, only certain people's dishes can affect me in that special way.

It all started with Alan. Before him, I was never much of a

housekeeper and the furthest thing from a housewife that you could get. I reveled in my slovenly ways, thinking I was exerting some backward feminist statement by being just as messy as the guys.

But in Alan's apartment, something changed. When I saw that huge pile of dishes soaking in his sink, something stirred inside of me, and I was drawn to them, almost magically, like Alice—only instead of a mushroom, my intoxicant was dishes. They weren't really soaking, most of them; they were piled so high that some spilled over onto the counter and stove. I could tell they'd been there for ages, and I just wanted to get started on them. I stared at them, entranced, ready for my first fix. But when I asked, he told me not to do them. "I couldn't have you do all those dishes, there are three weeks's worth there! Don't go to all that trouble; I'll just put them in the dishwasher."

I didn't bother to point out that if it was that easy, he'd have done it already, or that so many dishes wouldn't even come close to fitting in his dishwasher. I didn't say anything, just nodded, fingers crossed behind my back.

Now, if it were up to me, all the dishwashing companies would go out of business and start making microwaves or something. We could give everyone with a dishwasher a free microwave and be done with it. Who'd want a cold, impersonal machine doing this special, seductive job? Not me. In fact, anyone dissatisfied with the policy could come to me for a very personal dishwashing. And whoever invented the dishwasher should just be banished to some island and forced to eat only with his hands.

So even though Alan asked me to leave them, I ignored him. It wasn't easy, let me tell you, to have to wait two whole days for him to leave the house. I didn't want to seem too eager about him leaving—but when he was finally gone, and I'd made sure I heard him head down the stairs and slam the door, I did a little dance of glee before racing over to the obscenely piled sink.

First, I turned the hot water on, holding my hands under the heated spray. I let it wash over my fingers for a few minutes, getting them used to the heat. I don't use those icky yellow gloves either; they make my hands smell like rubber, and if I were going to do that, I might as well delegate the dishes to an evil dishwasher. No, I like doing my dishes with my naked hands.

I then went to fetch my shoes; I wanted to wear high heels so I could reach everything more easily. Also, something about this job just calls for high heels—especially for someone of my rather short height; it looks much nicer than balancing on the tips of my toes. I felt almost like I was being filmed, and I wanted to look the part. Some of the plates and utensils needed soaking, so I drained the old water, filled the sink up with new, hot water, and poured the liquid green soap into the mix. I lifted one plate, relatively clean, and lightly ran his purple sponge over it.

I smiled when I noticed the days-old coffee in a mug next to the sink; he'd probably been in too much of a hurry to finish it. I ran the tip of my index finger around the edge of the mug, thinking of him sipping the steaming brew with his soft lips, then slamming the mug down on the counter before rushing off to work. I lifted it to my lips and gently licked the rim, wanting to stay connected to him for just a little bit longer. I'd been making progress with the dishes, and only about half a sinkful were left.

In another mug, I found fresh remains of hot chocolate, and smiled indulgently. How adorable. I dipped my index finger into the sweet sludge, then slowly ran it across my tongue. A shiver passed through my cunt at the taste. *Mmm* . . . I took many more dips before plunging the mug underwater, erasing all remaining traces of chocolate.

By the time I reached the bottom, where there were mostly pots, I was really into it. For these, I'd have to work. I opened the cabinet under the sink, looking for a thicker sponge. I found a heavy-duty one, unopened, and ripped the plastic with my teeth. I attacked the first pot with as much vigor as I could. I had the water on full blast and was scrubbing away, so I didn't hear the door open.

All of a sudden, Alan was in the kitchen doorway, a scowl on his face. "What are you doing?" he screamed.

"I know you said not to do them, but I just couldn't help it. Please, please don't be mad. Actually, well, I didn't want to tell you this, but it turns me on. I've been doing your dishes for half an hour and now I'm covered in water and turned on. Don't you want to come over here?"

He stared at me for a good minute, taking in the way my nightie clung to my chest in the many areas where water had splashed onto it. I still held the purple sponge in my hand. He came toward me and pressed my back up against the sink. The sponge fell to the floor, but I didn't care. He lifted me up so I was sitting on the edge of the white counter. "So, this gets you turned on now, does it?" he asked, stroking me through my panties.

"Yes, it does," I said, leaning back with my arms on either side of the sink. I knew I'd be able to get him to see dishes in a whole new way, and I was right.

The next time, dishes helped me get the girl—at least that's what I told myself.

We'd been having a pleasant enough date, but one that looked like it was going to end with a sweet kiss on the lips and an "I'll call you soon." She was going to drive me home, but said she needed to take a shower first. Well, that was a weird sign, but short of asking to join her, I couldn't figure out how to spin that into her bed.

So, while she turned on the blast of the shower spray, I turned on the tap. I rolled up my lacy long sleeves, knowing they'd still get a bit wet. I didn't mind. I let the hot water run, no gloves, feeling its heat course through my body. I plunged my hands in, soaking them as I scrubbed. I thought of all the commercials I'd seen as a child, talking about dishpan hands, the dreaded disease of mothers everywhere. But I liked the way my hands felt after a good scrubbing—all wrinkly and used.

I worked slowly, savoring each dish. I rinsed the bowl we'd used for the salad, removing traces of oil-covered lettuce leaves. I found the knife I recognized as hers and slipped it into my mouth, savoring the tangy metal against my tongue. Finally, I slid it out and washed it properly, wondering how it would feel inside me.

I was nearing the end when she stepped out of the shower, wrapped in a robe, a towel atop her head. I sensed her pause on her way to her room and just watch me, but I didn't turn around. With the next knife I found, I again opened my mouth and slid it in, pushing it back and forth in a fucking motion that she'd have to be completely dense to miss.

She came closer, dropping the towel to the floor. She walked right up behind me and pressed herself against me. She reached for the knife and slid it into her own mouth, then pushed my head forward and trailed it over the back of my neck. I gave a startled jump, and she pressed it in tighter. She led the knife down the ridges of my back, slowly, while I tried to stand perfectly still. When she reached my ass, I couldn't help but move, and I spread my legs a little wider. She was now standing a few inches away, her attention focused on her kitchen knife. She tapped it lightly against my ass and I moaned, and she did it again, harder. I lifted my ass to give her better access, but she was beyond that. The knife was about to enter the place I'd fantasized about earlier. She turned it around, but the heavy end slowly entered my slick pussy. I moaned and tightly gripped the edge of the sink.

She slid a finger in alongside the knife handle and I felt like I would explode. She didn't move the knife too much, just slowly back and forth, but the whole experience pushed me over the edge. My body shook; I had to hold on to the sink harder and press my feet firmly to the floor to keep from collapsing in bliss.

She handed me the knife and steadied me against the counter. "Keep washing, we're not done yet."

I took a deep breath and turned the water back on. I held "our" knife under the hot spray for a moment, ignoring the ecological implications of wasted water in favor of watching it splash off the silver metal. She reached around and fondled my nipples. "Keep washing, remember?" she reminded me, twisting my nipple with her fingers. I kept the water going, moving slowly, determined to take as long as possible. She kept on twisting my nipples, occasionally rubbing my clit while I did my best not to drop the dishes. Sometimes she'd grab a utensil and fuck me with it, making a never-ending cycle of dishes that I was more than happy to play my part in washing, and getting dirty.

I smiled happily. Maybe tomorrow I'd start on mopping the floor.

Within a year, my dishwashing fetish gained me quite a reputation. I was frequently asked over to friends' houses after dinner parties, and they'd covertly imply that they wanted me to do their dishes, or ask me outright.

But this time, I was caught off guard. I'd spent the night at a kinky party shamelessly flirting with Alex, a dyke top who until now had seemed totally aloof and unapproachable. But tonight, while she whipped several other girls into nicely streaked creatures, their marks proudly displayed for any interested bystander to admire, she kept sneaking looks at me; I could feel them from across the room. I couldn't even look at anyone else, just kept crossing and uncrossing my legs, wondering how my ass looked in my black leather mini skirt. I drank so much soda that I started to get jittery, and had to keep going to the bathroom—which meant passing Alex. Finally, near the end of the night, she grabbed me on one of my return trips. "Are you coming home with me tonight or what, you little tease?" I don't know what came over me, but I kissed her, pushing my nervously bitten lips up against hers and rubbing the rest of me against her as well.

"I guess that's a yes. Go wait for me by the door." In a fog, I gathered my things and waited at the appointed spot. We drove silently to her place, her hand on my thigh for most of the trip. If we didn't get there soon, I was going to have to move her hand up a bit higher for some relief. After the longest ten minutes I could remember ever experiencing, we pulled into a driveaway. I didn't take in the scenery, just followed her up some stairs and into a large living room filled with thick white carpeting and a plush leather couch. I went to sit down on the couch, but she grabbed the waistband of my skirt and steered me in another direction, to the kitchen.

What I saw took my breath away. It was like the backup at Alan's—but much, much worse. This woman owned more dishes than I'd ever seen in one place, ever. And they were scattered all over the room, on every possible surface. It was like some surreal art exhibit, with honey and chocolate sauce and spaghetti sticking to each plate, cup, and spoon. It looked like a food fight had erupted amongst the edibles in her refrigerator, each one battling for the title of "able to do the most damage to a single kitchen."

"I've heard about you, Missy, so I had some friends make a little treat for Miss Dishes." She reached her hand under my skirt and pressed her fist against my cunt, the hard edges of her knuckles making me even wetter. "Now I know you're just dying to have me beat the shit out of you; I thought you were going to pass out watching me at the club. But as much as that hot little body of yours deserves it, you're going to have to make this kitchen sparkle before you get any of my treats. Do you understand? Now, I'm going upstairs to rest for a while. Don't bother me unless it's an emergency. When I get back, I want this kitchen perfectly clean, okay?"

I sucked in my breath and nodded; while she'd been talking, she'd been kneading my pussy in a way that brought me close to orgasm—but then she took that fist with her right up the stairs. I stared longingly after her for a minute, before trying to figure out how to tackle this mess.

The first thing to do was strip. I threw my clothes into the only clean corner of the room I could find, and set to work. I brought all the dishes over, close to the sink and stove, placing them in like order.

I started with the silverware, even though conventional wisdom says that with any major project you're supposed to tackle the larger items first. But that's never worked with me. For me, the silverware is foreplay. I can go quickly, stacking the shiny spoons and sharp forks, and listen to them jingle together. I like to build up the anticipation before I get to a really huge pot, one I can linger over and fondle.

But before I got anywhere near the pots, Alex came back. She stared at me from across the room, barking orders, telling me to work faster or to go back and redo a certain plate; how

she could tell the state of its cleanliness from ten feet away I
don't know, but apparently, she could.

As soon as she'd come downstairs, I'd started getting wet
(again), and was nervous that some of my juices might dribble
down my thigh. But her voice brooked no argument, and, truth
be told, that's exactly why I got so wet. She marched over, closer
to me. I noticed her holding a miniature alarm clock—it made
me feel like we were at boot camp. She set it for five minutes.
The sink still held an overabundance of dishes, and the kitchen
itself looked like a war zone. There was seriously no way I could
get it all done.

"Bend over, right here," she instructed, pointing to yet
another pile of dishes. "Since you don't seem to be doing too
well the traditional way, I'm going to have you lick these plates
clean. Go ahead, I want your tongue on that top one there." No
sooner had my tongue reached out than she lifted up my skirt
and started spanking me, first with a light hand and then much
harder. She meant business. My tongue lapped and lapped, wishing it was her pussy, working frantically to get through even one
dish. I did, somehow getting it to look relatively clean—though
who she'd get to eat off a licked-clean plate I didn't know.

"Good girl, now, let's get moving." She placed the clean
plate in its own new pile and presented me with more. Some
had chocolate sauce, but even that was hardening into an unap-
petizing mess. She took pity on me, opening the fridge to take
out some whipped cream, then covering the entire plate with it.

"Knock yourself out."

I plunged my face into the cream, not caring about making a
mess (what difference did that really make in this environment?),
eager for more strokes. This time, I went at it with gusto, and
the more I licked, the harder she spanked me. Then she slipped
her fingers into me, not starting with a delicate single digit but

pushing three fat fingers inside. I could barely keep up with my whipped cream but I knew I had to if I wanted to keep getting fucked. Just as I was about to come, the alarm went off. Had five minutes already passed?

"Okay, darlin', you're off the hook for now." She blew a whistle that had been hidden in her pocket and two sexy women in French maid outfits appeared out of nowhere. (I guess I'm not the only one with a cleaning fetish.) Alex led me upstairs and fucked me for the rest of the night, whispering dirty words about suds and sponges and silverware in my ear the whole time.

SECRET SERVICE

Some people go to culinary school with dreams of becoming the next Michelin-starred chef and reviving American cuisine. Me, I just wanted to make people happy, namely women, and the only thing that rivals food, to my mind, is sex. My plan all along had been to combine them in the form of one-stop shopping. I couldn't exactly blurt this out while attending the Culinary Institute of America, so instead I bided my time, working as a chef in top restaurants in New York, Miami, LA, San Francisco, and Seattle, taking note of everything that was done well and everything I thought could be improved.

I perfected my cooking technique, while also bedding plenty of my fellow chefs as well as servers, busboys, hostesses, and customers. Closing time took on new meaning as I kissed someone whose breath smelled of the food I'd just prepared, and that's when the idea for Secret Service was formed. I was living in Brooklyn by then and my inspiration came from Kokie's, a bar that closed a few years back, but before it did, did a brisk business in, yes, cocaine, in the back (Google Kokie's Place if you don't believe me). You could walk in, order a beer, then casually inquire about doing a bump, get whisked away, and emerge high and happy.

My friends and I had marveled at how such a business had managed to stay afloat at all, its name taunting all comers. Now, you couldn't just walk in and go up to the bartender, wave a rolled-up dollar bill and be given a mirror and some blow. It was more subtle than that, and it was the very subtlety, the sly maneuvering, that gave me my brainstorm: I wanted to open the Kokie's of cunnilingus, a restaurant that would offer a little something extra in the back, geared specifically toward women who wanted a few minutes to spread their legs, lean back, and get licked and sucked by an expert mouth.

The whole thing was kind of an in joke, to some people at least. But to my employees and customers, it was a brilliant merger of supply and demand. It was like the sexual equivalent of fast food; women didn't have to wait around for what they really wanted. Sure, most of them could've found a man to take them home and fuck them, but to take them home and simply focus their tongues on these women's most private parts, focused solely on their pleasure? That was rarer to find, and I knew there were plenty of women who would rather pay for their orgasm, while enjoying a fine meal. And I was right. From our opening night, we were a big hit.

I thought of it like the In-N-Out secret menu; we didn't post a sign or have something on the menu saying, "Sides: French Fries: $5; Cunnilingus: $20." That would simply be tacky. As distinctly modern as my concept was, there was something old-fashioned about how the gossip spread, and watching women emerge from the back room with that flushed sex high lighting up their faces made me glow with a satisfaction money can't buy.

Working at restaurants had given me a taste of what it meant to sell a kind of oral bliss; watch anyone dig into a truly superior meal, whether it's macaroni and cheese or tiramisu or even a plate of perfectly cooked spinach, and you will see a look that rivals orgasm on their face. By catering largely to women, I hoped to give them a space where they could enjoy the food as well as the extras in peace, without a care as to what their man, or any man, might think.

Don't get me wrong, though; word spread even before our official opening to the right kind of guy, the one who wants to see his woman satisfied, who gets hard thinking about his woman in the throes of ecstasy. My phone was ringing off the hook with men making reservations and subtly inquiring how they could comp their lady of the evening a turn backstage. Business was booming and opening night was booked solid two weeks in advance. I had planned an extensive advertising campaign, but found that I didn't even need it. The ones who needed it found me.

I would have loved to install secret cameras and watch what really went down back there, but my ethics wouldn't allow it, and I wanted the men I hired to feel uninhibited as well. How did I choose them? Well, I didn't have any ethical qualms about putting them on the restaurant version of a casting couch. I was too busy putting my business plan into action to really date, and, like many of my customers, wasn't interested in the whole wining and dining drama. I'd have time for that later; I wanted to cut to the chase, and while I have an extensive collection of sex toys, which I make good use of, they simply can't rival the human touch required for proper cunnilingus. I've been given head by dozens of exuberant men, as well as a handful of very talented women, so I think I know what goes into pussy-eating, even though mileage may vary depending on your preferences.

I set up timers so the women would have an idea of the limi-
tations of what they were ordering; if they wanted to continue
their private pleasure outside the restaurant, they were more
than welcome to. My employees were free agents, and many of
them wound up rolling out at closing time right into the beds of
women they'd serviced earlier in the night.

For me, the most important thing, the one element I can't live
without, is that the person putting my pussy where their mouth
is wants to be there, not just for the money or for what comes
afterward, but because that's what makes them horny. It's true
what they say: good eaters are good at going down; picky eaters rarely make good lovers. I trained my associates, making
sure they were comfortable with the job. There'd be plenty of
downtime, since I couldn't exactly ask my customers to make
appointments for when they wanted their happy endings, so my
staff could have to go down on several women in a row. "Could
you handle it?" I'd grill potential pussy eaters during interviews
as I fed them my special calamari or my roast duck. A free meal
or two was part of the interview process. I'd listen closely to
their answers, trying to get at the heart of why they wanted a
job that essentially boiled down to being a tongue for hire.

The men whose demeanors changed as they discussed the
pleasures of giving head were the ones who got a callback. I could
hear something in their voices, a tone that got more hushed,
an unmistakable reverence as they sang the praises of pussy as
intensely as they did the flavor of an imported olive oil. They
were true sensualists, and while their job wouldn't take place in
the kitchen, I wanted them to appreciate both kinds of services
my business would provide. Similarly, my chefs had to know
about the importance of the taste buds to arousal, of the connec-
tion between the two sets of lips. I wanted the joys my customers
experienced, whether the fiery spice of a chili or a mouth sucking

hard on their clit, the thrillingly sweet smoothness of the perfect gelato or a tongue caressing their innermost parts, to match, to complement one another. I'll admit, too, that I found my own sex pulsing with desire as those I interviewed talked. I employed a few women as well, in the kitchen and in back, because I wanted to appeal to as wide a range of customers as possible, and sometimes what a woman needs most is another woman to set her at ease and then shake her world so intensely she sees stars.

I liked the play on words that "Secret Service" conveyed, as well as the hiding in plain sight nature of the name, just like Kokie's before it. I secured my staff, and brought my friends in over the next two months for trial runs. They were more than happy to subject themselves to meal after exquisite meal, not to mention providing feedback on the oral offerings. I quickly realized we'd need to play our music on the louder side to cover up the women's screams of arousal; one room was an actual closet, soundproofed, for the real screamers. What I heard from my friends let me know right away that we had something big on our hands. My phone started ringing off the hook, my inbox exploding with requests for reservations from people who'd heard through the grapevine about what was really on the menu at my restaurant—or rather, off the menu. Except that in this case, I hadn't waited for my customers to request an amorous appetizer; I'd anticipated their needs before they had.

Tara, the publicist I hired, was instructed to not speak openly about anything other than the food, but she perfected the art of the double entendre. Having taken her own personal tour of every head-giver on staff, she knew whereof she spoke when she peppered her press release with words like "satisfaction," "orgasmic," "completely unique," and "female-oriented." Even so, the average reader wouldn't have a clue unless they heard from someone what (and who) was really going down. Opening night, I fluttered around nervously, hoping that advance buzz, curiosity, and general horniness would all work in our favor.

Reporters swarmed the place, and I knew from careful observation that more than one female restaurant critic had made her way to the back while waiting for her meal to be served, tucking into her order with the gusto of the freshly tongue-fucked.

But I was more curious about what the average woman thought; if she was happy, then so was I. I was busy, overseeing the cooks, making sure people were seated quickly, trying to look like I wasn't frantic. I must have failed miserably because Ed, my second in charge, pulled me aside. "Kate, you're making people nervous. You have to stop pacing. Come with me." He tugged me into one of the back rooms that happened to be empty. "You know what you need. This whole place is simply your fantasy writ large. Now keep quiet and sit back and relax."

He shoved me into a chair while I spluttered, my mouth open. "Not now. Later, after everyone leaves. I can't let you do this right now."

"Why not, exactly?" he asked, snaking his hand up my jean skirt and slipping his fingers into my waistband. I was wet against his touch even as I heard what could only be the sounds of a woman in the throes of orgasm from the other side of the wall.

I bit my lower lip, worrying it with my teeth as no good answer came to mind. There was little I could do at that point, anyway, and now that he'd gotten me so riled up, I feared I wouldn't be able to relax if I didn't get off immediately. "Plus, I bet you're dying to know what I can do with my mouth." He was onto me; I'd hired him in part for his impressive resume, but also because he had a goatee, big hands, and tattoos that made me want to tackle him and strip him naked. Now he was about to do the same to me, and I was about to let him.

I shut my eyes as he shoved my skirt up and then took a Swiss

Army knife out of his pocket and sliced right through my wet white panties, balling them up and shoving them in his jeans pocket. The click of the knife echoed in the air, but he kept it in his hand as he held onto my skirt and then placed his mouth against my lips. I'd expected him to dive right in, but he started slow, breathing in my scent, rubbing his lips gently against mine before allowing his tongue to make contact. "Relax," he whispered, making me realize that I hadn't fully done so. I let my arms go slack, my fingers tight against the chair's back, and rested my heels against Ed's shoulder blades as he showed me that he could've just as easily applied for a job on his knees, rather than in the office.

While in the rest of his life he's a blur of energy, as he licked me, he took his time, giving me slow lap after slow lap of his warm tongue. Then he started fluttering it, fast little flicks that made my nostrils flare as I bucked upward against him. He pushed my hips down, and I struggled to get closer. "Next time I do this, I'm going to have to tie you up," he said, and I melted back down, both at the idea that there'd be a next time and the image of me bound with black rope, unable to move.

His tongue pressed inside me, filling my hole as best he could, even as my hard clit silently begged to be touched, sucked, kissed. Slowly, every thought about the future of the restaurant, all the stress of the past few months, which had culminated on this monumental day, disappeared into his mouth, replaced simply by the need to come. That need was one I welcomed, one I treasured, for even though I'd made time for sessions with my vibrator, even sneaking a quiet one into my office for a few minutes of stolen pleasure, it wasn't the same as a man whose mission was to make me climax. Everything about Ed's actions told me he was as into it as I was, that his enjoyment fed directly from mine. He hummed against my sex, not as part of some new age sex tip he'd read, but to express himself, half hum, half "Mmmm," as he coaxed forth more and more of my juices.

He lifted his head at the critical juncture, making me jerk mine upward. "Don't stop," I panted.

"I wouldn't dream of it, Kate," he said, then gave me the lightest kiss, a peck, really, but one that let me taste my own saltiness on my lips. His thick thumb pressed inside me, curving down toward my ass, then swiveling up to press toward my G-spot. Soon the thumb was gone, replaced by other fingers, several of them, while his palm pressed on my lower belly. He curved his fingers just so and I bit my lip even harder, rocking my head up and down since clearly moving my hips wasn't permitted in our silent little power play.

His fingers twisted inside me just as my muscles clamped down, a sensual tug of war that ended when he pressed four fingers into me, stretching my poor cunt, opening me up as he sank down once again to devote his lips to my clit. In concert, his fingers and mouth serviced me, summoned me, scattered my senses all over the room as they delivered their two-pronged attack. My clit met his teeth, a feral greeting befitting my now-frantic state. His teeth held my bud steady as his tongue speared it while his fingers seemed to grow inside me, though I knew that wasn't technically possible. He made me feel so big, my pussy becoming a powerful giant capable of ruling the entire world, even as he narrowed mine to this singular sensation. When my climax finally roared from within me, I felt its power leap out from the mouth of my pussy like dragon's breath, fierce and dangerous, a five-alarm fire that clanged its way from my center outward. He stayed glued to me but gradually stilled, his fingers slackening, his tongue pausing, as he gave us both time to recover.

Eventually he pulled out, licked his fingers, then scooped me up in his arms, arranging me into a standing position and pulling my skirt down. "You've done good, Kate," he whispered in my ear, and I wasn't sure if he meant with coming or the opening. "And just so you know, if you're ever short a man back here, you can count on me."

The rest of the night passed in a blur, at least for me, a happy one as I floated around, helping out as needed, urging women who seemed reluctant to take even just a quick moustache ride in back. "It's on me," I told a few of them, sensing that this was the kind of freebie that would ensure some truly dedicated customers.

The looks they gave me were priceless—before and after. So many versions of the raised eyebrow, the quizzical glance, the knowing grin. Some women were clearly unsure of what they were getting into, but the true New Yorkers, the gutsy types, were willing to boldly go where their friends could only ogle.

The next day, the papers were abuzz about the outstanding service, the off-the-menu specialties, and the attention to detail. The food got high praise and the phone rang off the hook for the next month, ensuring a full house every night. I couldn't get Ed off my mind, and invited him back to my place after work one night to see what he could do in a more relaxed atmosphere. If I'd thought ten minutes with him was heavenly, try three hours. I was literally weak in the knees when he was done. It hadn't been a fluke; he was magically able to get me to relax, then get me to come, or keep me on the edge. His mouth made love to me in the most incredible of ways, without trying to show off or be macho, and certainly without a hint of asking for anything in return. Eventually, though, after I'd begged, he'd showed me the present hiding in his pants. My nostrils flared as I sucked in a deep breath at the sight. It was so tempting, but he told me he'd rather we kept our arrangement focused on me. "But . . . you like it, right? Eating pussy turns you on? This isn't just some job for you, is it?" I was horrified at the thought.

"Of course not," he said, stroking my hair the way I longed to stroke his cock. "I'm not saying I'll never fuck you, but for now, I want this to be about you. I want you to know you can trust me, with your pussy, and your business. I can do it on command, or I can do it like this, with you, where it's like a feast. I have to pace myself so I don't come in my pants like a teenager. I'm getting to know what you like, where you want to be touched, how soft, how rough. That's enough for me for now." No man had ever said anything like that to me. We'd always been in too much of a hurry to tear our clothes off. Yes, even on long, lazy vacations. We'd bake ourselves in the sun, then swim in the water, then someone's hands would wander and we'd almost wind up fucking on a public beach. Never had I met a man with more patience than me, especially when it came to sex. I sank back and let him work his magic one more time. I forced my mind to let go of everything it wanted to think, every thought it was tempted to send wending its way through my orgasm. I floated there, even with my body firm against the bed. Ed made me float, made me rise and soar and then sink back to the sheer delight of his tongue and lips, his heat and passion. He made me feel so special that night, allowing me to relax in a way I hadn't in longer than I could remember. Having him around has made even the most maddening moments of running a restaurant feel like no big deal. I just think about how calmly he approaches everything he does, how he always has a knowing wink, and, when need be, a lusty appetite that isn't sated until I am.

Some people have asked when I'm going to open a corresponding restaurant for men, and don't worry, I'm already working on it. It'll be called BJ's, and I can't wait to hang the "Coming Soon" sign on the door.

PUNCHING BAG

Kyle still wasn't sure, two years in, if he liked punching or being punched better, on or off the ring. All he knew was that boxing made him feel alive, lit up, excited, manly . . . and had even when he was a woman. He'd started lurking around the gym when he'd been Kim, binding his breasts, mostly using the inert punching bags. He was afraid of hitting another woman, but he wouldn't be afraid of hitting the block of muscle in a man's chest. He didn't even need anyone else, at first, to get that special high, one he'd never gotten from running or swimming or tennis.

There's an energy to a boxing ring that he had never experienced in any other sport, not even wrestling. This was pure, raw aggression, tempered only by the rules of the game and sometimes not even that. It made grown men and women drop all pretense and simply get down to the business at hand, and he liked the way it sliced away every false veneer society put on his shoulders until it was just his mind and his fists, working in concert.

Transitioning from female to male had made the process mostly easier, though he'd had to switch gyms. With his red hair, freckles, and still a bit of a baby face, no matter how flat and firm his chest, how bulked up his shoulders, he couldn't risk someone saying something and his ridiculer getting truly beaten to a pulp. He knew that if he'd been born a guy, he'd have gotten picked on, no question. He was only five feet six: decent for a woman but short, scrawny even, for a guy.

So he switched to an all-male gym, where the level of aggression, testosterone, and drive suited him perfectly. For the past year or so, ever since his surgery, he'd been trying to figure out so much about himself that dating had fallen by the wayside. People were easier when consumed on his computer screen, in flirtatious notes or all-out dirty chat sessions, where he could say things like, "Punch me. Pummel me. Use me," and go there, completely, in his head. He'd never wanted to get punched like that before—not for real.

He'd assumed that since he'd been mostly a dyke as a woman, going more for the athletic types than the overly made-up ones, that he'd continue to want that kind of woman, but something had changed somewhere along the way. He'd always assumed that he wanted to be the tough, brawny, roaring hulk he'd watched countless times in the ring and fought against once or twice. That was the kind of fantasy that, at twenty-eight, he knew was never going to quite come true; there wasn't a surgery he could endure to make himself taller, to make himself a completely different person. All he could do was make himself into the strongest, healthiest person he could be. Thankfully, he had savings he'd grown with some good investments in school, ones that had supported him ever since. He was finally ready to look for a job in computer science but hadn't wanted to go through a public transition on the job, with all the explaining. He was too private for that. For the moment, he could take his time looking for work, as he worked on himself. He got top surgery and he was taking T, and while he felt different, he was still sorting out exactly what that meant, and what that made him.

His heart, though, if it belonged anywhere, was in the gym. The energy there rippled in waves, flowing through him like a computer's motherboard. His first waking thought was no longer about his unruly body or his first cup of coffee, but for his gloves, the new black and red ones he'd had custom made. When he put them on, he felt invincible.

He woke up and stood staring at himself in the mirror, indulging a few minutes' vanity before showering, closing his eyes, and smiling at the muscles that seemed to have sprouted all over. They seemed to be telling him, on a daily basis, "You made the right choice. Here is your reward."

He didn't let himself admit, except in rare moments, how much he did miss the little intimacies he'd forgone in the last year; the kisses on the back of his neck, the spooning with his usually taller girlfriends, the flirtatious banter of a first date, the holding hands, the making a girl come with his hands. That, he thought as the hot spray blasted his face, was second to the sublime thrill of cutting the perfect right hook. And then he felt it, what would've been an extreme hard-on in what he was sure, if he'd been born with the right parts, would have been at least a nine-inch cock. He stepped back and let the luxurious spray blast his flat chest, now sprinkled with hair and bursting with muscles. He reached down and touched himself, shocked at how close he was to orgasm. When he came, he didn't think about getting his ass—or what had been his pussy—pounded. He thought about someone pounding his chest, slapping his face, using him as a personal punching bag. Kyle had to force himself to turn off the shower, step out clutching the sink, then drop, dripping wet, onto the toilet seat, lest he collapse with the sheer joy that image had brought him.

He went back to bed for a few minutes, lying damp and naked between the smooth sheets, mentally reviewing the guys he knew at the gym, considering which ones might be worth pursuing to live out this fantasy—because this wasn't the kind of fantasy he was willing to wait for. His mind flitted from one to another until he finally roused himself again. Maybe this wasn't his decision to make.

He went to the gym after everyone else's workday had ended, lurking, observing, but sticking to himself. There was still a sense that he didn't quite belong, not because of gender, but personality. Maybe he needed to be gruff and demanding, but that wasn't really Kyle's style. Hanging around proved useful, because eventually there were only four guys left. He'd seen the owner give James—a huge, hot, hulking white guy with a buzz cut, stubble, and a killer body—the keys. "Wanna spar?" James had asked. Kyle looked around and realized he was talking to him.

"Sure," he said, shrugging casually, like it was no big deal. And, in a way, it wasn't. He took a few minutes in the locker room to suit up and put on his gloves and mouth guard and psych himself up. He didn't have time to think too much about the man who was almost twice his size, or he might chicken out.

Kyle was totally into the match when he first sparred off against James. His new, gray tank top clung to his muscular body, loose red shorts hung to his knees. He was fired up, ready to dart and strike, to unleash, not fury, but energy and passion. When the first blow landed against his chest, he liked it a little too much, liked it in ways that weren't fit for a boxing ring, that had no way of translating into the ancient sport they were engaging in.

No, the way he liked it was all about another ancient sport, that of men sparring with men . . . in the bedroom or in his dreams. Only they were in public, and for perhaps the first time ever, Kyle was glad he didn't have a dick, because if he did, there'd be no way he could've hidden his erection. There was barely a way to hide the sensations now as his two urges battled, one to win, and one to chance another beautiful blow. Boxing was an eat-or-be-eaten world, and suddenly Kyle wanted to be beaten, slapped, choked. The sensation almost overtook him, but he hopped back, shook his head, tried to get a glimpse of James's eyes to see if he was the only one feeling this way. He hoped not.

They went on for a few minutes, but Kyle realized he'd have to throw the match if they were ever going to move on to the real thing, the best part. He didn't think, just then, about the fact that this was his true test of manhood: to be able to give up the mantle of macho, to abandon being in charge, to revel in the thrill he'd never dare try as a girl of going over the edge, giving himself to someone. He'd spent so long building himself up, pumping iron, pumping hormones, priming himself to be someone mighty and powerful, that he'd never let himself truly savor the possibilities.

He poised his body to take a blow, then fell, using the few acting classes he'd taken in school to make it look as realistic as possible. There were only two friends of James's watching, ones who were all too happy to call it for their pal. James leaned over him and tapped his face, sending another jolt through Kyle. "Hey man, you okay?" Kyle looked up into James's pale, piercing blue eyes, hoping what he saw looking back was a reflection of his own desire. He wasn't sure, but he nodded and stood. After James got pounds from his friends, the two men went into the locker room, where James quickly pressed Kyle up against the lockers.

"What the hell was that?" he asked. His voice wasn't angry so much as serious, wanting a real answer. Kyle wanted to ask, "What?" but didn't.

"I don't know. I mean, I do; I just don't know if I should tell you." James didn't answer, just stood hovering over Kyle, like he had all day to wait, but his eyes were patient, not menacing. Kyle flushed, looking down momentarily before looking back up into James's gaze. "I liked it, okay? There was a moment right after you slammed me in the chest that I liked it, the whole thing, the pain, the rush of the blow, the power behind it, the way it almost knocked me down. I liked the sensation and I wanted more. I want more. Now. From you."

The smile slowly crept across James's face, tilting first the corners of his lips, then moving up his cheeks to those mesmerizing eyes. "You mean you're a masochist, is that what you're saying?" Their gloves were off, but Kyle suddenly longed for something to shield his face with. He was new to actually engaging in BDSM; new, even, to truly fantasizing about it in such a deep way, so he didn't yet know that wishing for it to end while secretly wanting to prolong it was one of the best parts of being a bottom.

"Yes," he said, as his voice trembled. "I think so, anyway. This is new to me." He paused, not sure whether to keep going and reveal the even-bigger secret.

James stepped closer until one sweaty body was pressed against the other. "I know," was all he said, so much meaning imbued in five little letters. And with that, Kyle sank back against the lockers, yielding his body, his mind, all the ways he held himself together, to James.

"Get in the shower," James said, then turned his back on Kyle. *Here? Now?* he thought, but he knew this was his first test. He never showered at the gym, but no one else was around;

James had a key to lock up and his friends had gone off to some bar, so they were completely alone. Kyle had absolute freedom, at least, in this way; freedom from discovery and prying eyes. Some men might have been afraid to do their first scene with no one around at all to hear if something went awry, but not Kyle. The fact that they had the gym to themselves was a luxury he couldn't take for granted.

Still, he moved into the deepest recesses of the locker room and took off first his sweaty tank, then the shorts, then the briefs. He felt it again, that phantom hard-on, only not so phantom this time. He was excited, aroused, and it was centered between his legs, the area he didn't know what to call, the area he'd tried to ignore for as long as possible but no longer could. He looked up and saw James and his eyes immediately went to James's cock, one so big it almost made Kyle swoon. He hadn't known he was a size queen, but he couldn't deny that the mighty weapon made him long to get on his knees.

"Get going, boy," James said. "Boy." He'd learned it in one context in school, a negative, racist word full of hatred, but now, Kyle heard it differently, maybe because he'd never been one. He'd rushed to become a man and now had a few moments to regress, to be a boy full of the wonder of hormones, of sheer exploration, of going with his instincts. James seemed to be able to read him like a book because he slammed Kyle up against the tiles of the musty shower stall and grabbed him by the throat. "Your safeword is *girl*," he said, the irony nowhere in his gruff command.

The tears that sprang to Kyle's eyes came unbidden, and he didn't bother blinking them away. James raised a knee between Kyle's legs and he didn't protest. "Okay, boy?" the man asked, that word again making him shudder, and he suddenly didn't care what James's knee found there. James managed to keep his hold on Kyle while turning on the shower spray, blasting them both with water hotter than Kyle usually used. He liked it, or maybe he didn't, but he wanted it, because James wanted it. This was his chance to prove himself, as a boy, a man, a sub—as himself.

James's hand stroked Kyle's cheek once, sweetly, softly, before he raised it and slapped him hard, the wet handprint lost to the next one that followed. Kyle didn't try to stop the tears, couldn't have, releasing all the emotions he'd thought he'd been getting out in the ring. James was mostly silent, save for a few grunts, the sound of the spray loud in their ears as he pummeled Kyle with his bare hands, slapping his cheeks and nipples, punching him hard in the chest, then turning him around to thrash at his back. Kyle trembled, the pain secondary to the tenderness he could feel coming through with each slap. James knew what he was doing, Kyle could tell, and finally he had to do something he could never have predicted: without asking, Kyle reached down between his legs and touched himself. In many ways, what he felt was the same as it had been, but he knew he was different. He knew this wasn't his pussy, but something else.

James gave his back a few more hard, wet slaps, then let his fingers join Kyle's, making him turn around and stare right at him as his fingers invaded. James could've gone for his ass, Kyle thought, but he didn't, he went there, and when Kyle came, the climax roared through his body, making him dig his nails into the grooves between the tiles for purchase. He'd been so focused on the pleasure of giving in, going over, he'd almost forgotten about James's cock, and when he looked down, he saw it standing straight up, as if to say, "Yes, this is for you."

Kyle shut his eyes and reached for James's hand to remove it. He was done, at least, with that, but not with James. With the water still pounding them, he got on his knees, putting his hands behind his back. It was the ultimate submissive, servile posture, yet it made Kyle feel, like almost nothing else had, like a man. Not the kind of man he saw on TV or was ever taught about in school or even saw in the muscle-baring ads plastered around the gym, but the kind of man he was, the kind of man he wanted to be, one who could claim every inch of his manhood by owning himself. He knew the moment his mouth met James's cock, one so big he had to stretch his lips and even then could barely get it inside. James helped, grabbing him by the neck and pressing himself slowly into the recesses of Kyle's throat, and this time he made noise.

Kyle found he couldn't look up and see James's face, but he could picture it as he sucked, as his aching body screamed not with pain, but belonging. He knew they couldn't stay there all night, but they didn't need to. Kyle had found everything he'd come to the ring to find. He swallowed what James's cock gifted him, taking pride not only in being the bigger man's personal punching bag, but in knowing he was now, finally, his own man, the kind he was meant to be, one with a solid chest, a pounding heart, and a smile on his face.

FLYING SOLO

I've made sure my camera has plenty of battery left for this trip, because you're not here to watch me. I wish you were, but life sometimes keeps us apart. You didn't ask me to, but I want to send you photos of me naked, turned on, wet for you. Even though you're not talking up a storm as you usually are when we travel, I feel you with me as I pass through security, and especially as I head to the gate and start casually, quietly, discreetly looking around, the way we did on our honeymoon. Has it really been four years? They've flown by.

I'll never forget sitting with you and hearing you whisper, "Find someone to take back to our hotel room with us." You didn't specify if it should be a man or a woman, and although I'd never considered it before, the idea of being pressed between you and another man made me so excited I almost spilled the medium coffee I'd just purchased. You took it from my hand and blew through the small opening in the plastic top for me, raising your eyebrows. I giggled, then started looking. I reached for your hand for support; you squeezed it but then let me go. I fiddled with my wedding ring, twisting around the new gold band over and over, afraid I looked like a kid in a candy store.

You'd whispered to me again. "I'm just so madly in love with you, and I think this should be a new tradition; when we travel, we find someone to join us. Just for fun, no strings attached." I'd spent the entire time before we boarded perusing every adult sitting around us, mentally undressing them, wondering who had piercings or tattoos, who was kinky, who was the best kisser. I pictured the tall man in a suit, speaking rapidly in Spanish on the phone, with his cock in your mouth. I pictured the short, curvy beauty with her head buried between my legs while you entered her from behind.

"Well?" you'd asked, as they started to board the plane.

"I can't decide. And I certainly can't go up to any of these people. What am I going to say? 'I just got married and my husband wants to have a threesome?'" Yet even saying those unspeakable words made me wet, made my mind and heart race. I'd told you that I was bisexual after our third date, wanting to make sure you wouldn't have that awful, frat-boy, "That's hot!" reaction that even most seemingly sophisticated men busted out once I revealed I went both ways. You just nodded and let me tell you all about Simone, the gorgeous woman with the smoky voice and beautiful, curvy body I'd most recently bedded.

I'd fallen in love with you in part because you let me tell you anything, and in turn revealed some of your fantasies. We'd tried out many of them—bondage, strap-ons, hot wax. We'd talked about threesomes and orgies but only in a fantasy way, until that trip. For whatever reason, you'd never mentioned wanting to be with another man, but I liked learning new things about you just when I thought I knew it all. "Let's wait until we're on the plane," I'd said, and lucky me: my dream girl, the one whose face I kept returning to, was sitting next to me on the plane. You'd pretended to sleep while I made small talk with her, all the while working up the courage to say what I most wanted to. As it turned out, she'd been the one to whisper in my ear, "I wish I could be alone with you for an hour. I want to kiss you all over."

I'd stared right back at her, barely hearing the screaming infant behind us, or the blaring music from the woman's headphones in front of us. I just saw her, Katia, her ripe, naturally pink lips, her jet-black hair, the tiny diamond glinting from her lightly freckled nose. When I reached up and traced her lips, you'd stirred, gently knocking my knee with yours. "You can. Well, not alone, exactly. I'm with him," I'd whispered, getting close enough to make sure my lips grazed her earlobe. "It's our honeymoon, but he wants me to bring someone home for us to share."

"I'm good at sharing," she'd whispered back, and she'd proven exactly how good once we were settled into our suite. Fresh from a hot shower we'd shared, our kisses making me tingle all over, Katia had gotten you and me on our backs and eased her mouth from one to the other until I was absolutely dripping wet, desperate for more. "You get on top of him," she'd instructed, in the sweetest, silkiest voice possible. It was an order, but a gentle one. If I'd had a better plan, I'm sure she'd have gone along with it, but there was nothing I wanted more than your cock inside me, my body primed from her hot, hungry tongue. She eased you inside me and just as I moaned and thought I might come right then and there, her tongue was back, lapping between the cheeks she held open with those soft, delicate hands. Her tongue pressed against my rosebud, making me groan.

"She's licking me," I'd whispered frantically before burying my face in your neck. She worked me into a frenzy, one that your hard, driving cock only made more frantic. When Katia's fingers reached around me to circle my clit, I came, trembling against both of you, then biting your neck when her fingers didn't stop dancing against my hard bud. She raised her head, only to nip at the soft flesh of my ass while she coaxed another climax from me. But it wasn't until she lifted me off of you, pressed three fingers deep inside me, then eased them out and put them in your mouth that I really lost it. The look of sheer ecstasy on your face had me slamming down on top of you, fucking you harder than I ever had. You looked right at me while you sucked her fingers, and I came for the third time, something I'd also never done.

"Can I taste him?" she'd asked, and no sooner were the words out of her mouth than I was climbing off of you, wrapping my hand around the base of your cock, and feeding it to her. She didn't swallow the whole thing greedily like I would have. Instead, Katia was like a cat with a bowl of milk, her tongue slowly licking up the cream at the tip, one long stroke at a time. I'd never seen a woman give a blow job up close like that, and I didn't even think about what I did next—I just leaned forward and joined her, my tongue on one side of the ridged crown, hers on the other. Soon we were taking turns putting the head in our mouths, but I let her do the honors when you started to buck your hips up and down. I was too blissed out to give you the proper care and devotion you deserved, but Katia certainly wasn't. I saw her saliva glinting off the length of your shaft as she rose all the way up, opened those beautiful brown eyes to stare at me, then, keeping her gaze locked on mine, moved all the way down. When I reached out to stroke her hair, you grabbed my hand and we both put just a little pressure on her head, enough to make her moan. Soon you were fucking her face—there's no other way to describe it. She was grunting like an animal and you were lost in the feel of her mouth.

If someone had told me I'd spend the first night of my honey-moon watching another woman giving my husband head—and liking it—a few years before, or even a few weeks before, I'd have thought they were crazy. But in the moment, it was the hottest thing ever. There was no separation between us; we were all connected by our desire, our yearning to give and get pleasure all at the same time. When you came, I could tell instantly, even though Katia expertly sucked down every drop. "I think you should let Katia sit on your face," you told me.

Oh, my goodness. Of course. I lay back and soon she was on top of me, not writhing wildly, but slowly pressing herself against my mouth, enveloping my senses with her perfume. You got between my legs and ate me while I ate her, and even though your tongue distracted me from what I was doing, nobody minded. Eventually her languid movements weren't enough for me, and I pulled her tight against me, loving how wet she was getting, loving it even more when she came. She repeated her clit stroking as you kept your mouth on me, so I got to experience a fourth orgasm that knocked me out. Katia was gone by the time I woke up, but what she left us with was an insatiable sense of sexual adventure.

Since then, we've bedded men, women, and couples—only while traveling, never back home. Today will be a first, though, and I not only don't want to let you down, I'm curious what it'll be like. Though I've had more partners than most of my married friends, when I'm with you, it always feels like married sex, no matter how many people are in the room. This time, it's just me, and I have to imagine you watching, you whispering to me, you encouraging me. I still get nervous, as you well know, but I've loved every single one of our encounters, both in the moment, and how they spur us on later when we're alone.

I text you a quick hello along with a photo of me, and just

as I'm finished sending it, I see a man watching me. His head is shaved, and he towers over my five-foot-two frame. I can tell he's muscular from how his suit doesn't quite fit him, even though he looks amazing. He's taller and wider and probably stronger than you, but again, I know that if you were here, you wouldn't be threatened. Remember that pro football player we picked up, the one who not only bent me over and, with my head buried in the sheets, fucked me so well I squirted, but also fucked you?

I think about that when I'm alone sometimes. It was one of the hottest things we've ever done. I wonder if Mr. Muscles would ever want to be with a man like you. Instantly, I blush; I can never hide that.

You've told me that's one of the things you love about me—how easily I blush, how readily you can tell when I'm thinking something dirty. The muscle guy walks over. "Hi," he says, his voice deep yet somehow boyish. "You busy?"

"Just waiting for my plane. Going on a business trip," I say.

"Me too. Meetings, but not till three tomorrow." Our flight's at seven and is only an hour and a half, which means we both have a whole night free. "Look, I don't want to bother you if you aren't interested"—he nods at my wedding ring, which I only take off when I shower—"but I couldn't help noticing you."

"I'm interested," I say quietly. I've had this conversation dozens of times, but it's never easy to tell a stranger you're in an open marriage, and it's even more challenging without you by my side to help ease things along. "I'm . . . available. Tonight, anyway," I say with a laugh.

"Tonight works for me," he says. I motion to the seat next to me and we sit in companionable silence. I have an urge to lean my head on his shoulder, so I do. He strokes my hair, a seemingly gentle touch, but one that sends shivers running through my body. I picture you on my other side, and me snug between two men, one who sets me on edge and one who makes me feel safe—and sexy too. That's what you do, if you didn't know; I feel like I could take on the world in every way, knowing you're there for me.

I don't say any of this, though; it's too intimate to share with a stranger. It's just for you. I give the stranger a look after a few minutes, one of pure desire, conveyed through my lowered lashes. I don't need to talk dirty just yet; in fact, the silence makes our gaze all the more powerful. He puts his hand on my cheek, cupping my face toward him, but instead of kissing me, he runs his thumb along my lower lip, folding it back against my chin before pinching it. Tears rush to my eyes and I'm utterly lost in his touch. I still feel your silent, unspoken presence near me, but it's starting to recede just slightly—forgive me—as this man works his magic on me.

"I only need one night," he says, then pinches my lip even harder before moving it aside, reaching into his bag, and pulling out a notepad and pen. "Write down how you're going to suck my cock," he whispers, his voice as prim and proper as his words are not.

If his command is meant to shock me, it fails completely. Instead, it thrills me. I picture you watching me as I write, you who knows so well exactly how I suck your cock—and how I love it. I write down what I think I will do, what makes me most excited about this most intimate act, but I also know that sex is the most unpredictable act ever invented. Just when you think you know what to expect, someone or something or some emotion comes along to make you feel as giddy as a virgin again. It's like that with you, anyway, and I've given you at least a thousand blow jobs, by my estimate. My cheeks do grow hot, which means they burn red, as I write down my oral plans, passing the note to him and then looking away.

"Your husband is a lucky man," the stranger whispers in my ear as we board the plane. My nipples get so hard it's almost painful.

As luck would have it, our seats are next to each other. Once we're seated, I look out the window—toward you, my version of you. I wish you were here, not because I need you to be, but because I want you to be. I want you to smile with pride when I take him in my mouth, to tell him naughty facts about me while I swallow him whole.

I manage to make it through landing, though my panties are drenched by the end. I don't tell the man because he has to know by now. I've been tightening and releasing, taking deep breaths, alternating between thinking about him and you. "Ready?" he asks as the flight attendant tells us we are free to go.

Am I? Not exactly, but I'm ready as I'll ever be. I touch my phone in my purse and think about texting you, giving you a heads-up, letting you follow my actions vicariously. But I don't. I'm not sure why, except that maybe I'd rather tell you later and try to be in the moment. Instead, I nod, and then impulsively take out the camera I'd so carefully loaded, and give it to my new lover. "Show him how lucky he is," I say with a wink. My exaggerated flirting is silly, but he rolls with it.

We're in the baggage claim area now, waiting for our luggage. I pose suggestively for the camera—for you, but also for this man, who, when the conveyer belt starts to rumble, pulls me close and gives me a deep, sensual kiss. I can feel other passengers' eyes on me, but I don't care. I like that they have no idea what we really are to each other, no idea that my lips are right here, my body now curving toward this man, but part of me is with you. We break apart and I am hot all over. Thankfully our bags arrive shortly. I was going to take the subway, but he pulls me toward the taxi stand.

He beckons me toward him in the backseat as we're whisked toward Manhattan. He asks where I want to go and I say his hotel; my room is just for me—and you, of course. I unbutton my coat and toss my long red hair all around, grateful it's still sleek and straight after the plane ride. He takes photo after photo, which makes me want to share more of myself. I flash him my breasts in their lacy, hot-pink bra, laughing as I throw my head back.

Soon we've arrived, and I people watch while he checks in, smiling as I ogle a six-foot-tall woman I know you'd love to bend over for. She notices me watching her, and I smile. If you were here, maybe I'd do more than that. Instead, I follow the man upstairs, aware of how hard my nipples are. He slips the key card in the door and once it's shut, says, "You've had my dick hard the whole flight. I almost jerked off in the bathroom, but I wanted to save it for you. Show me those gorgeous breasts again." I drop my coat right on the carpet and unbutton my blouse until it hangs wide open. I peel down the cups of my bra and show him my breasts. This time, the camera stays in his bag while he moves toward me, hunger on his face.

He pulls me close and sucks my nipples one at a time, using not just teeth, tongue, or lips, but a combination of all three. It goes on and on and on until I want to buckle under him. When I reach for his cock, he holds me back, though. "Call him," he says, whipping out his phone. "I want him to hear you come." I freeze. This might be too much for you; it borders on being more intimate than you'd like me to be without you. Yet am I really without you if you're listening, maybe even touching yourself?

Hesitantly, I dial you. "Hey, baby," you say as I adjust the setting to speakerphone. "What's up? Where are you?"

"In a hotel room," I say. I turn around for a modicum of

privacy, but I can still hear him taking off his pants. "I'm with someone I met on the plane. A man."

"Are you?" you say teasingly.

"Yes. He wanted me to call you." I pause until the silence is more unbearable than my next words. "He wants you to hear me come."

"Oh, my goodness, Sunny," he says. Now the man knows my name, but I don't care because I can hear how aroused you are. "Let me talk to him."

I hand him the phone, but he adjusts the settings so I can't hear anything except "Got it," and "Will do." He puts the phone back down, and you say to me, "Be a good girl for him, baby. I'm listening."

Instead of pressure, though, all I hear is permission—to be myself, my best self, with you by proxy. He picks me up and throws me onto the bed, and in a few quick moves has my clothes off and my wrists tied above my head with my bra. I squirm, turned on in the way only bondage can make me. He fishes out the camera and snaps a photo, then says, "Spread those pretty legs for me, Sunny." I blush at his use of my name, and at exposing myself so blatantly, but I do it. "And open your eyes," he adds.

I stare back at him until he finally gets his fix then kneels next to me to show me his cock. "Your husband wants me to fuck you nice and hard, said that's what you like, so that's what I'm going to do." He gets a condom out of his bag and rolls it on while I wait for him. Normally I'd touch my clit before penetration, but I can't at the moment. He rubs the head of his cock against my clit for me, then the wetness along my slit, but when I start to thrust and urge him inside, he pulls back. "I was warned that you can be greedy," he says, pinching my clit instead. "Roll over. Now you have to wait for my cock."

No sooner have I managed to roll over, arms still bound with my bra, than he lifts me up and positions me across his lap. He spanks me hard, way harder than would normally happen the first time I'm with a new partner. You must have said something about how much I can take. The smacks are sharp and perfectly placed, my bound wrists hanging in front of me. He gives me two fingers to suck, and I am grateful for the distraction as the whacks get even harder. I whimper against his fingers, but not in protest. After a round of blows so intense they make me wonder if I need to ask for a break, he finally touches me. I'm dripping wet, so the three fingers sink inside fast.

"You were right. She responded very well to her spanking," he says to you in a loud, exaggerated voice, making me even wetter.

Then he slides the bra off my wrists, settles me on my hands and knees, ass in the air, and enters me. With only a few thrusts, I'm coming, my moans filling the air. "I love hearing you like that," you say, and I smile. Maybe this isn't so different from you watching up close and personal. "I want him to come on your tits and send me a photo. You'll do that for me, won't you?"

"Of course," I tell you. And of course, it's not just for you; I am a glutton for a man showering me with come. Yours is my favorite, but after the way this man just fucked me, I am ready to feel him give it to me.

He turns me over, removes the condom, and stands over me, cock in hand. He's going to make it rain down on me. "Do you want to taste it?" he asks.

"Yes," I say, panting. He strokes himself, while I stare up at him in awe. I can hear you doing the same thing. When he sinks down onto the bed next to me, his hardness mere inches from my mouth, I know it's time. I open wide, and soon he's spraying my breasts and face with his hot cream, his shout echoing in the room. We hear your frantic breathing and then the long exhale of release. The man runs his fingers from my breast up my chest and neck, pushing some of his seed into my mouth as I greedily swallow it, a little bit of extended bliss.

"Get his card, baby. Maybe next time we can all get together," you say before hanging up. Wouldn't that be wonderful?

SEXATHON

When Doug told me he wanted to enter the sexathon at our local sex club, at first, I looked at him like he was crazy. We've been together for ten years, and in many ways, it seems like a lifetime. I'm thirty-five and he's twenty-nine and most of our friends are only now starting to talk weddings and babies. They look to us as a model couple, and maybe we are. I often joke that we're like any old married couple—we tied the knot four years ago, finally—with each of us having our own spot on the couch, our pillow, our mug; in short, our places within our home. Yet, we both welcome those niceties, those symbols that go far beyond the solid gold wedding rings we exchanged during the ceremony. And we'd been monogamous, save for a few random threesomes we'd taken part in, which had been hot—don't get me wrong—but in general we were one-man men, focused on building our lives together, eager to share everything from sex to breakfast to road trips. The adventures we'd shared up until then, including traveling everywhere from

Belize to Alaska, as well as being godparents to our friends' son Peter, had only brought us closer together. We had our spats, sure, but I was certain that without Doug my life would be far worse off than the one we shared.

Doug explained that the club was having a fundraiser, but instead of a marathon or walkathon, it was a sexathon. You got points for everything from deep-throating a dildo to how far you ejaculated when you jerked off to how many partners you hooked up with, and people were supposed to pledge a dollar or more for every point you earned. Condoms would be mandatory. When he told me about the points and prizes—a trip to Paris, a big-screen plasma TV—I knew there was no talking him out of it. The thing about my man, though you'd never know it unless you were in a specifically sporting situation with him, is that he's incredibly competitive. Whether it's doing crossword puzzles, guessing the answers on *Jeopardy!*, playing bingo at our gay community center, or even taking part in pickup softball, he plays to win.

"What about me?" I asked. I'm not insecure, but even the most solid long-term relationship can hit its rough spots. Was he having a midlife crisis? Did he regret not having more partners in his younger years? We'd discussed this, and not just when we first got together. Back then, we'd been youthful and idealistic, and while we were definitely falling in love with each other in those days, we were also in love with the idea of love. I thought the men who picked up a different trick every night were fools. Who'd want a new cock when you could have a man like Doug: tall, strapping, husky, hairy; who could be by turns savage (teeth and nails clawing at me), and tender (taking care of me in countless ways)? Not me. And those kisses! The kind that went on forever, that left me breathless, that seemed to come out of nowhere and for no reason—he'd stop me in the middle of a sentence just for the pleasure of sticking his tongue down my throat.

Yet over the years we've each wondered, occasionally aloud, what else is out there? Who might we have missed by our focus on each other? So, on one level, I understood; this wasn't just about his cocksmanship or pride, but something deeper. Was he trying to test the waters? Was he looking for a fling or a new husband? I had so many questions, but my most vulnerable one was what I wound up speaking aloud, three little words that betrayed my nervousness.

"Baby," he said, pulling me close till our foreheads were touching, "I love you. I always will. This is just something I feel I need to do. I'll be safe, you know that, and you can come watch and cheer me on."

I thought it over for the rest of the day, but something about that scenario didn't sit well with me. I'm not exactly like Doug, which is what has made us so compatible in the long term. I'm more laid-back, whereas he's, if not high-strung, certainly excitable. I care less about winning than about doing things I enjoy; I'll get so involved in a crossword puzzle clue that I'll go research one of the answers and even read a book about the topic. I'm a detail man whereas Doug is about the big picture. But for all that, I knew immediately what I was going to do: I would enter that sexathon right alongside Doug—and hopefully win and raise even more money than him.

I came to him that night as he was reading a murder mystery. "I have something to tell you," I said quietly, as I took the paperback from his hands and curled up facing him.

"You're really pissed, huh?" he asked.

"No, not really. But I'm not just going to be there cheering you on. I'm going to be entering the competition too."

"You?" he asked, squinting at me, clearly surprised.

"What do you mean? Don't think I have what it takes?" Maybe he meant that since I'm a bottom, with him, anyway, almost all of the time—it wasn't always like that with other lovers—that I was somehow not as qualified. Or maybe he just didn't think of me like that; I was the one who'd rather watch everyone else climb a mountain than sweat it out myself.

"Of course, I just . . . I'm surprised. But I can't wait to watch you compete," he said with a grin, before tackling me, his cock already hard. I sank into the sheer pleasure of being with the man I loved, grateful he wasn't upset, and more than a little excited about the prospect of taking on new lovers and a new adventure.

This wasn't the kind of event we trained for. We fucked, certainly, but we'd always done plenty of that. Our sex was good: frenzied at times, slow at others. But we didn't go out of our way to try anything new or introduce any new toys or tricks into the bedroom. And we didn't say another word to each other about the sexathon; instead, we each hit up our mutual friends, along with select coworkers and other trusted acquaintances. We didn't share how much was pledged, though that would be posted on the wall at the event.

Time flew, and soon we were as ready as we'd ever be. Though we'd be naked for most of the event, we got to pick our starting outfits. Doug decided to wear a pair of snug new black-and-white-striped briefs that did a lot to emphasize his already generous package. He wore jeans and a T-shirt over the briefs, but once we arrived, he stowed those away. I went the opposite route, showing up in my favorite soft gray pants and an elegant, crisp white button-down shirt, my hair freshly combed, two days' worth of stubble on my chin. No underwear.

Our friend Al greeted us when we came in. "Well, well, well. You two are quite the catch. And the only couple who's signed up."

"Well, we're not a team today," said Doug. "It's every man for himself. Right, baby?" He grabbed my ass and gave me a kiss. It was a powerful kiss, but I could sense the tension thrumming through him, the uncertainty over what, exactly, was going to happen in the next few hours. I kissed him back and tried to reassure him with my lips. No matter what, he was the only man for me.

We were each given a number and told to report for duty. There were eight tasks, and we'd be graded on all of them. They were: deep-throating a dildo, rolling an extra-large condom onto an extra-large real cock, getting spanked, boot worshipping, coming as far as you could, getting a butt plug up someone's ass, and bobbing for cocks (think bobbing for apples). The final stage: all the contestants would be put in a giant room and compete to have as many partners as they could in an hour (multiple partners permitted, up to four).

This would be quite the test; some of the men, judging from a quick glance around, were hot, but some weren't my type. Many were wiry and thin, while I prefer, if not bears, more meaty guys. I had to remind myself that it wasn't about being attracted to them necessarily, but simply going for it, doing things I'd never done in any other circumstance. I'm not shy by any means, but pre-Doug, I'd always wanted to at least know the guy's name. Here the men were just numbers, myself included (I was seven while Doug was eight). There were twenty contestants and probably double that number cheering us, while various guys volunteered their services, as it were.

I felt pumped up with adrenaline, and in a weird way, even though we'd be competing against each other, it made me feel close to Doug. I'd never done anything like this without him, and now I was inspired by his team spirit, or rather, sex spirit. It made me want to let him tie me up, as he's always begged to do, and have his way with me fully, completely. But first, there was a sexathon to win.

There were some tasks I knew I'd be great at, and some that I'd never contemplated, let alone tried. First up was deep-throating. I do pride myself on being able to take all of Doug's wide nine-inch cock down my throat, so I figured this would be an easy task. But it's one thing to get down on my knees and sword swallow my best friend and husband, quite another to have my hands tied behind my back and have to open wide for a piece of silicone that smelled nothing like a human cock. Lined up next to me were nine other men, including Doug. Part of me was tempted to peek at him, but I knew that would throw me off track—others had the same idea, because I did glimpse a blindfold or two—so I shut my eyes and, when I heard the bell go off, opened wide and started sucking. The dicks weren't being rammed down our throats, but were held in place by a man who'd be judging us on technique, attention to balls, saliva control, and so on. At first, I almost spit out the dick, but then I harkened back to my college theater roots and simply pretended the cock was Doug's.

Then it was easy: I lavished attention on the head, pretending its owner was patting my hair, moaning, and praising me, then started to slide my wet lips along the length of the toy. I'd actually given head to toys before, prior to their going up my ass, and the more I did it, the more into it I got. The room was filled with slurping and sucking sounds and the occasional grunt or sigh or exclamation. I was quiet, studious almost; I usually let Doug make the noise when I'm sucking him off. Before I knew it, a bell went off. We'd find out how we'd done later. My jaw was a bit sore, but it had been fun—though not as fun as getting a mouthful of Doug's cream on my tongue.

Next up was condom-rolling. I figured this was the easiest

task, except that Doug and I had been fluid bonded for so long and save for those threesomes, hadn't had to use condoms. I figured it would come back to me, like riding a bike, but it didn't quite work out that way. The condom was slippery, and we only had one minute total; the first three to complete the task got bonus points. They'd switched things up from the first round—instead of the rubber going on a fake cock, we got the real thing. I was putting a condom on a stranger, and I couldn't help but blush. His dick was big and thick and the sight of it was entrancing. I didn't dare look up at him as I held the base in one hand. First, I started rolling the condom down the wrong way, then I had to quickly shift gears. I got his cock covered just before the buzzer went off.

Then we were led into a room with ten padded spanking benches and instructed to bend over and hold on to our ankles. "You will be spanked with a hand, a ruler, a paddle, and a belt. You may use the safeword *pussy* at any time, but points will be deducted for that. All our tops have been trained to provide the same amount of sensation, for twenty lashes each. Are you ready?"

We murmured our agreement. I wasn't just ready; I was extremely hard. I love getting spanked, and the novelty of having someone new spank me was arousing. My competitive streak kicked in, because I knew that this round would be a challenge for Doug. He's 100 percent top; he just doesn't have a submissive bone—let alone boner—in his body. I held on and got ready. A hand covered my right asscheek, then when the whistle blew, it began to smack me methodically: right, left, right, left. I got used to the rhythm of the smacks and was eager for the ruler when it started. The man hitting me used the ruler to strike both cheeks at once. A few times, I clenched my bottom and he rapped it against me to get me to unclench and be fully in the spirit of what we were doing. "Give me that ass," the man whispered in my ear, and for some reason, I wanted to. I shuddered as his words traveled through my body and I relaxed into the bench so he could properly pound me. The whacks were stronger, making my skin tingle. I was grateful we didn't have to count out loud because there was so much noise in the room, it was easy to lose track. I preferred to savor each wave of heat coursing through my bottom, sending pleasure right through to my dick.

I was fine with the ruler and paddle, but the belt was a lot for me to handle. I focused on taking deep breaths and again thought of Doug, not whimpering in pain, but praising me after I'd lain across his lap and taken my blows like a good boy. Despite my resolve, a few tears managed to escape my eyes and travel down my neck. The man gently wiped them away when he was done and offered me the belt to kiss. It was an oddly tender moment as slaps rang out across the room.

Then it was time for boot worship, and again, my oral prowess came in handy. I love using my tongue—or having it used—and I was so consumed by the feel, smell, and taste of the leather that I forgot to look for Doug among the others. I got lost in the sensation, hoping, in those minutes, only that the recipient of my tongue-lashing enjoyed it. From the groans he was making, I was pretty sure he did.

Then we got a bit of a break in the form of masturbation. Doug and I stood next to each other, and in this case, it helped me. Our goal was to shoot as far across the room as we could, something I'd practiced out the window of my college dorm late at night, so I was pretty good at it. Nothing so far had involved my cock, save for getting spanked, and I was ready. I'd deliberately pulled back from Doug that morning when he'd wanted to fuck me for good luck. He has a faster recovery time than I do, and I didn't want to jinx things. I snuck glances at him as I worked myself, then at the other men, realizing that regardless of who won, it was a treat to be in a room with nineteen other men beating their meat. I figured my advantage would be in holding off as long as possible to see where the competition landed. As it turned out, watching stream after stream of come erupt from men's cocks is extremely exciting! I managed to wait until it was just me and Doug, and I was so horny I couldn't stand it, and I let loose, almost spraying a guy who apparently didn't think I could make it all the way across the room—or maybe he did and he wanted some. "Oh, Matt," Doug said, watching me and then shooting a lot of come, but pretty much right in front of him. Despite his showing, there was a huge smile on Doug's face when he was done.

Next were the butt plugs, and we were given a bucket from which to choose: slim or fat, black or red or silver or purple; there were all shapes and sizes. I chose a red one with three ridges, since part of what we'd be judged on was how much pleasure we brought our partner, along with size, amount of lube, speed, and accuracy. We were all paired with guys who loved getting fucked, and though I didn't know the man's name, his beautiful olive-skinned asshole spoke to me. He was on the ground, on his knees, his hands reaching behind to hold that sweet hole open just for me. I added some lube to my thumb while around us the judges took notes.

I'd only done Doug back there a few times, because he's not that into it but occasionally let me because I like it. Here I couldn't really engage in an extended dialogue with the guy, so I had to go by his body language, and from the way he was pressing back against me, I knew he wanted me to get going with the toy. I withdrew my thumb, slightly reluctantly, and then heard Doug's voice coaxing his bottom to let him in. "Oh, yeah, you dirty boy, give it to me, you slut," he said. For a second, I was jealous, but then I remembered the words he'd used that morning to try to coax me into bed. "You're going to be punished for teasing me, Matt." Oh, I hoped I would be. I hoped that any jealousy this event incited would serve to bring us closer together, because the truth was, I'd have left butt plug guy there waiting if Doug had approached me right then. I looked at him for a few more seconds before returning to the task at hand.

The plug was easily swallowed by the man's hungry anus, which sucked it right in. I teased him by twirling it around and pulling it out, only to slowly shove it back in, making sure he felt every ridge of the toy. When time was called, twenty male asses were faceup, on display, all but one stuffed with a plug; the guy who'd missed had apparently chosen a toy that was too big for its intended recipient.

Then, I got to stick my face in what felt like a sea of cocks. There was no water, but there were men crowded together, their hard dicks bobbing and weaving as they jerked them slowly, while I tried to capture one in my mouth. We'd each be given this chance, so the men were instructed not to come. It was exciting to feel so many penises within reach of my tongue; at one point I just trailed the tip of my tongue along the heads before finding one I wanted, and I guess my lips felt good enough that he forgot he was supposed to be evading me. I swallowed all of it, then rose and teased the head, feeling his body jerk until he pulled it out and slapped it against my face. Then my time was up.

We were ushered into the waiting area where there were light snacks and sodas. I smiled at another contestant. "How's it going?" I asked.

"Great, man, just great. I've been having a dry spell so when I heard about this I signed right up. But you two—wow! I don't know if I'd have the courage to do what you're doing."

I pondered what he'd said. I hadn't thought of it as courage per se, but it was a sign of us having faith that our relationship wouldn't be derailed by a little extracurricular fun. I knew that at that moment, the only man I really wanted to fuck was Doug, my familiar, sexy, tough, gorgeous Doug. He walked into the room and came right over to me. "You were amazing out there," he said, like I'd been race-car driving or something.

"You watched me?" I asked.

"Of course; I couldn't get enough. And now I'm going to watch men fuck you."

"What about you?" I asked.

"You know what? I realized that I'd really rather watch. There were a few hotties, but only one I want like that," he said and pulled me close for a kiss. After our tongues had gotten reacquainted, I pulled back.

"Do you mean you want me to drop out too and are just being polite?"

"Not at all, babe. You go get 'em, just save a little something for me." At that moment, my heart, not to mention my cock, swelled. Doug was not only the sexiest guy I'd ever known, but he was going above and behind. He wanted to see me take the gold, and I'd be damned if I wasn't going to make him proud!

The room was filled with men in tight red spandex shorts, who would be our pool of partners; we could also add on other contestants but then we'd each get points. Hand jobs got you one point, blow jobs two, rimming three, fucking four. We had twenty minutes. I strolled in totally nude and immediately set eyes on a guy about ten years older than me, though I only surmised that from his white hair. Otherwise, he was strong, his muscles showing through. I eyed him up and down and he peeled down his shorts to show me the impressive cock waiting for me. I turned back to look at Doug on the sidelines and he gave me a thumbs-up.

I grabbed the man's cock and while I did, reached for a kid who had to be just over the twenty-one-year-old cutoff. I snapped his shorts and he turned, looking for a moment like he didn't know how he'd gotten there. The truth was, neither did I, but I wanted them both. I pulled him over to me and soon I was sandwiched between them. "Let me fuck you while you rim him," the older man whispered in my ear. I'd never done two guys at once, but I was game. The boy got on his stomach and spread his legs and I didn't stop to think, just lunged for his balls with my tongue while the other man lubed me up, and then I felt his condom-covered cock pushing into me. Soon his cock was inside me, his thrusts shoving my face into the young guy's ass, while around me the smells and sounds of sex filled the air. It was hot, for sure, but my cock was hard for one man only. "I'm gonna come," I heard the older guy say, and I braced myself for his jizz.

When he was done, and the younger one still showed no signs of coming, I flipped junior over and jerked him off while pressing two lubed-up fingers up his ass. That did the trick, and he gave us all a delightful treat as he came all over his chest. I had already found my next partners, two men who looked achingly alike, who were holding hands. "I want to jerk you both off," I said. "Over there," I added, pointing to where Doug was sitting.

They obliged, and I found that in this context, I liked being in control, rubbing their dicks together, making one get on top of the other when my hands were tired, then blowing both of them. Doug clapped softly next to me. The rest of the free-for-all was a blur of hands and tongues and cocks and toys. I wound up wearing nipple clamps and sporting a giant erection. When the buzzer sounded, I raced over to Doug, who held out one of our soft, plush towels from home for me then carefully took off the clamps, while the judges told us they had to calculate. "Your time is your own until we're ready."

"You're gonna win," Doug said

To which I replied, "I don't care."

"Well, I do. I want to show you off next time we come here, parade you around with your winning medal on your chest—or your cock." He laughed, and so did I, and then his hand was on my cock and I couldn't think about anything else but the way he was touching me. It was the same as hundreds, maybe even thousands, of other hand jobs he'd given me, yet it felt different, more special for us having gone through a sexual marathon (mostly) together. Fittingly, I was coating his hand with my cream when they came in to announce the winners. When my name was called, I burst out with a cry of excitement, then leapt up to collect the gold cock statue and, yes, a medal. I couldn't wear it on my flaccid cock just then, but I looked forward to hanging it above our bed—and trying new things with Doug whenever one of us got the urge.

"Speech! Speech!" the guys filling the room cried out.

"Okay, okay," I conceded, standing and putting my arm around Doug. "I wouldn't be here if it weren't for the love of my life, Doug, who is the best husband a guy could ask for. Maybe next year there should be a doubles category, like in tennis, because I don't want to even think about trying to fuck anyone without him." The applause was deafening, almost.

I still heard Doug when he whispered, "I love you," in my ear.

A FIRST TIME FOR EVERYTHING

"Are you sure you want to do this?" Chip asked me.

"As sure as I'll ever be," I said, feeling surer even as the words came out of my mouth. After all, what kind of tease would I be if I backed out of the bukkake party I'd organized for myself?

It all started with Truth or Dare. I'm a wordy girl and will always pick truth over dare, even though I consider myself pretty gutsy. But without truth, without words, without syllables spilling out into sentences, dares don't make any sense; they're just reckless actions of the sort performed by drunk boys in late-night race cars, rather than the magnificent grace of a tightrope walker or bungee jumper. I want to be the daredevil superhero girl of sex, boldly going where few, if any, of my peers have gone before. If I go with a dare, it's of my own making, one that really does push me right up to my limits, not just where an envious partygoer would like to see me go.

The truth is, I'm a thrill seeker. I'm the girl who's been there, done that, and gone on to relish telling the story over and over again. I've had sex with men and women, in groups, in public, in dungeons. I've had all manner of sex toys, real and improvised, shoved into my pussy. I've been fucked underwater and spanked on camera. I've said yes to things simply to shock other people. I've used a violet wand, a Magic Wand, and a TENS unit. I've had all my toes shoved into a greedy bottom's mouth, and I've sucked two cocks at once. I've made a girl profess her love to me the first night I met her, all because of the way I wielded my fist. I'm only twenty-four, but let's just say I get around. I prefer being single because it gives me room to play the field without worrying about hurting anyone's feelings. I like to come home at six a.m. once in a while, do the quick two-hour catnap, shower, and change, using the memory of the night before to fuel me when the lack of sleep threatens to kick in. I'm the one my friends call on for advice, even referring me around to curious but shy friends: "Oh, call Caitlin, she'll know." Yes, that's me, the girl who's done just about everything (and everyone), whose little black book is actually a massive journal scrawled with names and stories and phone numbers and Polaroids, a glorious jumble of limbs and cocks and breasts and lips, ones I've never sought to try to untangle into a neat, chronological history.

Sex has always been the starting point, never the end, to any inquiry about who I am. It's the gateway drug to, well, more sex, to finding out more about how I operate, what buttons I like having pushed and which I set permanently to caution. This utterly carnal lifestyle is balanced by the hours-days-weeks-years' worth of fantasies that must jumble together until I'm compelled to act. I'm not just an ethical slut; I'm a thoughtful one too. The time I spend thinking about sex, pondering its every nuance and possibility, far exceeds the time I spend engaging in it, and I'm perfectly happy with that uneven ratio.

So, when Sally asked me what my deepest, dirtiest, darkest fantasy was during what had, up till that point, been a rather tepid game of Truth or Dare (bra size and taking one big bite of everything in the refrigerator among the highlights), I told her— and the whole room. "I want to do bukkake. I mean, be on the receiving end. I want to be lying naked on the floor and see a circle of cocks, all pointing at me. I want a round of boys to want me so badly they'll get naked in front of each other, press their dicks up in my face, while I beg them to come all over me. I want them to take turns shoving their cocks down my throat, slapping them against my lips, rubbing them on my skin, in my hair, doing whatever the hell they please. Maybe I'll be tied up, though then that would deprive me of the pleasure of giving two hand jobs at once. I don't know exactly how it would work, but it's been a mainstay of my fantasy life for years."

I paused, mentally highlighting my vision in my mind where they all started to spurt at once, barely giving me a chance to open up and say, "Aah." I swallowed hard and blinked rapidly, trying to get back into the present. "Yeah," I finished quietly, breathless, my eyes closed, almost ready to cry. Some fantasies are too primal, too out there, too real to ever admit—even to ourselves. But it was true; just thinking about all those anonymous cocks close enough to taste, close enough to smell, close enough to swallow, had my panties soaking wet.

I wasn't the only one who was intrigued with the idea. Everyone started asking me logistical questions, their eyes lit up, the tension in the room palpable, but I shushed them. "It's just a fantasy. You asked for the truth and you got it. If you really want me to go through with it, catch me next time I say 'dare.'"

I didn't mean to sound so haughty, but then again, I hadn't meant to reveal something so intimate when everyone else was only sharing the most superficial of details. I hugged my arms to myself, beyond blushing. What does it say about a girl that she dreams of jizz raining down her face, dreams of being a sex object in the most extreme fashion in the way that some girls dream of getting married? What does it say about me that after I went home, the idea just wouldn't go away? I'd thought it was one of those fantasies that could never come true, and even if it could, that it would be pushing things, even for me. Whoever heard of women willingly submitting to bukkake outside of porn? Maybe gay men, but that was okay. They'd be pigs among pigs (in the best possible sense of the word, of course). But who would I be in such a scenario? Could I ask men to degrade me and respect me and get off on me, literally, all at the same time?

Apparently, I could, because my gay friend Chip called me the next day and tried to sound casual about bringing it up. "God, Caitlin, when you said that, everyone in the room got a hard-on. Even Mikki," he said, referring to our most vanilla, conservative friend, who just happened to be a lesbian (but would never call herself a dyke). "Seriously. It wasn't just that we were getting off on the idea, but your voice got so breathy when you said it, like you were literally seeing yourself doing it in your head, not just spouting off some story you tell all the time to impress people."

"Thanks, I guess," I said, wondering what kind of can of worms I'd opened up. "But it's nothing, really. It's a fantasy."

"But what if . . . ?" His voice trailed off.

"What if *what*?" I hissed.

"What if you could actually do it? What if I found you hot, straight guys—big cocks guaranteed—who were into it? I'd so do that for you. All I'd ask is that I get to watch."

"Whoa, whoa, whoa . . . slow down there. You? Watching me? And where would these guys come from?" I was supposed to be suspicious, supposed to protest, but I was intrigued and knew from the pounding in my pussy I wasn't going to stop the thoroughly filthy path this conversation had taken.

"I know people, Cait, guys who'd love to jerk off over your pretty face."

"Like who?" I just couldn't imagine anyone we knew would actually volunteer for such a task, in the presence of other guys.

"Rob, for one."

"Rob? Hot Rob? Really?" My nipples hardened at the thought of bodybuilder Rob, always so brooding, silent, and hunky, being naked before me. I'd tried flirting with him in the past, but he seemed so stiff and quiet.

"Yes, Rob. I already asked," he said.

"What?" The word came out as a yell, but inside I was starting to get totally wet.

"And Rob can bring Jeremy and he said he has at least two other friends who are interested. They've all been tested and are single, so there'll be no jealous girlfriends butting in. And I have another friend, Omar, who wants in on it. I'll arrange everything; you just have to show up."

"Really? You'd do that for me? I mean . . ." I trailed off, not really sure what I meant since I'd never been in a situation remotely like this one before.

"Really, Cait, trust me. And it's not for you. Well, it is, but it's for us too. Believe me." We hung up and I slid beneath my quilt, letting my fingers plunge deep inside my wetness as I contemplated saying yes to making my fantasy come true. The answer was obvious.

I wound up letting Chip plan the whole thing, and when he was done in a week's time, he had five guys willing and eager to cover me in their come. It wasn't quite the dozen-man orgy of dick I'd fantasized about, but the fact is, we live in New

York, and a twelve-cock circle jerk along with spectators, and me, would probably have been too much to ask for. Five was manageable, a nice, albeit odd number, just slightly above four, which was still a respectable configuration. What we were about to embark on could even be called a sixsome, if that's a word, I told myself, and then Chip.

"Caitlin, let's face it. This is your big slutty night. Whether it's five or fifty cocks, it's still bukkake. Be proud, girl! Everyone I've told about this is totally jealous. You're gonna have the time of your life; don't downplay it. This is your chance to live out a fantasy you never thought you'd get to."

He was right. As his words burned in my ears, I went about cleaning up for what promised to be the party to end all parties. I had a few days, but I'd need them.

The night of the party, I was the perfect host. I prepared a spread of hors d'oeuvres, light snacks like veggies and fruit, some chips, some candy, and laid out soft drinks and a few beers, though I kept the alcohol light. I offered plenty of lube, flavored and not, condoms, in case one thing led to another, and some sex toys, including handcuffs. I'd thrown in the restraints I sometimes get shackled to my headboard with. Yes, I'd decided to do it where I'd be most comfortable, on my bed. Chip was there to oversee things and to get off on the spectacle. "What about this?" he asked, rummaging through my toy chest as only a gay man can, coming up with a red blindfold my ex had gotten me years ago. I didn't even know I still had it.

"But I want to *see* all those cocks," I said, already picturing the guys wanking away just for me. That was the part I liked the best; the men wouldn't just be jerking off, they'd be doing it with a purpose. I'd be the center of attention *and* get to feel wave after wave of hot come splashing across my face.

I'd always loved the depravity of shutting my eyes and submitting to that most intense of sensations. Even more than swallowing a lover's spunk, having him grace my cheeks, lips, even my hair with it made me feel at once worthy and degraded. I'd had lovers refuse to do it, unable to see me as the filthy whore I sometimes longed to be. One ex had chickened out at the last minute, able to paint my breasts creamy white but otherwise wanting to come only on my insides, not my outsides. Knowing men were being handpicked for this activity, men who'd want to be there, who'd know just how much I wanted it, was a truly special thing to contemplate. Utterly perverse, utterly fucked up, and utterly arousing all at once, all the more so because they weren't just horny beasts off the street but men I admired and respected enough to welcome into my home to defile me. Unless you know the thrill of pure submission, those two things may sound like opposites, but believe me, they're not. It takes a special, enlightened, intelligent kind of man to treat a slutty girl like me just right.

"Well, I'd recommend keeping the blindfold handy, both for you and for them. They may not be able to go through with it with you staring up at them. Plus, think about how your other senses will be enhanced by not being able to see." I shut my eyes and pictured myself surrounded by cock, pure cock. We were expecting the five guests who'd RSVPed, so that would be five dicks, five sets of balls, and hopefully five hot blasts of come streaming over my lips and the rest of my face. It was like a gangbang, but even better.

"Okay," I whispered, already feeling my body respond to the mere thought with an intense ache.

What does a girl wear to her very own bukkake party? I pondered, flipping through my closet and then my dresser drawers. Nothing seemed quite right, considering, but I didn't want to answer the door naked. I settled for a simple, sheer nightie in mint green, and almost as soon as I'd put it on, the doorbell rang. Chip had been urging me away from my makeup, against my natural instincts (how could I host a party with a bare face?), but now the doorbell had decided it.

The first guest to arrive was hot Rob, wearing basic jeans, sneakers, and a white T-shirt. He'd brought a friend who could've been his twin. Both were equally delectable.

"Welcome," I said, giving a small smile to the newcomer and a flirty wink to Rob. "I'm Caitlin," I said, sticking out my hand.

"Joe," he said, reaching forward and enveloping me in a hug. My body responded to his sheer size, and I wondered if his cock would match his heft.

Rob seemed to want in on the hugging action, and as soon as Joe put me down, he swept me up. "You look beautiful tonight, Caitlin," he said, possibly the longest sentence he'd ever bestowed on me.

"Rob," I said, smirking slightly, "you don't have to butter me up, you know. I'm a sure thing, tonight anyway."

"Look, I know that. And if you want the truth, I'm a little nervous. I've never been in a room full of cocks before."

"Well, if it makes you feel any better, neither have I," I said. Well, that wasn't strictly true; I'd been to orgies and sex parties where naked couples abounded, but none where I would be so close to dick, and I couldn't wait. "And . . . I've been especially looking forward to seeing what you've got under there," I said to him, lightly running my fingers over his package. He stirred beneath my touch and as a reward, I lowered the nightie so my boobs popped out. Rob leaned down and began sucking one nipple while I moaned. The doorbell rang, but I figured someone else would get it. I wasn't sure about proper bukkake party etiquette, but that seemed like an oxymoron if I'd ever heard one.

We continued to kiss and fondle each other, and I just shut my eyes and focused on Rob. That lasted all of a minute or two, until Chip was pulling me aside. "Save some room for the main course," he whispered. I giggled, then winked at him as I twirled around before clapping my hands and calling everyone to attention.

"Okay, boys, I guess we're ready to get started. I just want to thank you all for coming *(ahem)* and tell you how excited I am." With that I paused and made eye contact with each of the men whose cocks were soon going to be right up in my face. "The only rule I have tonight is that we're all here to have fun, and I want to make sure you're all comfortable. Does anyone have any questions?"

One guy, Jaime, raised his hand. "Can we come anytime we want?"

This was something I hadn't considered; I'd sort of assumed that they'd all jointly have the urge to splatter me with their jism . . . just like in the movies. But the question also granted me the power to answer, and thereby control his orgasm, and my pussy responded to this unexpected opportunity. "No." I looked directly into his eyes, then walked toward him, reaching under his shirt to twist his nipple. He whimpered, and I smiled. "No, Jaime, you're all going to come when I tell you to. Just because I'll be lying there aching to suck, lick, and feel your cocks doesn't mean I'm not in charge. If you want to stay at the party, you'll have to learn to wait."

The collective mood in the room went from excited to practically orgasmic as we all realized that this wasn't a prank but that we were all about to engage in something we'd only dreamed of. "Okay, then, I'll give you a few minutes to get naked. I'll be right over there," I said, pointing to my room. I wasn't sure how they wanted to handle that process, so I let them be while

I slipped out of my lingerie and looked down at my naked body. The slight curve to my belly felt sexy, and I slid my hand down over it to my mound, which sported just a few tufts of pubic hair.

I walked over to my bed, the scene of the crime, as it were, and lay down on my back. Chip placed the blindfold and a bottle of water near me, then kissed me on the cheek. "All those cocks are soon to be yours," he whispered to me, and I opened my eyes long enough to see that his own cock was extremely aroused. I began playing with myself, lightly stroking my clit, then running a finger along my slit, trying to be patient. As I glanced at the men as a group, they ceased to be individuals distinguishable by voice and looks and conversation. They were all equal, their cocks together forming a whole that would transport me into another dimension, or so it felt. I let myself sink fully into that fantasy, losing whatever shreds of propriety I was clinging to in order to make the most of this momentous opportunity, for that was what it was.

The first man to saunter over was Jaime, and I immediately felt a frisson of arousal as I looked at his cock. It was already hard, fat, and delicious-looking. I smiled at him, then rolled over to the edge of the bed, turned onto my side, and brought my mouth within sucking distance by way of greeting.

Without saying a word, he offered me his dick. Well, the head of it, anyway. His fist was wrapped around it and he fed it to me slowly. As I took the rounded tip in, then let my lips move down over the crown, I shuddered. Nothing makes me more aroused than wrapping my mouth around a man's hard cock. Today it didn't matter whose cock it was or what he thought of me or even how he was feeling. For once, it was okay for it to be All About Me, though I was sure the men would enjoy themselves as well. I immediately had to keep stroking myself as I swallowed Jaime's cock, his hardness making me frantic. Before I could really start bucking up and down though, he wrapped his fingers in my hair and pulled me away. His forcefulness combined with my now-empty mouth turned me on even more.

"Baby . . . if you want me not to come, you can't suck me like that. I'm only a man, after all," he said, taking a step back. I looked up at him, begging with my eyes, running my tongue over my lips, but he shook his head, seeming to take delight in withholding it. "Later," he murmured, and when I turned onto my back, I saw that another man was next to him and three more were on my other side, perched on the bed so they could be close enough. They were each stroking their cocks, almost tentatively, as if waiting for a cue from their comrades that they could go faster. I'd given up trying to distinguish whose cock was whose, because at that moment it just didn't matter.

I moved so I was facing the trio, my back toward Jaime and his pal. I opened my mouth and two men brushed their cocks against my tongue. I looked up and all I saw was dick, dick, dick, literally, as another one appeared near the others, trying to get inside, though as talented a fellatrix as I am, that would've been impossible. I could hear heavy breathing and pumping on the other side and Chip clapping in delight. "Give it to me," I said, stretching my mouth as wide as I could so those first two cock heads could fully enter my mouth.

This was much farther than I'd ever gone before, for even the largest cock I'd swallowed, and there had been some that had made me truly stretch my mouth, gag, and strain. That didn't come close to having two dicks jockeying for position. Soon I pulled back and kissed the three tips. I took the dildo I'd placed beside me and began working it into my pussy. I had lube nearby, too, but found that I didn't need it. I knew this wasn't the traditional version of this kind of gangbang, where the men's pleasure was paramount, but since I'd orchestrated this scenario, I wanted to reap the rewards. Far from being humiliated, I was overjoyed at getting to arrange this affair to my exact specifications, and the wetness I found between my legs proved it.

I was torn between closing my eyes and focusing on the feel and smell of so many cocks and seeing them in action. I sat up on one elbow, dildo inside me, and we all jerked off communally, grunting and grinding, hands flying over skin, slamming and jerking, violent words for harsh actions yielding dizzying results. I'd always found it to be true that a light touch may as well be a tickle; I need firm, steady pressure, and gazing upon these men with cocks in fists, apparently, they did too.

Under my observation, the men seemed to jerk their cocks faster, moving in sync almost. Someone crawled behind me and I lowered my head down to the sheet so his penis could rub against my forehead. That gave the others entrée to slide closer, hover directly on top of me, and slap their dicks against my face. I fucked myself with the dildo, wishing I had a vibrator because soon my hips were rising and crashing down against the mattress, my eyes tearing in ecstasy as all those penises suffused my senses. I turned my face slightly to the left and took the nearest dick into my mouth, easily swallowing its long, swollen length. Just then, I felt the first jet of cream land on my back, and I whimpered as best I could with a mouth full of cock. I looked up into the eyes of Rob, and he cradled the back of my head gently in his hand as I sucked him. This may sound crazy, but it felt spiritual to me, a moment of bonding that went far beyond the mechanics of sex. Or maybe I'm just the rare girl who can have a holy moment with five gorgeous cocks surrounding her.

I gave everything I had to Rob, slamming the dildo so deep inside me it bordered on pain, the best kind of pain, as I let him invade my mouth. I'd wanted this invasion, asked for it, negotiated it, and now I delighted in it, all of it. I moaned against his mouth, urging him to come down my throat, and my man of the moment obliged. The stream of hot liquid surged into my mouth and I swallowed, my cunt contracting around the dildo at the same time. Rob's release freed me to lean back and simply let the men take over. I surrendered to the glory of this unique situation and watched as one, then another, then yet another dick let loose until I was coated in sticky, white, beautiful come. I reached up and smeared it all over my face, and kissed whoever's lips moved forward to kiss mine. I didn't want to get up just yet; this sex spell was too beautiful to be broken. I lay there and smiled up at my suitors, my good-time guys, my bukkake boys, a grin covered with come, basking in pure bliss. It sure beat the hell out of most of my other sexual firsts. Chip winked at me, and I winked right back, reaching out my hands for whoever wanted to grab them.

BELTED

You'd never know the belt is there by looking at him. It's lost between his shirt and his pants, tucked away, hidden, pulled close, serving a dual purpose. You'd never know it's there, unless he made it a point of showing you. And he does, often, a hand resting there as a reminder in public, an intimation of what will happen in private. You have no idea how many other girls he makes a point of showing it to, but the reason you keep returning is that when you're with him, you don't care about the other girls. There could be hundreds, thousands even; as long as he looks at you the way he does when he unbuckles and unfurls the soft, worn, brown leather, then coils the belt purposefully around his hand, you can let yourself believe he wears it just for you.

This isn't the first belt that's been used to strike you. There was the boyfriend in college who had you bend over, skirt around your ankles, camera flashing, and belt lashing against your skin before plunging his oversized cock into your unprepared ass. He was all flash and no finesse.

Your lover is the opposite, or rather, flash and finesse mixed together in a dizzying way, with plenty of substance to back them up. He holds the belt like it belongs in his hand, like it's an extension of him. He tells you that he thinks about you every day when he loops it through his pants, when he touches the cool metal buckle. Alone in some room or another—never either of your bedrooms—your body reacts before you have time to consider its wisdom when you see him reaching for the buckle. After all, you know from experience that could mean anything—he's giving you his cock to suck, he's going to shackle your arms behind your back, he's going to pull your hair hard and slap your face until you cry, he's going to beat you until your skin is heated from the outside in. All of these are possibilities, and all of these bring you pleasure, but you hope it's the latter.

The belt is able to speak in ways that even the both of you, wordsmiths by trade, cannot always do. The belt is not a "toy" for "foreplay" but a separate part of your sex life, one that may appear at any moment. Its presence lurks while you casually sip your drinks at the bar, hidden but powerful; your fingers are itching to stroke it, if only so they can be slapped away. You never know if he will bring it out, how he will use it, how much of the belt and himself he will give you. You try not to be greedy, but you hope it'll be a moment like this: You're sore from having his cock inside you, from him holding you down, from his hand crushing your neck. Sore in a good way, so you almost don't even miss the belt—almost. You never have much time, can never stay overnight, have to steal hours out of other people's schedules to accommodate this affair, so you learn to take what you can get. You're wondering when he will have to leave, when this spell of lust will fade back into real life, when he reaches for the belt from the floor. "Turn over," he tells you, and you roll onto your stomach, your pale backside before him.

Your face is turned away from him, sunken into the softness of the pillow, freshly washed hair now tousled and messy. The tip of the belt rests against your newly shaved lips as you hear the words, "Spread your legs." You do, because you always do, because this is what your relationship is about: he orders, you obey, and you both like it like that. Your hands instinctively curl around the pillow, long nails digging into the cotton and feathers as you wait. The belt strikes the air and you shiver, feeling a breeze that may be a phantom one or may be very, very real. The next sound you hear coincides with a strike of the belt on your cheeks, both of them, a slice that takes a moment to process before you say the words almost automatically: "Thank you."

There's never a "You're welcome," or rather, not a verbal one. It's implied by the next stinging strike, by the fact that you're deemed worthy at all. He doesn't talk then, is almost solemn as you wait for it to be over with equal parts dread and glee.

But those kinds of smacks aren't what make you come. No, that's saved for when he makes you cry. You turn over and open your eyes for a moment to look at him, hovering over you. You marvel that you can feel so close when he's not touching you with his body at all. The belt is capable of magic. You start to shiver once you realize what's going to happen, that the belt is not just teasing your lips with a kiss, though you pucker up when it approaches.

Then the belt moves on to its real work, kissing your other set of lips harder, the equivalent of a shove-you-against-the-wall, bruising kiss. This kiss is merely an introduction, a warm-up. You know what's coming and even though you want it, you press your legs together involuntarily until he barks at you to put them back. You shut your eyes because you know you can't watch this. Your hands are twisted above your head, clinging to each other for some kinky version of safety. You focus on keeping your legs open, all of you exposed. When the belt strikes there, right there, you don't quite scream; it's more of a strangled, garbled cry. Your hand automatically goes to cover the sting, to cradle yourself. You finally get a "Good girl."

You try to turn over, to curl into a ball, but you're not allowed, or rather, your desire to prove yourself wins out over your desire to stop what's coming. You didn't travel for hours just to shy away from the pain. But you almost forget that when the next blow strikes. You wonder how the tender skin between your legs can stand that force, and then you stop wondering when the belt moves upward, to your breasts, your pebbled nipples no match for the blows. You arch your back and thrust upward, even though inside, you want to cower. You reluctantly remember telling him you wanted bruises there, marks you could proudly reveal with a hint of cleavage, a well-timed reveal as you lean over on the train. You still want the marks but breathe deep through your nose, twist your fingers more tightly around each other, to get through them. You bite your lip as the sweet pain of the belt heats your chest and wanders downward. You almost get used to the rhythm, your nipples stubbornly rising after each blow.

Then it's back down, back to the place that no longer feels like your cunt, not the way it's being set afire again and again. These lashes aren't as swift as the ones against your breasts, but they are sure, steady. He's not twice your size for no reason, and each slap strikes precisely where he wants it to. The tears finally appear in the form of sobs, traveling fast through your body, a current of energy you use to sustain yourself through the last few lashes. You'd think the pain would be a little more subdued, the pussy's diminishing law of returns, but no. You feel every ounce of force he uses for each stroke, every bite of the leather into your inner thighs, against your wetness. You have a vision of the belt wrapped around your throat, the buckle cold against your skin as you stare deep into his eyes, but that was another time, another place. The next blow has you thrashing so much he has to hold you down.

Is it the belt that makes you come? The leather, the thrash, the pain, the jolt? Is it the force behind it? Is it the noises he makes as he does it, the hitches of breath that are nothing like your shuddering sobs but are music to your ears nonetheless—is that what makes you finally go over the edge? Is it him holding you down, him promising you pain that may or may not come?

Maybe it's all of it, all the forces combining to make the orgasm nothing like what you were expecting, the kind where your body bonds with the belt, giving back some of its life force, only to have it beaten back into you. Though you know that logically, rationally, it's impossible, you hope the belt has absorbed some of your tears, has taken them and held on to them for next time, has put the pain that you mostly wanted, but kind of didn't, somewhere for safekeeping, somewhere he can hold next to his skin any time he desires.

Oh, it's not like you really have time to think all that or think anything, not then. The belt is reminding you, lash by lash, that you must stay open, stay ready, stay through the moments when you don't know how you will get through it, stay through the times you don't have a chance to take a bracing breath or perform any other magic tricks to turn the pain into something else. By now even the light touches, the strokes of the belt's rough edge against your fleshy inner thigh, the dance of the musky leather against your cheek, are enough to make you shudder, like when he raises his hand to smack you but stops right before his fingers reach the finish line. The effect is the same.

You breathe through your nose, a more refined type of breath, one granted you by the momentary lapse before the belt

is between your legs again, crashing hard, calling forth wetness you didn't know you still had. Pain, pleasure, obedience,
pride, love, hate, and fear ride each other along the waves of
your body until you hardly know who you are anymore. You've
moved beyond some simple goal of taking it into somewhere
else, somewhere you're afraid to look at too closely lest it prove
to be just a mirage.

And then, almost too fast, it's over. The belt lies limp on
the bed and you're allowed to press your legs together again, to
admire the bruises on your chest that you will wind up keeping
close like a secret. You wipe the tears from your cheeks, embarrassed but secretly pleased. What happens after that hardly even
matters, because that is what will remain, not the belt or the
pain or the marks, but the beauty of being transformed by each
of them into someone new, blossoming like the bruises on and
under your skin; traveling with him somewhere far away, somewhere magical no one else will ever visit, where each strike of
the belt serves to bind you together in this sensual cocoon, seal-
ing you in with its heat long after the physical marks drift away.

You hope it'll be something like that, but with him, you
never know what you're going to get, and you wouldn't have it
any other way.

I'LL HAVE
WHAT SHE'S
HAVING

S ome restaurants hire professional greeters, buy advertising, offer two-for-one deals, or make outrageous dishes designed to lure in tourists and those craving the latest culinary concoctions. I didn't do any of those things when I opened Sizzle, but I did hire Pam after watching from two tables over as she dined with her boytoy, Brad, one afternoon over a particularly languorous brunch at a low-key bistro I frequent. It was a holiday weekend and most New Yorkers were away, so I got to stare at her as she consumed a meal fit for a king—or a person twice her size. A fluffy omelet was brought out, along with a side of bacon, followed by a fruit and cheese plate, and waffles. Brad was sipping a cup of coffee and nibbling on a Danish, but like me, mostly he was watching Pam. And no, she didn't go in the bathroom and puke any of it up.

What Pam did was eat her meal with more gusto and sex appeal than I'd ever witnessed anyone consume anything. She had a serene glamour to her, and each bite of every single dish was savored obsessively, in the manner of a true foodie, with her eyes closed, her head tilted slightly, like the food was taking her to another planet, or maybe another dimension. She wasn't so much ignoring Brad as giving every ounce of her attention over to the meal. The chef in me was riveted, and the man in me was very, very aroused.

I wasn't the only one staring. Brad, who I'd later meet, eventually gave up on his Danish as Pam gave a performance that would've gotten Meg Ryan replaced on the set of *When Harry Met Sally*. Her sleek black bob shimmered in the light playing off her pale skin, her eyes were closed, and her head tilted back so we could practically see the food being swallowed. A quick survey of the room proved that many other diners had found their afternoon's entertainment, right in front of them, at no extra cost.

When Pam paused to take a sip from her lemonade, she used a straw, sucking from it in a way that made her cheeks pull in and imitated what she'd look like with her mouth stuffed full of cock. Whether she was trying to attract attention or not, Pam had almost all the eyes in the restaurant on her—I saw a waiter drop a whole tray of empties as he turned back for just one more peek at her.

Sizzle was all about the hot, the new, the now. I not only wanted the food to be spicy, bold, and edgy, but also to have the restaurant itself stand out in any way it could, from the flashing neon pink sign outside to the black-and-white décor inside. I wanted it to be a place where one could see and be seen, where the surroundings were as noteworthy as the food.

I approached Pam when Brad went to the restroom. "Hi," I said, slipping her a card. "I'd like to hire you to work at my new restaurant." I put my hand up and cleared my throat. "Before you object, let me assure you I don't mean as a server or hostess.

Those jobs would not come anywhere close to maximizing your talents. I want you to be the centerpiece of the restaurant, a bit of advertising genius. Your job will be to eat, just like you did today. If you didn't know already, everyone in here was staring at you. They were drawn to you. I want you in my prime window seat, looking sexy and glam and powerful and hungry. All you have to do is eat, slowly and deliberately. Think of it as performance art, if you'd like, and feel free to dine with whoever you like as long as you are constantly putting something in that beautiful mouth of yours. Your boyfriend is more than welcome," I concluded, even though, if I were to be honest, I already wanted her mouth for myself.

I finished my pitch in a rush of words and then realized I hadn't even told her my name. "I'm Alan Oliver, by the way."

"He's not my boyfriend, just a man with a very beautiful cock I like to play with. And yes, I recognize you," she said, and didn't need to elaborate; I'd done a few stints on *Top Chef* and was hoping to ride that buzz for my latest endeavor. "Well, apparently this is my lucky day. I just got fired from my design job and have been trying to figure out where to go next, not to mention stocking up on pasta and peanut butter. This was a little escape. I'm familiar with your work. I'm into the idea . . . but this sounds a little outrageous. How much would I have to eat? I don't want to get fat." She managed to say all of that, from "cock" to "fat," without losing an ounce of her calm assurance.

"I'll buy you a gym membership, and we'll do small plates, whatever you'd like, on the menu or off."

After just a little negotiating, I hired Pam for a regular forty-hour workweek, telling her she should bring a guest, unless I'd lined someone up, so it wouldn't look odd to see such a gorgeous woman dining alone repeatedly. I placed her in the prime seat from day one; she was our first customer, much to the chagrin of an eager-beaver middle-aged balding foodie who showed up right on the dot of eleven on opening day, tossing a look Pam's way as if to say, "Who'd she blow to get that table?" The truth was, all she'd blown on was the steaming bowl of cauliflower soup I'd just served her along with a salmon tartar salad and glass of jalapeño lemonade. Her friend Andrea joined her soon thereafter, dressed in an orange pantsuit that billowed, drawing even more attention.

I didn't have time to stare at her every minute, but I could tell that just having her in place was enough to draw curious passersby from the street, and to keep their attention once they entered. If a woman as beautiful and glamorous as Pam was glued to her seat, with waiters serving up seemingly nonstop delights to her table, they might just have to check out the hot new restaurant for themselves. Brad joined her for dinner, and I watched her lean back while he cut her steak, a move of either gentlemanly deference or submissive training. Either way, it made her power over me complete.

The place filled up quickly that first day and soon we were booked a week in advance. As we got into the swing of things, I let Pam rotate her position, trying out the bar and other seats, but wherever she was, she failed to blend. She stood out even when she switched her normally bright red lipstick for a pale pink or retro white. She had the magic touch, and the gossip columns were even starting to wonder who exactly this elegantly appointed, sexy, middle-aged woman with the black bob, designer outfits, and nonstop appetite was. She made it into Page Six with a cup of Starbucks coffee and a doughnut in her hand; "Sizzle style maven slums it" read the headline. My plan had worked! Of course, maybe Sizzle would've been a stunning success without Pam—I'll never know—but with her there, I not only had an on-demand food tester but the most gorgeous eye candy I could imagine, something that came in handy after a long day putting out fires, literal and otherwise.

One day I got an unexpected request. An older businessman, his salt-and-pepper hair and deeply tanned skin probably putting him at sixty, asked if Pam was available as a dining companion. "What do you mean?" I replied, trying to play it cool. Was it that obvious that she was an employee rather than simply a very enthusiastic customer? And exactly what kind of companion did he have in mind?

"Well, I've seen her here every time I've walked in and she looks like she'd be a delight to dine with. I'd pay for the meal, and for her time. That's all I want, truly. I'm divorced and don't tend to meet women so easily these days." His look turned urgent. "I've never done anything like this before, but I'm drawn to her. I watch her every time I eat here and, well, let's just say it's enhanced my dining experience." I let my eyes roam out the doorway to survey the room and indeed, most of the men and many of the women were watching Pam, their gazes flickering toward her as she consumed each bite as if it were her last, her only. She ate everything from her spicy shrimp gazpacho to her poached halibut to her lemon meringue tart and fruit and cheese plate with a theatrical flourish. My own cock twitched as she speared a raspberry with a fork and popped it between her lips. She smiled at me as if we shared a secret as she sprinkled some sugar on her strawberries.

"Excuse me for a moment." Her friend had left before dessert, so I was able to catch Pam alone.

"You're a very popular girl tonight. That man in my office wants to have dinner with you. Right here, right now. Well, I'm pretty sure he wants to do more than have dinner with you, but that's what he's asking."

"So, I'm good at oral, is that what you're saying?" She

laughed loudly enough to fill the space around her, and let me
see her tongue stained slightly red. "Don't worry, I'm not going
to say no. I'm happy to have some company. Brad found someone a little more available. But I think this calls for a special
request from the kitchen."

"Anything you like, my dear." Her brown eyes twinkled at
me, flirting. I knew she knew I was hard; the truth was, I hadn't
fucked anyone since I'd hired her. While in the kitchen dreaming up new recipes, I'd picture her eating them, or rather, picture me feeding them to her, picture that orgasmic look on her
face when she tasted something truly divine.

"I'm pretty easy, actually," she said. "I'd like some turkey
meatballs in spicy tomato sauce, a side of your wonderful sau-
téed spinach, wasabi mashed potatoes, and then a rich dark
chocolate mousse for dessert."

"I don't know if I'd ever call you easy, Pam, but that is certainly something I can whip up." One thing I'd come to appreciate about Pam's palate is that she was game for trying my most
ambitious concoctions, and would give me her honest opinion,
while maintaining a poker face as she sat in public, but could
appreciate hearty, homespun meals as well.

"What's the man's name?"

"Peter," I said, then paused. "You don't have to do this, Pam.
It's not in your job description."

She took out a compact and sheer lip gloss I'd seen her apply
repeatedly over the course of the last month; she'd told me she
used a long-lasting lipstick to keep her lips red throughout her
meals. "I know I don't have to. I want to. I like eating the food
you make. Even when you just tell someone else to make it." The
look she gave me pierced me; she was clearly saying so much
more. "Maybe we could eat together sometime. Not here, not a
work thing," she said. "I could even cook."

I walked closer, the hum of the restaurant fading in the background. "I'd like that very much," I said, longing to touch her shiny hair for myself, finally, to get lost in those glorious lips. At first, yes, I'd pictured her on her knees, using those lips to take my cock between them, but after watching how she held herself, my thoughts had drifted. Now I wanted to taste her, kiss her, devour her all over.

First, though, I had to take care of my customer. I returned and told Peter that Pam would be happy to dine with him, then relayed her requested menu. "That sounds wonderful," he said, his eyes taking on a far-off look.

"No funny business," I warned, even though it wasn't my place to dictate that, especially if they left together. I hoped it would come across sounding protective, paternalistic even, rather than perverse. I was her boss, nothing else, yet it felt like a more intimate relationship. I'd spent so many stolen moments staring at her as I surveyed Sizzle or sat taking a meeting, my gaze drifting toward her. She was never overly loud, and even those times when she should've blended with the rest of the crowd, she never did, not for me. Without being overly dramatic, she still managed to command attention, as if she were sending out signals to other diners to indicate that they may be sharing the same food, but she was enjoying it infinitely more than they were.

"I wouldn't dream of it. I'll leave her to you," Peter said with a knowing look. Okay, my jig was up, but I would still get the pleasure of watching the two of them together. Never had my voyeuristic side been quite so engaged as it was when I watched Pam—and watched others watching her. It was a ripple effect, and seeing the joy she brought others not only enhanced our collective dining experiences but made her seem like a special prize, a woman whose lips were in much demand.

I oversaw the preparation of the meal, whipping up the special sauce myself, adding some rare spices for a kick I knew Pam would appreciate. As I tasted my red, bubbling concoction, I wished it were me sitting across from her, feeding her, watching so many emotions play across her face as she dined. I set the dish of meatballs, the sides, along with the mashed potatoes, on a tray and brought it over myself. There was a smile on Pam's face already that caused me to look below the table; they were playing footsie!

Rather than be jealous, though—after all, I was twenty years younger than Peter and ran my own set of successful restaurants—I was again aroused by proxy. "Thank you," they both said at the same time, and I was forced to retreat. I went into my office and watched on the hidden camera I'd installed; I wouldn't go so far as to record conversations, but I had the pleasure of seeing Pam's face in black and white as she dished out meatballs, mashed potatoes, and spinach evenly among the two plates. She nodded her head to indicate he should eat first.

Then Pam cocked her head slightly, awaiting her companion's impression. Only after he smiled did Pam set about starting her meal, while I again marveled at her stomach's ability to put away enough food for three women and still remain trim. As she ate, I watched closely. She lacked a poker face, so each mouthful made a significant impression on her face, and when she closed her eyes, it was clear she was trying to deconstruct the meal in her mouth, to break it down to its component parts, solve the culinary mystery even as she savored the mix of textures and flavors. I wondered what she would taste like; I'd been close enough to smell her coconut-scented skin a few times, but what about her lips, her tongue, her mouth, her sex? Were they warm and spicy and delicate like flowers? Was she reminiscent of our chilled cucumber soup or more like our mole sauce?

I found my hand going to my cock, grateful for the privacy of the small room, as I watched her taste each and every part of the meal. When she held a forkful of spinach up to her nose and simply sniffed, I was a goner. I came in my hand, then looked around for a way to clean up.

I wiped my hand on a towel and pressed the intercom to tell Greg, my most handsome waiter, to serve the dessert. I'd made extra chocolate mousse, not because I had anything close to an appetite, but because I hoped she'd like it and would want more.

Finally, their meal was over, which was my cue. I went to shake Peter's hand, telling him the meal was on the house. He looked like he was in a food coma, his eyes slightly glazed over, as he thanked me profusely and promised to return very soon.

Dinner hour was winding down and Pam's official duties were over. I hoped she would still want to share herself with me. "Well, you sure do know how to follow orders, Alan," she said.

"I do?"

"Yes. Maybe you're so used to giving them that you know what it's like. What I'm trying to say is the food was delicious." She just sat there, smiling at me. "But I think you're going to have to fire me. Because otherwise we might wind up engaging in some improper workplace behavior."

"Like what?" I asked like an idiot. I thought she wanted to cook for me at her place.

"I can't wait," she said, as if reading my mind. "I want you now. Sit down." Even though we were still open, I followed her command. "I'll have to cook for you another time. Right now, I want to watch you, since you've been so studiously watching me. Yes, I've noticed." She laughed, a sound that immediately cut me down to size—but didn't cut down on my erection in any way.

She then signaled a waiter and reeled off the priciest dishes on my menu, including the fifty dollar hamburger—not that I

cared. I'd happily pay just to be in her company. I could feel
the stares of everyone around us. Then I felt her foot in my lap.
"Rub my feet while we wait. I want you to be on display for a
change. I've been thinking about what you look like naked . . .
maybe coated in chocolate mousse. What a pretty picture that
makes," Pam said, her voice dreamy with desire. "And by the
way, I want a raise. I know exactly what's going on here, and I
think your business would go way down if I wasn't sitting here
doing my best to eat as slowly as humanly possible. Don't get me
wrong, your food is divine, but still, a girl wants something else
in her mouth once in a while."

I tried to focus on her feet, on digging my knuckles into her
skin, wanting to see if I could make her lose her cool, even just for
a minute. I knew that even though we were mostly hidden, there
was still an air of danger in what I was doing; should someone
notice my hands moving, or pick up on the sexual tension between
us, I could be in trouble—but Pam was worth it. Instead of breaking her calm, though, she just stared at me. The burger arrived but
I had no appetite, not for food—but I couldn't refuse it without
losing her and looking like I was the type of chef who preferred
McDonald's. Under her gaze, I lifted the burger, realizing this
was the first time I'd truly gotten to sit in my own restaurant and
relax. Well, relax may be overstating it, because my senses were
on high alert, but I wasn't thinking business, just pleasure.

I had to shut my eyes eventually as her stare became too
intense—and because her foot was pressing against my cock. I
took several slow bites of the burger, relishing the mix of tastes
on my tongue. When I opened my eyes, she was offering me a
fry and licking her lips. This was food as foreplay, no doubt
about it. Disregarding everything around me, I let her feed me,
her fingers brushing my lips and tongue.

I was sure everyone had to be watching us when that

happened, because even that simple act Pam managed to imbue with so much eroticism, I felt like I was eating something much more sensual than a fried potato. She savored the act as much as she savored each bite of food, making each second count. I was suddenly sure that even if someone were watching us, like Peter my customers would fall under Pam's spell just as surely as I had. "How do you like it, Alan? How do you like having everyone watch every bite you eat, thinking about your mouth, what it tastes like, how warm and wet it is? I know that's what you think about. I see you watching me."

"I like it," I said. "I mean, I like you. I've wanted you since that first day I talked to you. I'll fire you if I have to. I just want to taste you, to smell you, to savor you." I couldn't hold the burger in my shaking hands so I sliced off a piece to stuff in my mouth before I embarrassed myself further. Pam signaled over her head and soon my plates were being whisked away.

Greg was saying, "I'll take care of things, sir." How she had signaled all of this to him with a wave of her fingers, I didn't know, but I followed her out.

She didn't speak to me as we walked two blocks to a high-end hotel, where, after requesting a room with a window facing the busiest street, she stepped aside and I whipped out my credit card. She handed me her purse to carry, even though it was a light one; I'd have crawled on my hands and knees to follow her into the room. Turns out, Pam's an attention-magnet even when she's not eating. She slipped the key card in the door and the minute it was closed she had me on my knees right in front of the giant glass window. We were on the sixth floor, high enough that probably no one could see us very closely, but low enough that they could guess what was going on. "Put your hands behind your head. I just want your mouth, the way you just wanted mine," she said.

Then she hiked up her skirt and pushed down her black mesh lace panties. I barely had a minute to glimpse the strip of dark pubic hair against her pale skin before she was straddling my face and giving me the meal that had inspired my cooking ever since we'd met. No, none of my dishes were exactly reminiscent of the slippery wetness of her pussy, of the salty tang of her sex, but the tingling I felt on my tongue and throughout my body was exactly what I'd been looking to evoke with my menu. Pam grabbed my short hair and rammed my tongue deeper into her. "Harder," she commanded.

That made sense; a woman like Pam wouldn't want a slow, sensual licking, the way she took her time eating the food I prepared for her. She was done being slow, and so was I. I grabbed her hips and sucked her clit between my lips, then my teeth, loving the way she trembled above me. Now she was holding on to me so she wouldn't fall, and I dared to add a finger to my oral explorations, followed by two. Soon my tongue was slithering into her cunt along with my fingers, when I wasn't feasting on her clit. Her hand moved to my cheek, slapping me and making me almost come in my pants.

When she realized how much I liked it, she kept slapping me, even going so far as to ease my face out from between her legs so she could look at my glossy lips and give my cheek the full force of her hand. The thought of a stranger seeing that through the window made my whole body buzz with excitement. It's one thing to be owned by a woman, to be fully at her mercy, but it's another thing to have the whole world, or even a slice of it, know that. I'm not sure how many times I made her come, only that each climax worked its way through my body too, from my nose to my lips on down. I shuddered right alongside her, my mouth glued to her until she finally pushed me away.

"Now for dessert," she said, and proceeded to drag me by

my cock over to the full-length closet mirror. She took it out and we both watched in the mirror as she wrapped her hand around my shaft and jerked me with firm, even strokes. She put my hand where hers had been and then took off her blouse and bra, leaving her natural breasts hanging there, the nipples hard and firm. She wrapped her breasts around my hardness and I was soon enveloped in the softness of her beautiful flesh. When she told me to come, I had no choice, even though I could've stayed in that glorious position for hours, it seemed. I watched as my cock let out streams of white cream all over her breasts, painting them. And then she stood and once again brought my head down, this time to lick up my own come. I'd fed it to girls, the horny kind who got off on it, before, and had taken a stray taste or two, but had never been with a woman like Pam, one who was adamant about me being an equal opportunity come drinker. I licked off every drop until her breasts were again bare, with only traces of my saliva to show what we'd just done.

She hummed to herself as she got dressed. "I'm going to keep the job. But I want my own menu item. I want to share myself with your customers. I want you to call it, 'I'll Have What She's Having.' I want it to be something so rich, so amazing, so much of an aphrodisiac that it'll make them have a mouth orgasm and be so turned on they'll have to leave as soon as they finish it."

"It's a deal," I said, before rushing back to the restaurant, which my staff had locked up for me, in order to concoct my most perfect recipe yet.

HANDS DOWN

Gretchen and I have a pretty conventional relationship, on the surface at least; we're in our late twenties, got married after a year of dating (three years ago), we plan on having kids, we both work high-pressure, high-power jobs in media, which often require late nights to meet deadlines. On the surface, we look like young, fresh-scrubbed, all-American white yuppies— at least, that's what my brother in Santa Cruz, a tanned surfer with blond stubble and a laid-back attitude, tells me, when I see him at Christmastime. But what he doesn't know, and very few others do, is that beneath our sunny surface, we have a dark side. Well, maybe dark isn't the right word, exactly—kinky is. We like to play, and play hard, and after a long day, few things soothe me more than a nice cold beer and watching Gretchen writhe when I tie her to the bed, or a chair, or simply order her to stand against the wall while I beat her, and if she dares move, I shackle her wrists together and use a spreader bar to keep her in place. She loves playing just as much as I do, if not more.

Recently, though, I decided I wanted to do something a little bit new for us by taking our bondage play out into the world—well, the world of hip, downtown New York City. I would get to see a new side of my gorgeous, kinky wife, and to see what happens when I unsettle her, shake things up, show her just how mischievous I—and she—can be. I didn't want us to be one of those couples who falls into a rut, even if it is a rut filled with spanking, bondage, dirty talk, and rough sex. I wanted to bring our kind of sexy fun into an unknown arena, and our upcoming date night was the perfect place.

We settle in at Joe's Pub, but as Gretchen's hand reaches for the menu, I tug it down under the table, as surreptitiously as I can. It's pretty dark where we're sitting; I'll need the candle to read the selections, not that I really care. My cock is getting harder by the second as I reach for her other hand and smoothly slip out her wrap-around silver bracelet, the one I've tucked into my jacket pocket, winding it around her wrists. Ever since she'd bought it a few weeks ago, I'd been intrigued with its erotic possibilities, and I'd held it in my hands, twined it around my own wrists, marveled at how pliable the coils of silver were. It was almost as if the jewelry maker had known the potential "trouble" it could cause—if by "trouble" I mean the most naughty of pleasures.

Before Gretchen can process what I've done, her hands are secured in her lap. She looks at me like she wants to laugh, or stick out her tongue, but I give her a calm smile and reach over to pinch her inner thigh. "I'll take care of you tonight; you just sit back and relax. Don't drink too much, though, because you're not getting up until the show's over." Of course, I'm bluffing; if she's on the verge of having an accident, I'll let her get up, but she'll have to beg.

I make a deliberate show of reaching for the menus and spreading Gretchen's open before her, since she's incapable of doing so herself. "You just tell me what you want," I say with a wink. I often advise her to tell me what she wants when we're in bed; she knows that ultimately, I'm the one who will decide if she gets it or is made to wait. The look on her face is priceless; she can't decide whether to whine in protest or indulge in the arousal I'm sure is already starting. I tap my fingers against the table as I turn my menu over to look at the cocktails. Just the act of immobilizing my wife has me hard, like the air around us has changed, becoming charged with the tension my simple yet powerful act has provided. I'm tempted to twitch the tablecloth so the couple at the next table over can get a peek. Instead, I make my own selection and lean in close for Gretchen to tell me what she wants, but she just lets out a little moan.

"Like that, don't you?" I ask, even though I know the answer. "Just so we're clear, if you really need to escape, I'm sure a smart girl like you can figure out how to, but I'm also pretty sure a smart kinky slut like you wouldn't want to deprive herself of having me take care of you all night." The words make her breath catch, and I reach for her inner thigh and pinch it to emphasize my warning. Feeling her smooth, soft skin with the pads of my fingers while the back of my hand brushes the bracelet makes me let out a deep breath, an image flashing in my mind of Gretchen bound with her hands behind her back sucking me off under the table while I guide her with a hand in her hair. That's the thing about playing with her—one naughty action always leads to another, a dirty domino effect that I can't stop, not that I would want to.

Gretchen's eyes bug out even more when our waitress walks over, her waist-length black hair flying around her, revealing a glorious array of ink along her shoulders and back. She places

water glasses on our table. "What can I get you?" she asks, pen
poised at the ready.

"I'll have the antipasto platter and a mojito," I say, "and
my wife will have the deviled eggs combination and a sparkling
raspberry cosmopolitan." There are other items on the menu
I know she'd have enjoyed, but these I can feed to her easily
and inconspicuously, unlike the pasta or spinach salad, what
she'd normally order. The waitress smiles at us and hurries off
to place our orders, none the wiser to our little game, I don't
think. I scoot closer to Gretchen and smile at her; the lighting is
dim, but I can still tell she's blushing. "Having fun?" I whisper
in her ear, keeping my mouth there so I can breathe against the
sensitive area.

"I'm going to get you back for this," she says, though I'd bet
money she doesn't mean it. Gretchen's a Type A powerhouse
at work, and sometimes it's hard for her to let go of work even
when we're enjoying a night out. My job in our relationship is
to force her hand—in this case, hands, literally—to relax. One
thing I've learned about bondage over the years is that it doesn't
work, in any form, if you tense up. For it to work its full magic,
seducing both parties into the glorious give-and-take of posses-
sion and surrender, you can't fight it, which is one of the things I
love best about restraining such an eager bottom; I'd never want
to engage in bondage with an unwilling participant. Gretchen,
though, was seemingly born for bondage. All it takes is a little
bit of restraint, and it's like a switch is turned and she's ready
for anything. The very act of keeping her still, locking her in
place, prompts her mind to slip out of overthinking mode and
her body to slip into full feeling mode. I'm not sure if she knows
it, but there's a visible difference when she crosses over, submits
not only to me, but to the adventure bondage promises. There's
a little bit of her good-girl nature that resists every time, until

the overwhelming need she has to be taken, controlled, and cor-
ralled wins out. If we were in a cartoon, this is when the light
bulb would go on over her head.

Sometimes I don't even tie her up at all, just order her to stay
still, and then have fun with her. I'll tickle her, or spank her—
sometimes I lick her pussy until she screams, as long as she stays
in place; one small move on her part and I instantly stop, even if
it pains me to do so. I can't do any of those things right now, so I
take an ice cube from the glass of water in front of me and slide it
along the side of her neck. "Don't want you to get overheated," I
whisper. She giggles softly, and I'm thinking about how quickly
this cube would melt if I placed it between her legs. Instead, I
trail it along her cheek for a moment before casually slipping it
into her lacy bra, the delicate lilac one I saw her slip on as she
got dressed and had to grab her and bite each nipple through
the lace before letting her return to getting ready. Thankfully
her black top has enough coverage that I can get away with it
without exposing either of us as inveterate perverts.

I pull back just as the lights go all the way down and the
singer steps forward, pure glam with bold red lips that beckon
to every corner of the room, blonde hair piled atop her head,
what seems like a ball gown on, complete with a slit up the side,
as she greets her audience. "I bet she'd know what to do with
you," I whisper to Gretchen as I pick up another ice cube, this
time slipping it under the table and into the palm of her hand.
I press my palm against hers, feeling the dripping water melt
against our skin.

If we were home, I'd surely take an ice cube and slide it along
her pussy lips, tracing them until she squirmed and moaned,
then press it inside her. I've done it before and it never fails
to amuse me to watch her squirm, tightening around the cube,
seeming to want to both draw it deeper and expel it, process-

ing the cold assault on her senses. And surely if, right now, her hands were free, the right one would be between my legs, teasing me, making me harder; she's as skilled at the subtle art of semi-public displays of affection as I am. I maneuver up her thankfully short skirt and manage to deposit the ice cube into her panties, just as I did with her bra earlier, and bring my fingers back to hers. She clasps one, digging her nails into my skin. The sharpness spikes its way through me, and I lean against her as the singer oozes seduction as she starts to sing—and strip. She's down to a gorgeous black camisole, black panties, and garters attached to leopard-print stockings by the time the first song ends, and I raise my hands above my head to clap, a sharp contrast to what Gretchen can do.

"Didn't you like that song, baby?" I ask softly, just as our waitress appears. Our water glasses are in the way, and I deliberately move each one as she sets the plates and cocktails before us. The waitress lingers for what feels like a moment too long, and the tension passes from Gretchen to me, but I know that for every actual bit of fear she feels, there's even more excitement. And it's not like we're doing anything illegal or even dangerous; she knows she can get away if she truly wants or needs to, and that I would help her do so if there were a fire drill or something. I would never do anything to harm her, and in fact, it's her willingness to do this even when with a rustle of our tablecloth someone could easily catch on that makes me truly excited.

I take Gretchen's drink and bring it to her lips, watching them part just enough to pour some chilled red liquid into her mouth. I picture the singer taking a turn feeding my beautiful wife and then it's no leap to picture my cock pressing between Gretchen's gorgeous lips, the singer stroking her hair. I set her glass down and take a sip of my own drink, before picking up my fork.

"Hungry?" I ask as my fingers drift into her lap, brushing against her makeshift bonds—I can't seem to stay away. The show only lasts an hour and a half, yet I'm the one finding the delicious agony almost interminable. The longer we sit here, the more I want Gretchen, in ways that are fully unfit for public consumption.

"I'm starving," she says with a smile, as the next set starts and the singer is back in a pale pink sheath dress that clings to her perfectly. Gretchen and I have only had a threesome once, but talking about and checking out hot women sets her off. I pick up a deviled egg and bring it to her lips. As she takes a bite, out of the corner of my eye I see a woman at a nearby table looking at us, and I whisper as much to Gretchen. Whether or not this woman knows Gretchen's hands are secured in her lap, my feeding her is clearly risqué, even for this hip crowd.

"Do you want the whole thing?" I ask as she savors the creamy confection. She opens wide and I push the rest of the egg between her lips, her tongue brushing my fingers in the process. I smile at the woman who was watching us, then give my full attention to the singer. She's beckoned a man onstage to help her change into an elaborate pair of heels, and he kisses the tops of her feet as he exits.

We keep watching as the blonde bombshell swoons and flirts her way through everyone from Marilyn Monroe to Britney Spears to Beyoncé. Gretchen doesn't know it, but I have a surprise for her when the singer asks for a female volunteer. Suddenly, I raise Gretchen's bound hands above her head, and immediately, the whoops and hollers from the neighboring tables cause her to look up at us, followed by a spotlight. "Oh, my," giggles the singer. "You with your hands tied, get up here," she says. I pull Gretchen's hands down so I can undo the bracelet, but I quickly coil it around her arm and send her down to the stage.

I watch proudly as she gets a whooping round of applause, and the singer admires the bracelet and even sticks out her wrists so Gretchen can show her how it works. Then they go behind a screen and the singer changes outfits while asking Gretchen questions, using the microphone so we can all listen to her responses. Hearing my wife confess to having had her hands bound beneath the table almost makes me come. When Gretchen returns, I don't care who's looking anymore, and I give her a full-on tongue kiss.

The show is thankfully winding down. We get the check, which also contains a note from our waitress saying, "HOT!!" I give a generous tip and lead Gretchen outside. "Let's take a cab," I say, even though we'd normally walk. I've already flagged one before she can protest. "Ladies first," I say, and once we're settled in, knowing I only have a few minutes, I reach for the bracelet and bring her hands behind her back. Soon her wrists are secured there, her body turned so she's facing the window, her back toward me.

"You were so damn hot in there tonight," I said. "I bet you had all the women jealous."

"I just hope nobody we know was there," she says, as if she really has some problem with it.

"So what if they were?" I ask.

I breathe hotly against her neck, and maneuver myself so she's close enough to feel how hard I am. We pull in, and I give the driver a twenty-dollar tip on a seven-dollar fare. "I'll come around and let you out," I tell Gretchen, and then do so, lifting her up and keeping my arm around her, nudging the cab door closed with my hip. I walk behind her, my hand on her lower back, and guide her up to the elevator and into our apartment.

"You're wearing too many clothes," I tell her, easing down her skirt and panties. She wiggles out of them, and I can't resist reaching between her legs to make sure she's as wet as I've been imagining. No—she's wetter, and I ease two fingers in and out a few times until she moans and starts to buck back against me. "Later," I growl, and instead of going into the bedroom, I pull her onto the living room couch. "Now you get to see what that did to me," I say, as I slip off my pants and briefs to reveal my cock at full mast. "You're going to suck my cock the way I thought about you doing under the table tonight. Maybe next time I'll have you actually do it." I guide her to the ground, and pull her toward me so she's in the perfect sucking position. Watching her ease her tongue up my shaft, knowing she is achingly wet, hungry to have me fill her up, and she can't do anything about it, adds to my arousal. I let her get my cock nice and juicy, but when she goes to deep-throat me, I pull her upward by the hair. "Just the tip, baby," I order, and she dutifully runs that sweet tongue along the hard ridge of my cockhead. Her mouth is wet, too, the saliva dripping onto me, and the heat so intense I might come before I'm ready. When the sensation is almost too much, I pull her off of me and slap my cock against her cheek, making her moan.

The look she gives me is one of pure longing. "I know you love feeling me fuck your mouth, but I want to fuck that hot, tight pussy of yours." I'd been planning to finish in the bedroom, but I can't wait. I lean down and lift her up, settling her legs on either side of me, her wrists still secured behind her back. We've never fucked quite like this—usually she's bound to the bed, spread eagled, but this is wickedly arousing too. I lift up her shirt and bite her nipples through the lace of the bra, while Gretchen raises her hips and slams herself down onto me. I bring my mouth to kiss her lips, her tongue racing to meet mine, and reach for her bound wrists behind her. I don't need to order her to come; I can feel the heat and trembling building inside her, and I crush her fingers in mine as the sensation builds before she collapses against me. "That's it, good girl," I tell her before I explode inside her. I ease the bracelet off her arms, letting it drop on the couch next to us, then pick her up and carry her into the bedroom. I pull her close, kissing her wrists, fully aware this has been one of our hottest date nights ever.

Later, before we drift off to sleep, I say, "You'll have to tell me the name of the store where you got that bracelet. I want to see what else they sell."

We both know we don't technically need any additional toys to embellish our bondage fun. All we really need is each other, but some extra help can never hurt. Plus, I know the perfect pair of nipple clamps she can wear while we shop. Now that we've ventured into "playing" in public, I certainly don't want to stop. The fun has only just begun.

THE END

It doesn't help that she looks more beautiful now than ever. Her face glows with a natural tan and the sweetest smile I think I will ever see, her blue eyes shining at me with need and want and love and pain. I want to feel as if we are our own entity, existing in a private universe that nothing and no one else can pierce. That life is all about looking at her, in her, nothing more, nothing less. Without makeup, she is the perfect combination of girl and woman, and she fills me with a need to hold and protect her that leaves me raw and open and more vulnerable than a person should ever be.

I know all the right moves to make, the ways to touch her, the strokes that will make her melt and move and clutch me as if she will need me forever. I know how she wants it. I need to feel as if I'm the only one who can give it to her. I live for those times when she grabs me and looks as deeply inside me as I am inside her.

As she lies there, so small, so seemingly fragile, her doll's body looks like some alluring creature, one that I might break if I handle it improperly. I can easily forget the core of strength and stubbornness she possesses. Spread out in front of me, she is truly the girl of the dreams I never knew I had. I slide my fingers inside her, pushing deep into her core, knowing just where to curve and bend to get to where I want to be. I've never known another woman's body quite like this, navigating her pussy as easily as I trace my fingers over her face, reading her like a well-worn page of a beloved book, instantly, easily.

At this moment, with her hair messy and tangled like an over-worked Barbie's, I want to grab it as I've done so many times before, to pull fiercely and then bring her head down into the pillow, to live up to the violent promise of this situation. I almost pull away, because I am not that kind of girl. I'm still getting used to being the girl who wants to hurt someone else, who feels a distinct kind of awe when I hear the sound of my hand slamming down against her ass. I'm still getting used to being the girl who likes giving it rough, who likes to claw and scrap, who sometimes wants to slap her across the face. The girl who got the slightest thrill when she cried the other day while I spanked her.

I see the collar next to the bed glittering brightly. It meant everything when I fastened it around her neck those countless weeks ago, transforming the airport bathroom into our own private sexual sanctuary. Now, it is too bright, too accusatory, a mistake in so many ways. Like the sweetest of forbidden fruit, her neck beckons, so white and exposed, pulsing with veins and life and want. Now when I see her neck, tender and ever-needy, I can barely go near it. The pleasure would be too great. It would be too easy to press a bit too hard, to enjoy it for all the wrong reasons, even though I can feel her angling toward it, begging me to obliterate her for a few blessed seconds. I know what it does to her, and for the first time I don't want to know. That's never been the kind of power I've wanted, even though she'd gladly give it to me, give me almost anything except what I need the most.

I want to slide back to that simple starting point, our bodies blank canvases on which to draw magnificent works of the most special kind of art. Maybe there is still some power left in this bed, something that flows from one of us to the other rather than simply inward, something that binds us together. The ways I thought I knew her have all vanished, lost in a mystery too complex for me to solve. Too many silences and unspoken thoughts war for space between us. She is just as much a stranger to me as she was on our first date, perhaps even more so now, her mind locked away in a box with someone else's keys. Knowing only her body leaves me emptier than if we'd never even met, giving me a hollow victory, a prize I'm forced to return, underserved and unwanted.

My fingers grant me nothing except access to a disembodied cunt, separated from all reality, the way the old-school feminists described pornography, parceling out body parts at random without context or meaning. I wish I could erase my sense memory of how it feels to fuck her, love her, and know her all at the same time, in the same motions. I am somehow back to square one, vainly hoping, praying, that I can make her happy.

Only this time, we have so much more to do than just fuck, than slide and scream and bite and whisper, than twist and bend and push and probe. The stakes are so much higher that no orgasm will ever be enough, but I try anyway.

No matter how far I reach inside, I cannot crack her. Those eyes are a one-way mirror, reflecting a surface of something I cannot see and probably don't want to. I want to tell her I love her, show her everything inside me, but I open my mouth and just as quickly close it. I can feel her body shaking, the tears and pain rising up like an earthquake's tremors, and I shove harder, grab her neck and push her down, anything to quell the rising tide that will be here soon enough. This may look the same as all those other times, my fingers arching and stroking, her eyes shut or staring at me, needy, grabbing me when I touch her in just the right way that is almost—but not quite—too much. But it is nothing like those other times, nothing like anything I've ever done before. It is like touching something totally alien, someone I never even knew, someone not even human. I feel lost as I touch her, my heart so far away I hardly know what to do or how to act. I can see that this is not bridging the gap, but I can't stop myself. I try to pretend that her moans, her wetness, these external signals of desire actually mean she is truly mine. There is no way to make her come and erase the other girl's touch entirely. I am not yet thinking about her and the other girl, wondering how she touches her, not wanting to know but needing to, drawn to that deadly fire with a car-crash allure, though that will all come in time, in those freestanding hours of numbed shock, those lost weekends when she invades my head and will not leave.

She has written me a letter, as requested, given me exact blueprints for how to fuck her. How to take her up against the wall, how to tie her up, tease her, taunt her, and hold out even when she protests. I want nothing more than to be able to follow these instructions, which by now I don't even need because I know how to trigger her, how to get her to go from laughing to spreading her legs in the briefest of moments. I know exactly how to touch her now, where to stroke and bite and slap to give both of us what we need, but that is no longer enough. I don't have it in me to be that kind of top, to blank out all the rest and fulfill only that viciously visceral urge to pummel, pound, and punish. That urge is too clearly real, too close to the unspoken pain, the words that will come later, the ones right underneath the tears. I know when I hit her what it means. There can be

no erotic power exchange when she holds all the real power. I
have enough soul left in me to know that sex should not be a
mechanical obligation. It should not be the only thing you can
do to stay alive, compelled with the force of something so strong
you're powerless to resist.

I reach, reach, reach inside her, desperately searching, hoping to wrench us back to wherever we are supposed to be, back
to where we were—a week, a month, a lifetime ago. I draw out
this process, watch myself, as if from afar, as my hand slides
inside her, as I lube myself and try to cram all of me into her,
making a lasting impression. I have my entire hand inside her,
yet I feel more removed from her than I have ever felt. She might
as well still be in Florida. She might as well still be a stranger;
this might as well still be our first date when I laughed so much
because I was so nervous. I'd rather this be any of those nights,
even the ones when I was so drunk and afraid, so powerless
and unsure; anything would be better than this slow death, this
slow withering until we are nothing more than two girls in a
room with tears in our eyes and an ocean of questions and scars
and hurt between us. I can't predict what will come after this
most pregnant of silences, can't know the depths of pain that
will puncture me beyond the horrors of my imagination, can't
know that I will regret everything I might have, could have,
done wrong, or did do wrong.

She turns over on her stomach, face hidden from my searching eyes, and I fumble to reconnect, to slide into her as if nothing is wrong, as if it's just a matter of finding a comfortable
angle. I finally have had enough, cannot keep going with the
charade that pressing myself against her will fill all the gaps that
still exist between us. But for whatever twisted reasons we need
this, this final time. And this is the last time, because nothing
is worth feeling so utterly and completely alone while you're

fucking your girlfriend before you break up. No power trip or blazing orgasm, no heart-pounding breathless finish, no sadistic impulse or mistaken nostalgia is worth this much pain.

I don't know how to say what I have to, what I'm terrified to, how to ask questions whose answers I know I won't want to hear. There's no book I can read that will teach me how to make her G-spot tell me her secrets, tell me those fantasies and dreams that don't come from her pussy but from her heart. The end, it turns out, is nothing like the beginning. There is no promise of something more, some grand future of possibility, the infinite ways of knowing each other just waiting to be discovered. There is no hope that we can merge, in all the ways love can make you merge, into something so much greater than the sum of our parts. The end is like what they say about death, when your whole life flashes before your eyes. I see moments, fragments— my hand up her skirt on the street; taking her in the doorway of a friend's apartment, so fiercely she can barely sink down to the ground; her on her knees in the bathroom, surprising me as she buries her face into me, no room to protest; grinding the edge of a knife along her back; slapping her tits until they are raw and red—but they seem so far away right now, like a movie, like someone else's pornographic memories. They don't make me smile, and I don't want them anymore. I want to bury myself in her and never let go, hold on to something that has just fluttered away in the wind, fine as the glittering sparkles she wears on her eyes, miniscule and almost opaque, too minute to ever recapture. But all I can do is back away, as slowly as I can, so slowly that it seems as if I am hardly moving, and before I know it, I, and she—we—are gone, almost as if we never existed.

SPECIAL
REQUEST

I love my job as a hotel concierge, because every day is utterly different from the last. One day I might be called upon to have a treadmill, exercise bike, yoga instructor, or Reiki healer sent to a room, another day it might be a pet snake or exotic foodstuff. My hotel specializes in offering anything a customer wants, for a price, and I'm the go-to person, the professional procurer.

I'm paid handsomely for the job—as I should be, considering it involves crazy hours and traversing all the hidden nooks and crannies of Los Angeles, and sometimes other parts of California—but that's not what I love best about it. I love it because I'm a people person, and there's no better job for meeting new people every day than catering to the demands of a high-end hotel's ritziest, most demanding customers. I graduated with a degree in sociology but quickly learned the best way of studying human beings isn't by studying them, but by interacting with them and being privy to their secrets. I was like a special combination of therapist and magician, ready to listen to the oddest

of requests and produce the desired results, while sparing my
clients any of the tedium of decision-making. All they had to do
was decide they wanted something, and I made it happen.

I'd been doing the job for five years, on a lucky break fresh
out of college after applying for the job and being sent on what
amounted to a scavenger hunt. I received a hefty bonus each
year and was treated as a key part of the team. I was at every
important meeting, and while my name didn't appear in the
hotel's literature or press releases, the fact that we offered every
amenity one could imagine was clearly stated. My existence was
a little bit under the radar, but word got around, and often I'd
be requested by name by clients who wouldn't part with the
information about their needs unless we were in a locked room
and they'd made sure nobody else was listening. Basically, I'm
paid to be discreet, discerning, direct, and thorough, to listen
without judgment. As long as the client can pay our fees, they
can have anything flown in from anywhere; they can buy goods,
services, and even sex—for the right price. I'd even signed
a noncompete, and while I knew I hadn't seen everything, I
thought I'd come pretty damn close—but nothing had prepared
me for Claudine.

Usually, the people making the requests were men. Rich
men, sometimes Hollywood stars, since we're located in Beverly
Hills; sometimes athletes, sometimes politicians or princes, or
just your average millionaire or even wild-card billionaire who
wants the fluffiest towels, a new designer bathrobe every day,
private access to the hot tub, and a pretty woman to fluff the
towels, not to mention fluff him if desired. I don't mind even the
most obscure requests, since at the end of the day, I know I'm
helping brighten someone's visit, and giving them the kind of
full service no other hotel can match.

Sometimes it's a couple desiring my services, the husband

busy with meetings while the wife wants a guided tour of the best shops and spas, or a partner to hike mountains with. Maybe she'll be dripping with diamonds, and ask for her food to be steamed and spiced to perfection, but with no fat. I'd sought out tattoo artists, feng shui specialists for long-term guests, nutritionists, manicurists, Japanese hair-straightening specialists, and more. But Claudine wanted something entirely different.

"This is all confidential, right? You don't have the room bugged or anything, do you?" she asked as I sat in a chair and watched her, my face professional but utterly curious. She was clearly not a lady who lunched—at least, not at any of the high-end see-and-be-seen restaurants my clients usually requested. Her elegance wasn't about designer labels, but an air of both entitlement and sexual power; she radiated her body heat across the room, so I knew it was going to be one of the racier requests I'd handled even before she spoke.

"Of course not. Your privacy and satisfaction are of the utmost importance to us. To me." I was surprised at her cautiousness. She was younger than I'd expected, not a wealthy widow or CEO, but a girl, really, who looked close to my age, twenty-eight. Her clothes were simple enough on the surface, though the jeans were designer, the white blouse clearly silk, the lacy white bra beneath it sturdily sculpted, showcasing her beautiful breasts, and the five-inch leopard-print heels were fierce, proclaiming her a woman not to mess with. There were no flowers in her hair or on her clothing; she was a woman who meant business, even though her business was of a kind only a woman like me could provide.

"So, I booked this room because I'd heard from a friend that you will do anything to fulfill your clients' wishes. I've been unable to find anyone who could meet my exact specifications, but you look like you'll know where to find what I need. And my wish is for, well, an orgy. Tomorrow night. I want a room full of hot men and women to pleasure me and each other. Not professionals, just regular sexy people looking to have a good time. And I want you to join us. That's a must. As a guest, off the clock. Confidentially of course—I must make sure not a word of this gets out," Claudine finished with a Cheshire catlike smile.

I'd just finished telling her I could get her anything she wanted, so I couldn't refuse—not if I wanted to keep my job, not to mention my pride. Instead, I just stared at her, agog. I'd brought in ladies of the night, fetish specialists, pro subs and dominatrices. I'd had people ask me to personally pour them baths full of champagne, and I'd even sipped a little as a recent Oscar winner had extended his gorgeous body into his suite's sumptuous tub while I'd popped cork after cork until he was fully submerged. He'd asked me to join him and while I was very, very tempted, I declined save for the luxury of pouring the chilled bubbly over his shoulders, then splashing the last few drops onto his face and indulging in one of the hottest kisses of my life. I was pretty sure he had a cell phone full of numbers of women who'd be more than willing to slip into his tub, so I'd left him to them.

I did, in fact, have the numbers of plenty of escorts and dominatrices handy, friends who specialized in high-end clients who I trusted implicitly for their discretion and ability to do their job well. But Claudine wanted real people, not professionals—except for, well, me. She wanted people who weren't acting like they wanted to share her bed, but who would be overjoyed to worship her leopard-print heels, not to mention the rest of her. I could tell that she wasn't so much a voyeur or exhibitionist as she was used to being the centerpiece of any encounter, erotic or otherwise; she'd never be so crass as to say "gang bang" but she wasn't going to be satisfied unless all those hands and mouths were focused on her at some point in the night. I wasn't sure if I was doing my job or relegating my duties when an image of Claudine with men nibbling on her toes and a woman buried between her legs flashed in my mind.

"Now, if we understand each other, I'm going to slip into a bath. I need to soak my feet." Claudine smiled at me, her glistening red lips curving upward, her brown eyes dancing over my surprised face. She unbuttoned her blouse and dropped it on the bed, then casually reached behind her to unhook her bra, letting her large, clearly natural breasts hang heavily against her, before pausing to finish her instructions.

"I'd love a couple, and maybe some college kids, a girl with some tattoos, a man with a huge cock. A boy I can tie up. With you as my dessert," Claudine added with a laugh before stepping toward me, placing her hand at the back of my head, and giving me a full, passionate kiss, as if that were something she were used to doing with her minions. Her mouth tasted minty and sweet, and her tongue was as possessive as the rest of her. It was the kind of kiss I was used to from men, not women. Her breasts pressed against me, begging me to touch them. I was still in shock, but my pussy clearly wasn't, because it responded to her touch, to her tongue darting against mine. She pulled away, then slithered out of her jeans and panties, before waving goodbye and sliding into the bathroom, where the sound of rushing water greeted me. I rubbed at my lips, hoping to remove the lipstick as quickly as I could.

I left and went to my office, opening up my notebook and writing her name at the top. I couldn't believe this. Why would a woman like her come here? I mean, yes, we promised full service, but she was taking that slogan to its grandest possible conclusion, aside from requesting a mountain of coke to roll around in or a chauffeur-driven Lamborghini Aventador. I would've been well within my rights to refuse, or to simply refer her to someone better suited to meeting her needs, yet I didn't want to. It wasn't just the challenge of Claudine's request, or the probable tip, or anything of a professional nature; I *wanted* to be there, as me, Francine, the woman who'd just been kissed by a woman who went after exactly what she desired. I wanted to see, feel, taste, smell, and simply luxuriate in being at such a hedonistic event, at my workplace.

This task was naughty yet dutiful, and being either of those was a surefire way to turn me on; combining them was already sending my libido through the roof. I'm not submissive in real life, and barely call myself a sub in the bedroom, but I do like serving, pleasing, providing. It makes me good at my job, and adds a frisson of sexual energy to my day, not to mention making me glad I contributed to the world. No, I'm not off lobbying Congress or anything, but I like to feel that what I put out into the universe is positive, that my existence feeds others', sometimes literally. Plus, there was the mystery factor. I wanted to find out, up close and personal, why Claudine was so eager for this, since she was clearly a woman who could probably walk into any bar, smile, snap her fingers, and produce a round of admirers.

I'm not a quitter, but it was more than my work ethic at stake. I liked who Claudine had turned me into in those few minutes alone together, the kind of woman who gets selected and seduced, who other women wanted for real, not just for a quickie make out session at a bar. I'm mostly into guys, but beautiful women have a seemingly magical effect on me. Plus, I'd always wanted to host an orgy myself but had never had the guts to orchestrate that particular fantasy. I'd been to a few, sure, but they'd never quite lived up to my vivid imagination. I had a feeling that even if I invited total losers, Claudine would find a way to spin them into the equivalent of sex-party gold; I was just the conduit.

Alone in my office, I immediately texted my best friend, Tracy, as well as Henry, our mostly gay but into the occasional woman pal, and a couple I knew who made documentaries for money, and documented their own wild swinging sex life for fun. All of them were free Saturday, and Tracy was planning to bring her basketball player boyfriend, while Henry had a hot young thing he had a date with that night; at the very least, they'd provide some entertainment for the rest of us. He referred me to a queer dyke couple who were more than happy to come once I promised them a free room.

I explained to each of them that this wasn't my idea, but Claudine's, and they were not only sworn to secrecy, but part of the bargain was that they'd have to be amenable to helping Claudine have the best time possible. I didn't want to lose her as a guest, not just for the money, but because I prided myself on retaining our most demanding customers, some of whom had been staying at our hotel for over twenty years, since long before my tenure.

I went to bed that night and deliberately didn't masturbate, wanting to save myself for the following night. I woke up early from a feverish dream in which Claudine had wrapped a slim silver chain around my neck and was leading me around by it, taking me on a tour of the hallways I walked purposefully in my heels every day, while I simultaneously reveled in being potentially seen by customers and blushed at the thought.

I was in full party-planning mode, and each action only made me wetter. I bought lube and gloves and condoms; nipple clamps, dildos, butt plugs. I filled a whole basket at the sex toy store, causing even the jaded clerk to raise his eyebrows at the large bill, and my use of a corporate card to pay for it.

Normally, I have little patience with nosy clerks, but this time I sized him up and decided on the spot to offer him an invitation. "I'm hosting a party. Well, my new friend is. It's at this address, in this room. You're invited, if you think you can handle it, Patrick," I said as I signed the bill. He looked a little stunned, but he smiled and stammered and said he'd try to make it.

I bought a selection of snacks and sodas and alcohol, programmed my iPod and made sure the rooms on either side of Claudine's were free. One of them opened up to a suite, and as for the other, I didn't want to risk someone booking it and them being subjected to what surely wouldn't be a quiet crowd. Then it was my turn to get ready. What does a girl wear to an orgy? I sifted through my outfits, then my lingerie drawer, finally concluding that what I wore, aside from a smile, didn't really matter. It was more about bringing the real me, the woman who wasn't a Type A perfectionist but was a woman, one who wanted to please and be pleased, to make herself happy by hearing Claudine moan. And, yes, I wanted to see Claudine crack a little, wanted to see the cool veneer of rich-lady power crumble into a screaming orgasm, or five.

So, I simply wore a lacy black slip over a lacy hot-pink slip, with a plain black coat that covered each. My five-inch heels accentuated my calves, including the string of pearls tattooed onto the right one. The half-open oyster shell near my hip was hidden, but would soon be revealed. "Calm down, everything's going to be fine," I said out loud, a mantra I'd taken to repeating when my world seemed to be collapsing.

I put everything I needed into my trunk, drove to valet parking, and told Marc to bring everything to Claudine's room in a few minutes. Then I spoke with Gerald, the manager on duty, presenting him with a firm guest list. "No one else, including staff, is to come up to her room unless you clear it with me first.

Got it?" He looked at me searchingly but didn't ask questions. That's what I liked about Gerald; it would've made him a poor detective, but he was a valuable employee to have on your side.

When I knocked on her door, I got a sudden chill. I knew Claudine would like the motley crew I'd selected for our evening's entertainment; how could she not? But what about me? Would I be a bit player or her costar? And which did I prefer? Claudine peeked around the edge of the door. "Come in, my sweet," she said, and shut the door right after me. She was completely naked, and up close, I could see she had at least a dozen years on my twenty-seven, and in all likelihood was in her late forties, but her body was beautiful nonetheless. I was impressed that, unlike me, she hadn't tried to adorn herself; her naked body simply said, "Here I am, ready for the taking."

"Let me get a good look at you," she said, whisking off my coat when my fingers fumbled with the buttons, then instructing me to twirl around, then lift the hem of my slips. I'd no sooner bared my thong-adorned ass than there was a knock on the door. I reached for the coat, but Claudine ordered me to sit on the bed. She opened the door the same way she had with me, and Marc entered, pushing a luggage cart and almost dropping the bag in his hand when he saw me nude. I winked at him, and he continued unloading everything, earning him a tip that Claudine made sure to stuff down his pants. Once the door had closed behind him, she said, "Now, where were we? Oh, yes, you were showing me your outfit." Her laugh filled the room. "Show me again."

Claudine stepped closer and I searched her eyes, wanting to please her. I was doing something bold, but inside I felt shy as I pulled up the slips to reveal the outline of my pussy lips, spared from view only by a small strip of fabric. "Take those off," Claudine said, her voice huskier, and under her watchful eye,

I slithered out of the thong, letting it land on the carpet. Claudine shuddered, then reached for the nightstand. As she moved
toward me, I saw she had a silk blindfold heading for my face.
Letting her put it on would be the ultimate test: could I be in
control of my job, of the party I'd organized, while submitting
to someone else's control? The questions must've been written
on my face, because Claudine said, "Yes. Yes. Give yourself to
me, Francine."

I decided this was a case of something being worth doing
only if you went all the way with it. Besides, I wasn't really in
charge at all; Claudine could kick out all my guests if she wanted
to. She could report me for some made-up transgression. She'd
been in control since that first kiss. I was immediately rewarded,
because once the blindfold was on, the white noise in my head
dissipated, as if by not being able to see, I couldn't hear all the
worries and fears that usually clamored for space in my psyche.
Instead, all I heard and felt were Claudine's movements. She
positioned me so my head was back against the pillows, my
arms above my head. Soon she was fastening cuffs around my
wrists. "How does that feel?" she asked. I tugged and smiled,
because I liked that too. I was submitting, surrendering, and
getting wetter by the second.

"You probably thought I wanted to be the star of the party,"
she said, once again uncannily reading my mind. "I'm much
more of a voyeur, my dear, though I do plan to participate. But
if anyone's the star, it's going to be you. I want to watch the
pretty boys and girls having their way with you, touching you,
taking you, filling you. I want to make sure you thoroughly
enjoy this hotel room that I'm paying for. You deserve it. And
so do I." I didn't ask why that might be the case, because I
soon heard a buzzing sound, followed by the press of a vibrator
against my clit. I dropped my knees wider and was so lost in the

sensations of being bound and being buzzed that I barely heard
the door. Claudine wrapped my hand around the vibrator and
left to answer it. Voices soon filled the room, and part of me
wished I could greet people in a less exposed way. But Claudine
was smart: being blindfolded meant I couldn't see the reactions
the others were having to me, couldn't assess whether my outfit,
my body, measured up to theirs.

"Sweetie!" Tracy said, rushing over to kiss me on the cheek
and grant me a dusting of perfume and powder. "You look like
you're enjoying yourself." I was, and I kept on enjoying myself,
until someone took the toy from my hand, and someone else
started sucking on one nipple. I knew I'd only invited nine people, but it felt like I was in the center of dozens of hungry men
and women.

"She's gorgeous, isn't she?" I heard Claudine pronounce, as
if displaying a piece of very modern art she'd sculpted herself.
Perhaps she had, because this version of me, the one sprawled
naked across a bed in my place of work getting filled and fondled and kissed and sucked, wasn't someone I'd ever have pro-
duced on my own.

I turned toward her voice and smiled, suddenly hungry for
her. She'd turned the tables on me thoroughly, tricking me into
thinking she wanted to be the star, when really, she wanted to
be the director of her own personal sex show.

I could hear Tracy murmuring near me, then gasping, as
Alex, her boyfriend, did something exquisite to her. "Can I have
a turn?" Claudine's voice said near me. I wanted to see what
she was going to get her turn doing, but just then my legs were
spread even wider and something big and slippery with lube was
pressed against my center. At first, I strained to listen and to
decipher what exactly was going on, but I figured out fast that if
I relaxed, the toy would not only enter me farther and faster, but

I could fully immerse myself in the many sounds and sensations going on around me.

"I think Francine deserves a raise, don't you?" I heard Claudine asking someone even as the sounds of hard spankings rang through the air.

"Yes," Tracy let out, and then I heard more than one hand slapping skin, and remembered Tracy telling me that Alex sometimes liked to strike her across the face, and she'd quickly grown to love it. Tears rushed to my covered eyes, tears of pleasure, especially when someone rushed in and used nipple clamps— likely a pair that I'd purchased—and fastened them on my buds.

There was a knock at the door. "Whoever could that be? Well, Francine invited everyone, so she should answer," Claudine said, and shifted her body to lick along my neck. The toy eased out of me, but the blindfold and clamps stayed on.

I walked to the door and called out, as casually as I could, "Who is it?"

"Patrick. From the store."

Damn. Well, I couldn't turn him away, so I opened the door as carefully as I could and said, "Hurry."

I wished I could see his face, to see if he was grinning at me, but I couldn't. He handed something to me. "Thank you," I said automatically, then paused. How to explain my outfit—or rather, lack of one?

"Welcome," called out Claudine. "Please feel free to set those chocolates out, I'm sure they will be greatly appreciated, as are you, pretty boy." I blushed, and smiled at where I thought Patrick was standing. "Francine, come back here," she called to me, and I did. "Do join in. An orgy's not truly an orgy unless everyone's participating, don't you think?"

"Sure," he said, sounding slightly uncertain, which endeared him to me. If I was in over my head, I had no choice but to keep going. You can't exactly kick everyone out when it's not really your party. Besides, it was fun, when I let myself enjoy it. Then Patrick pulled me close. I knew it was him because he told me. "You look beautiful, even better than you did at the store, and that's saying something." His breath was sweet, minty, his mouth warm. He kissed me like we were alone, his tongue slowly slithering into my mouth. He climbed on top of me, and I figured the other orgy-goers were occupying themselves because nobody seemed to bother with us. "Is this okay?" Patrick asked as he started to take off his pants.

"Yes," I said. "I want to feel you." I almost added, "I don't normally do this," which, while true, was unnecessary. There's no room for modesty at an orgy.

Our private moment was interrupted by Claudine whispering in my ear. "Are you enjoying yourself? I am," she said, then kissed all along my earlobe, my neck, my cheek, then my lips. She fed me each breast, her necklace dangling in my face as Patrick entered me. I was more than ready, having been primed by the dildo. I could tell he was wearing a condom, and I could also tell he was big, wonderfully so.

"I am enjoying myself," I said as she kissed me for a long time, before shifting so I could lick her pussy. Claudine rubbed herself against my tongue, and the more she did, the more I liked it. The room was filled with the sounds of sex, and spanking, and kissing. The noises swirled around me as I ate Claudine, then shifted so that both Patrick and I could pleasure Claudine.

Only after we'd exhausted every possible position was I allowed to take off the blindfold. The familiar room looked different, and not just because there were so many naked bodies strewn across it. Then I looked down at myself, at the lipstick smeared on my body, the metal clamps tight on my nubs, my lingerie on the floor. I was the one who was different. I'd procured, and been procured. I'd more than met Claudine's demands, and in return she'd tipped my world on its side. I knew that from that moment on, I was never going to look at my hotel in the same way again.

BETTER LATE
THAN NEVER

After I got divorced, I resigned myself to a fairly lonely existence. Well, not entirely lonely, but sexless, certainly. Even before the breakup, Stella and I had become little more than roommates, and the truth was, though we had managed to get it on occasionally, I was never all that into it, so this seemed like the usual state of affairs for me, except now I was living alone. At thirty-seven, I wasn't fresh meat, but I wasn't totally over the hill. Friends, many of whom came out of the woodwork after the split, tried to set me up on blind dates, but I wasn't interested. I liked having our Upper West Side apartment to myself; it had seemed to grow overnight, morphing into a more masculine environment without her delicate female touches dotting everything.

There was about a month where I walked around in a fog, missing her, missing her company. I'd come home after a long day selling jewelry, something I'd somehow found I had a knack for in college and had parlayed into a lucrative position at Tiffany's, and settled into the silence. Friends invited me out for drinks or dinner, sometimes with their families, sometimes on our own, usually at bars crawling with people a good ten years younger than me. What was strange was that when women would catch my eye, or a friend would bring a single woman over, nothing happened. I'd smile and buy her a drink, listen to her lilting voice, but nothing was happening down there. I'd even walked one woman home and she'd leaned in to kiss me, smelling of peaches and vanilla, but I dodged her for a quick hug.

I figured that I just didn't have a high sex drive, that my friends and my softball team and my job and occasional noodling on the guitar were all I needed to keep me occupied. And the truth is, they were. Unlike my buddies who'd been devastated by their divorces, or the ones who had the opposite reactions, becoming consummate playboys, I was pretty much neutral. I missed Stella's presence, and her cooking, but that was about it. Our sex life had dwindled from its earlier passion to a half-hearted blow job from her here, a late-night quickie there, but we'd never really talked about it. I'd assumed sex was something you forgot about in a long-term marriage, and I truly hadn't missed it much.

I was surrounded by women most of the day, wealthy customers wanting jewels draped around their necks and wrists or hanging from their ears. Often, they flirted as they waved around tens of thousands of dollars' worth of diamonds, telling me what the gifts were for, slipping double *entendres* into their rich laughs as they twinkled before the mirror. I liked helping them look more beautiful, but I didn't want to fuck them.

And then about two months after Stella was gone, my libido came back to life. Except it was like one of those movies where bodies get swapped, because all of a sudden, it wasn't women who were reviving my dick from its long dormant stage. In some

ways, I was a teenager again: I started having wet dreams. I'd
be asleep and I'd wake up remembering someone sucking my
cock. The face and body would be anonymous, fuzzy, but the
lips, and occasional stubble, and my own intuition, told me that
these lips were not female. A man was sucking me off in those
dreams, a man with a cock as hard as mine that he was either
stroking or waiting for me to stroke. These unconscious blow
jobs were always the best head I'd ever received. The dreams
only came to me occasionally, and I'd wake up either having
jerked off in my sleep, or needing to when I awoke, but they
were so realistic, I felt almost like I'd gotten laid.

The dreams were starting to consume me, making me take
after-work catnaps, hoping they'd return. I decided to see what
would happen if I chose a more conscious route to accessing
this brave new fantasy world. I picked a guy I worked with,
one who I knew was gay, even though he never talked about it.
You'd have to pick up some very subtle clues to know, but I've
always had excellent gaydar—except about myself, I soon came
to realize. He wasn't what I'd have guessed would be my type,
but who knew anymore? He had shaggy dyed-black hair that
fell into his eyes, extra-pale skin, overly full lips, and thick black
hipster glasses. He wore funky skinny ties and spoke softly, so
you often had to lean in to hear him.

I spoke his name out loud: "Kevin." I felt myself open up,
felt the fantasy step up a notch into something that could actually be possible. "Kevin, I want you to . . ." I paused because
I honestly wasn't sure what I wanted him to do. But I knew if
he'd been in the room, I'd probably be tongue-tied. I pressed
on, though, determined to see what might happen when there
was more than a nameless face in my big gay dream. I had
never thought about what Kevin was into sexually. I tried to
dredge up a story from our chats, but he was too circumspect

for that. I decided, maybe because he was tall and skinny and probably weighed less than me, that he might like to be held down, maybe have his wrists tied together. Then his dick would be mine. I pictured it tall and skinny, like him, just perfect for my first time.

Sucking someone else's cock was totally different, even in my head, than getting my dick sucked. It was better, in a way, because I was in control; with my fantasy man's lips around my hardness, I couldn't control when I'd come, could only wait in perfect agony for him to work his magic. I shut my eyes and pushed two fingers into my mouth, trying to suck them in a sexy way, rather than just gulp. I whimpered, tears coming to my eyes. This was nothing like going down on Stella. Sucking Kevin's imaginary cock made goose bumps form all over my skin. My nipples hardened, my senses coming alive. I started moving my fingers slightly back and forth; even if Kevin were tied up, he could still raise his dick if he wanted. It was over pretty soon, because while I may have been in control of my mouth, my cock had other plans, and soon spurted a giant load of come.

I knew it wouldn't be long before I sucked my first real cock.

Seeing Kevin at work was a little awkward over the next few days. How do you come out as . . . newly horny for guys, probably gay, when you've been known as the married, straight, rather boring colleague for years? I couldn't pin on a rainbow flag at work, and in every other way, I was still me. It wasn't like people could tell just by looking, and I had a feeling if I confessed my fantasy to Kevin, he'd shoot me a look of great horror and scamper away. We weren't destined to become lovers, and I wouldn't have wanted to mix business and pleasure, anyway. Still, I observed him on the sly, wanting to be more like him, so at ease with his carefully coiffed hair and bee-stung lips, not caring who knew he was into boys, not girls. I felt in limbo, with my new desires loud and clear, while the rest of my life stayed stuck in the past.

One day, coming home on the train, reality caught up with my fantasies. My dick stood to attention when a sweaty young man rushed between the subway doors, fresh from a round of basketball. His brown curls clung to his head; his muscular calves topped by thighs that made me ache. I lifted my gaze and tried to read a subway ad for chewing gum, but my eyes kept darting over to him.

A seat opened up behind me and I sat, almost stunned at the visions swirling through my head. I reached for a copy of *Time Out New York* and placed it over my lap to try to hide my erection. When I looked up at the basketball player again, his eyes locked on mine, and he casually made his way over to stand right in my line of vision. His crotch was right before me, the outline of his cock visible when I took a quick peek. I flipped a page in the magazine, and he shifted so his leg was brushing mine. I probably looked a little bit crazy, a middle-aged man in a black designer suit, smooth shaven, surely blushing as I sat there with an aching dick hidden by a magazine as a young man, probably a college student, made me hard by brushing his knee against mine. Finally, my stop arrived and I stood, inevitably brushing against him. In a flash, he took my hand and let it trail over his cock. The whole thing took maybe two seconds, and I'd say I imagined it but I know I didn't because my dick shifted in my pants, responding instantly. You'd have to have been staring intensely to think it anything other than two passengers shifting to make room for one of them to exit, but my face burned with the truth as I rushed home.

I stood before the full-length mirror in my closet and jerked off, holding my cock and wishing it were the sweaty subway guy's, wishing I could've taken him in my hand, wrapped my fingers around his firmness for more than a single moment. I reached behind me and started to gently stroke my anus, which heretofore had been a sexual no-strike zone. I had so little experience with anyone's back door, but my finger there felt good. I pressed harder, knowing I'd need lube to get the job done right, but being too caught up in the sensations to pause for even a moment. I kept stroking myself, moving my fist up and down, thinking of the sweaty basketball player's face back there, licking me, opening me up with his tongue. "Yes, harder," I cried out and then opened my eyes and watched my dick shoot a veritable waterfall of jizz.

Then I met Felix. I can't honestly say I was looking for him; we were both on line at a Starbucks on the Upper West Side at eight in the morning on a Saturday, surrounded by strollers and families in what could have been Middle America. I was behind him, thinking about what I should do with myself that day. I still wasn't used to planning entire weekends. Then he turned around, just for a second, and I gasped. I just knew, the same way I had just known, in my earlier life, with Stella: God was speaking to me, telling me He had hand-delivered this fine specimen for my pleasure. And for all I knew, maybe he had. Felix turned and gave me a killer smile, perfect white teeth gleaming from a tan face with sexy stubble I suddenly wanted to rub my face against. "Hey there," he said in a sensual Southern drawl, and I returned his smile. There were a few people ahead of us, so we had some time for chitchat. He was friendlier than most folks you meet randomly in New York, perhaps because, as I soon learned, he'd just moved here from Atlanta three weeks earlier.

He was a fresh-faced twenty-five, but that didn't stop him

from flirting with me, standing closer than necessary, and giving me this smile that, while blindingly white and seemingly wholesome, felt like it was speaking straight to my dick. Whereas I felt like a tongue-tied teenager at first, Felix was all confidence.

We walked outside and found a bench to sip our respective coffee and tea. I teased him about his English Breakfast with milk and sugar ("Do real men drink tea?") while he teased my decidedly nonmacho option of a caramel macchiato. I found out that he was looking for work, doing anything; he had two months until law school started and wanted to have fun and make some cash, but nothing too high pressured. I told him the briefest of details about my job, and finally, after a pause, he asked the big question: "So, are you single?"

He wasn't asking if I was gay, and I realized that by my having coffee with him, it was simply understood. I liked that; just by being me and talking to a stranger, I could be taken for gay. It gave passing a new meaning. "Yes, at the moment. I was with someone for a long time." I wasn't ready yet to give him the whole story. I did, however, give him my card, and he leaned over my shoulder, resting his chin on it as he dictated his number. "Nice to meet you, Mr. Perry," he said, all mock formality as he extended his hand. I gripped it and had the overwhelming urge to hug him, to smell his hair and hold him close. It was a different impulse than my cocksucking fantasy.

He emailed me the next day, a casual, *Want-to-have-lunch?* missive.

Let's make it dinner. Tomorrow night. I'll cook. The words were on my screen and then whizzing their way to his before I could rethink them—or overthink them. This wasn't the time to beat around the bush, not when my future depended on it. I needed to know whether I was really gay, whether this was just a rebound fantasy or something real.

I found out very soon. Felix replied and wrote, *You're on. I hope you can handle me. F.*

I wasn't sure what he meant and didn't want to ask. I took the next day off because I knew I'd be a wreck at work thinking about trying to get my place ready and planning a meal. I made chicken with eggplant and garlic, my specialty. For a minute, I considered leaving out the garlic, but I like the taste of it, and hoped I'd be tasting it on Felix very soon. He arrived promptly, bearing a bottle of champagne. His tan looked even deeper, but his smile was just as easy and relaxed. I went to hug him hello, then just put out my hand for him to shake.

Even that simple touch made me tremble in a way I wasn't sure I ever had before. This was now far beyond simple arousal; it wasn't just my cock that wanted to get close to Felix. "Would you like something to drink? Or a snack?" I asked, pointing to the plate of Brie and crackers I'd set out.

"A snack? Like this?" he asked, then leaned down and kissed my neck. Being shorter than Felix, even by just a few inches, along with the whole gay virgin thing, made me feel like I was the younger man. His lips on my neck sent vibrations through my body, and I had to lean on the counter for support.

"Felix . . ." Just saying his name, one so different from the one I'd gotten used to saying, felt rougher, more forceful than "Stella." Just like him. Felix turned me around and kissed me right on the lips. His tongue probed my mouth and I opened up for him, letting him take me.

I was hard, and no longer cared about our meal. "Take me to your bedroom," he said. I did, holding his hand all the way. I was glad we were skipping the preliminaries, because the last thing I wanted to do was dwell on the fact that this was my first time. That would be my little secret.

"Steven," Felix said throatily. "Take off your clothes. I'm

going to help you relax." I did as he ordered, sensing him watching me. When I was undressed, he told me to get on my hands and knees on the bed. "Head down, ass up." My cock was so hard, my mind racing, my body buzzing, I'd have done anything for him. The difference between being an adult and a fumbling teenager was that I wasn't about to come before things got interesting.

That's when I felt it—a smack on my ass. I'd heard of S&M, but my sex life with Stella had been strictly by the books, and I don't mean *Story of O*. I'd never thought much about it one way or another, and there was no time for thinking now. Felix kept smacking my ass, the right side, then the left, once again so sure of himself. I grunted in response, the pain a mere flicker before heat took over; heat that warmed not just my ass, but my entire lower half. "You're getting more comfortable, aren't you?" he asked.

"Yes. Yes, sir, I am." I had no idea where that came from, but there it was. Felix kept going until my backside burned, my fingers curled around the sheets, my teeth clenched. I wasn't sure whether to be relieved or excited that he had stopped.

"Now kiss me again." Taking orders from Felix was easy, even though I'd never done that before, either. Letting someone else run the show and tell me what to do, wondering what would happen if I disobeyed, all lent my otherwise drab bedroom an air of naughtiness. I'd say it was like an out-of-body experience, but I was there, 100 percent. I was there as Felix kissed me, there as he pushed my wrists down onto the bed, there as he hovered over me, pinching my nipples. I was there when he ordered me to keep my hands above my head, then brought his cock to my lips. "Take it, take it all," he demanded.

It was like in my dream, but a million times better. I wanted all of Felix—not just his cock, but his being—and the way to get it was to take him inch by inch down my throat. The smell drew me closer, then feeling just how hard he was. I opened my eyes to see the last inches of his hardness disappear between my lips. Then Felix reached his hand back to manipulate my dick.

"No," I halfheartedly protested, not meaning it. Of course, it felt good—hell, it felt incredible—but I wanted to focus on sucking him.

"Learn to multitask," was all he said, and I couldn't really talk with a mouthful of dick.

So, I did, enjoying his slowly pumping hand and his faster-pumping cock. I shut my eyes, knowing that there would be no going back. Felix's cock was speaking to me, and it was saying: *Welcome home.* He only lasted a few more thrusts before he was coming, right in my mouth, on my tongue. I'd been expecting it, but it was still a surprise. I'd stopped comparing everything he did to Stella—we were in our own world now—but tasting another man's spunk was a revelation. I'd tasted my own, but no one can ever be a good judge of that. I gave Felix's five stars for fine dining.

"Your turn," he said, and I watched as he jerked me off. We both looked on as I ejaculated far enough to hit the wall on the other side of the room.

I tried to downplay my response to what we'd just done. I didn't want to look foolish in front of Felix, or worse, to seem like the inexperienced straight guy looking just to get off. But our conversation over the delayed dinner was easy and comfortable, and I knew by the end of the evening we'd be getting together again soon.

It wasn't until a year later, on our anniversary, that I fully fessed up to my straight past. Felix wasn't mad, just curious, and we spent the rest of that night talking. The others we've spent otherwise engaged. You can only imagine (at least, I hope you can). I haven't exactly racked up huge numbers on my bed-post (though Felix promises to take me to a sex party soon), but I've learned that quality is quantity when it comes to sexual partners, and that when enjoying the finer things in life (*i.e.,* cock), you're better late than never.

A SLAP IN
THE FACE

Jade strolled into the bar, walked straight up to Amber, who was leaning against it wearing a slinky leopard-print slip, ripped fishnet stockings, a see-through black top along with a sheer black bra, and dangerously tall black heels, her red hair gleaming even in the low lights, and slapped her across the face. The sound was louder than Jade had expected, the sting in her palm stronger, both of which she liked. Amber didn't smile, not with her mouth, anyway, but Jade knew exactly how much she'd liked Jade's slap. She could read it in the way Amber shivered, the way her eyes skittered from the ground and, for a second, up to Jade's, from the way her body radiated a heady combination of fear, awe, and desire.

This was not a kinky bar. It wasn't a dyke or queer bar, either. It was your average Brooklyn dive bar, filled with its mix of colorful high-glam hipsters in everything from hot pants to schoolgirl skirts, older white guys with huge beer steins who seemed like they'd been sitting there since before either woman was born, parents stealing a late-night cocktail before the baby-sitter came home. And Jade and Amber, who'd shared a stormy, kinky relationship of six months, one that Jade wanted to last even though she had no idea if they would blaze through all the intense passion zinging between them too fast and have nothing left, or could find ways to keep it going. She was trying to live in the moment, and this scene was part of her new mission. She kept any trembling she felt on the inside steady as she stared down at the girl who'd given so much of herself to Jade, but was always looking to give more.

To anyone watching, it would've looked like what it was: a slap in the face, a blow across her cheek, something at least a little mean, harsh, powerful, something that must have hurt and brought tears to Amber's eyes. And it was, certainly, all of those things—Jade would never have denied that it was one of the most powerful ways you could strike someone—but it wasn't unwanted; in fact, Amber thought it was the hottest thing she'd ever done, and she'd been to, and participated in, her share of extreme play parties. She looked up at Jade and realized that her fantasies had been fulfilled, technically, but not all the way; her face tingled in anticipation of the next slap. She suddenly wished she'd worn her matching leopard-print panties, the silky ones that rode up her ass, because her wetness was starting to trickle down her thigh. She liked it, even more than when Jade slapped her at home; she liked it so much she was torn between step-ping between Jade's jeans-clad legs and pressing their bodies tight together and what she wound up choosing, looking right up into her girlfriend's eyes, letting her see the tears that shim-mered there.

"You want me to slap you again, don't you?" Jade's voice was low, deep, quiet enough that only Amber could hear. Jade kept the tremor out of it, the awe that this creature was letting her do the most wicked things to her and kept wanting to push the envelope.

"Yes, Jade, I do." Amber let a tear fall, because she didn't totally understand why she liked it, she just knew she did, and she wanted people to know. Well, that wasn't strictly true. She couldn't honestly say she wanted people to know about her predilection for being smacked, but the fact that now, finally, they did, after so many months of fantasizing, made her pussy feel like it was both tightening and expanding all at once.

This time, Jade tenderly held her hand against one of Amber's cheeks, the pristine one, and with the other raked her short nails down the edge of the other. She waited, toying with her, trying to ignore their surroundings, because the exhibitionism was really Amber's thing, though she couldn't deny she got a small thrill from being so controlling in so public a location. Then, she did it again, a smack that reverberated through her palm, skin striking skin, and again. Jade stepped forward and shoved her knee between Amber's legs, pressed her mouth against her ear. "Thank me for it, or I won't do it again."

"Thank you, Jade. I love you." Amber hadn't meant to say that, but it came out in a rush. There were moments when she was afraid of Jade, but she liked those moments, she liked the way those moments spurred her on to be more daring, to let herself get pushed farther off what felt like a precipice, until everything she had was Jade's for the taking.

"Let's go," Jade said, plucking Amber's half-full glass from her hand and placing it on the bar, then rushing her outside, while Amber scrambled to put her pink fake-fur coat back on before they entered the chilly night. Jade would've stayed, but what was bubbling up inside of her was too fierce for public consumption. There's no way the patrons of that bar would ever have understood what she wanted to do to Amber; the truth was, she hardly understood it herself, but she knew it filled something primal within her, something that made her feel like she was enacting an ancient ritual, a hunt-or-be-hunted animal-istic desire to go for the kill. Slapping Amber, beating her, tying her down, choking her, all took Jade's breath away as much as they did Amber's, though she didn't have the freedom to show it quite as much. "Why are you shaking?" Amber had once asked after a particularly cruel, intense scene. Jade had just shaken her head, not having any further answer.

This time, she wanted Amber quiet, even though she usually loved the noises the girl made. She pulled Amber into an alley she'd scoped out beforehand. The wind whipped around them as Jade pressed Amber against the brick, then slapped her face as hard as she could. Amber let out a cry, her nostrils flaring, her body straining against its own desires. Jade knew there was a part of Amber that was horrified at just how much she liked being slapped, and an even bigger part that was in awe of how little it took for the sensitive skin on her face to make her diz-zyingly wet. Amber liked to be hit all over her body, but there were some spots she liked best. Her face. Her pussy. Her tits, especially the nipples, all areas Jade had mostly shied away from with her previous play partners, by request.

Amber wanted it, and the first time she'd done it, Amber had come with a ferociousness Jade had never seen, while her own arousal had been different than anything that had come before. "I want you to walk up to me at a bar and slap my face, so everyone can see," Amber had emailed her a month ago, and ever since, Jade had been fantasizing about doing just that. Now that she had, she wanted so much more. She wanted someone to help her, but that would have to happen another time. For now, it was just the two of them, ready for anything.

"Put your hands above your head," Jade said, partly to see

if Amber would do it, partly to watch her breasts thrust forward with the movement. "Good girl," she told her. She looked
closely at her girlfriend's beautiful face, so pale, so sensitive.
The wind was competing with her hand in coloring her flesh,
but Jade didn't mind. It had taken her a while to get used to
the fact that she liked slapping Amber, liked hurting her, liked
seeing the tears rush to her eyes as she looked up at her so
desperately.

Amber was biting her lower lip, and Jade used her fingers to
pry the lip apart. "You told me you want this, Amber. If you
flinch or fidget or look like you don't, I'm not going to do it."

"I do want it," Amber exclaimed, the words tripping over
themselves. "I want you to slap me. I want you to hurt me. I
want you to slap me so hard my ears ring." Amber kept looking up at Jade, even though Jade sensed she wanted to close
her eyes, to pretend that somehow it wasn't her saying those
perverse, filthy words. Because they were extremely perverse;
asking to be slapped made it all completely real. Amber couldn't
pretend Jade was some dominating brute, at least, not entirely.

Jade liked it when Amber watched, when Amber saw her
hand coming, when she anticipated the pain. "I have a present
for you," she said, and reached into her jeans pocket, the jan-
gling of the clamps loud in her ears. Amber's eyes widened, and
the hint of fear Jade saw, the hint that warmed her heart even
as she prepared to tighten them around Amber's nipples, made
Jade smile. Amber was so open, whether by choice or design or
a little of both; she could never hide her feelings, not like some
girls Jade had played with who only truly let go when they were
under the most extreme erotic distress. Jade could play the too-
cool-for-school game too—but she didn't want to.

She leaned down and pressed her body tight against Amber's,
kissing her roughly. "Take out your tits," she said, "and hurry,

or I'll have to do it for you." They both knew that "do it for you" was code for "rip your top off and send all the tiny buttons flying to the floor," because Jade had done it before, with a hundred-dollar top (though she'd bought a replacement for Amber later).

Still, Amber rushed to unbutton her blouse and take out her breasts as soon as Jade stepped back to give her room, and the sight floored Jade, even though she'd seen those glorious globes so many times before. There was still something awe-inspiring about their weight, their eagerness to be touched and abused. Amber's tits were like works of art, and were Jade's favorite part of her body. "Pinch those nipples for me," Jade said, allowing Amber to bring her hands down. Amber started to lightly grab them between her thumbs and forefingers, much too lightly for Jade.

"No," she said fiercely. "Pinch them. Like this." And with that she slapped Amber's hands away and pinched and pulled at the same time, then twisted, watching Amber's face contort as she did, knowing it was making her wet, knowing too that the longer she did it, the more Amber was contemplating using her safeword, "strawberry," a fruit she hated but ate when it was the only polite thing to do. Similarly, Amber hated to have to resort to her safeword, and only had once, when her leg cramped up.

When she was done, she let Amber's breasts go, watching them bounce lightly before settling where they should be. Then she clamped one hand over Amber's mouth and slapped her tits, slapped them hard enough to feel the sting in her right palm, to see the marks on Amber's breasts, a defiant red. This brought out the wild beast in Jade, the one who wanted to claw and bite and grind Amber into the ground, the one that liked watching her struggle, feeling her lips pressing against her hand as she then switched to flicking her middle finger against her thumb and then right at the bull's-eye of each nipple.

She finally let go, both of them breathing heavily. "Now you're ready," Jade said, and Amber gave her another of those almost painful looks, one that seemed to beg her not to put the clamps on while also swearing she'd leave her if she didn't. Jade took Amber's now-sore nipples, one at a time, and attached the clamps, pushing the rubber-covered lever just a little bit higher than she knew Amber would have, before taking the metal chain holding them together and shoving it into Amber's mouth. "Bite down hard, sweetie, because if you let go, I'm out of here." She slapped her face again, to see what Amber would do. She bit down harder on the chain, breathed in deeply through her nose.

And then she went to work on Amber's pussy. She hadn't intended, originally, to go this far in public. They'd been outside long enough that they could, reasonably, be noticed, and Amber was a knockout even when they weren't doing anything out of the ordinary, drawing catcalls and sometimes a little too much attention. But Jade couldn't have stopped herself from reaching between her girlfriend's legs and slipping her fingers inside her if she'd wanted to. Of course, Amber wasn't wearing panties, and of course Amber was wet. Jade looked up, looked at Amber's eyes—full, wide, riveted on hers, her teeth clamped around the metal chain, her body saying, in a language that needed no words, *Take me.* And Jade did, no longer on quite the power trip she'd been on before, but now intent on giving something back.

She worked her fingers in the familiar ways she'd grown to learn Amber liked, navigating her insides, feeling her press back against her in response. Usually this was when Amber let out a stream of dirty words, or Jade did, or both of them did, but this time, Jade was silent as she pushed three fingers deep into Amber's pussy, and then four, because she needed to be as far as she could go. She felt a slight twinge in her wrist as she shifted, sinking to her knees so she could peek up Amber's skirt; the sight of her hand in Amber's cunt never failed to make her swell with pride. She kept going, not needing to rattle the chain, not needing to slap or hit or hurt Amber any more, because she knew Amber could still feel the glow of the pain, the sweet sting from getting exactly what she wanted. Then Jade couldn't resist, and pressed her head against Amber for a quick taste of her clit, a quick suck on her engorged bud that had Amber twisting her hips in response.

That was what did it; that stroke of her tongue had Amber coming hard, coming so hard she crushed Jade's hand just the way she liked it. When Jade felt Amber relax, she pulled her hand out, then got out a handi-wipe, because she was a top who came prepared. "Let go," she said, taking the chain from Amber's teeth with her own, both of them still hungry. She released the clamps slowly, heard Amber's loud gasp as the blood rushed back into her nipples. Jade untied Amber's wrists and pulled her clothes back in place. They'd been out there maybe ten minutes, Jade guessed; not long, but enough time to do what she needed to do. Jade took Amber's hand and led it between her legs. She was packing. She kept it there as they walked home, where it would be Jade's turn to get exactly what she wanted.

SECRETARY'S
DAY

The day of my interview with one of the top law firms in New York City, I'm sweating through my brand-new designer suit, desperately mopping at my brow as I try to look composed. I'm fresh out of Rutgers, making my way through round after round of Manhattan office buildings, steep high-rises filled with bankers, lawyers, editors, and businessmen. Being a male applying for a job as an administrative assistant in the year 2007 is no easy task, let me tell you. Sure, we've said that we're all about equal opportunity, but to the minds of most bosses, the job is still that of a secretary, and she should be wearing a suit, heels, and pearls. I've done plenty of temp work, can type one hundred words per minute, and am prompt and efficient, not to mention having edited the school paper, but so-so grades and a major in American studies have landed me here today.

Well, that and the fact that women in suits make my cock hard. Unbearably hard. So hard it's almost painful. Women with power, the power to tower over me, to snap their fingers and make me obey; women who need their phones answered, need coffee brought to them, need a man "ready for anything," as the classic David Allen business book advises. The kind of woman who's got so much going on, who's turbo charged and needs someone to keep her action-packed, meeting-filled day running smoothly, those are the ones I dream about.

I've never told anyone about these fantasies, but I've had them for as long as I can remember. While my buddies went for the hot cheerleader types or the sweet girls-next-door, I was after the valedictorian, Audrey Hayden (and occasionally fantasized about our very prim and proper English teacher, who was actually British). With Audrey, I loved the way she raised her hand so knowingly in class, the smug look on her face when she finished a test, and, most especially, seeing her in her interview suits. She looked so efficient, so strong, like she could take over the world, become president or an ambassador. Power wasn't something she questioned, but something she owned, and rather than wanting power of my own, I wanted her power unleashed on me. With Audrey, I never got up the courage to tell her how I felt, just looked longingly at her from afar.

Aside from my fetish, the fact is, if I want to move out of my parents' house in Hackensack, I need to get a job fast. I've been grilled about my background, ambitions, and educational history, usually by creaky older guys who look like they could barely get it up in the sack, let alone submit to a woman if they were smart enough to know how exciting it would be. Or could be, I guess I should say, since I've never actually realized these fantasies. I'm just starting to drift off into my go-to jerk-off material, where I'm down on all fours getting my ass inspected by a woman with sharp, spiky heels, bright red lipstick, and a voice that could cut glass, when I hear my name called . . . by a woman who looks like she's walked straight out of my naughty daydreams.

"Matthew Brick!" she calls, my name ringing out amongst the other, all female, applicants. I stand up uncertainly; I definitely arrived after a few of the women here, and we all signed in on a clipboard. Some of them sigh, chomp their gum, blow their bangs huffily off of their foreheads. They've noticed this preferential treatment too. But I look up at the woman with gleaming black hair done up in a bun, wire-rim glasses, an off-white blouse, navy skirt, bare legs, and four-inch heels, and I follow her, doing my best to look professional. "I'm Ms. Davis," she says, and something about the way she introduces herself— the inscrutable Ms., the lack of a first name, the clipped tone— further sets me off. "I'm the senior partner here and in charge of overseeing the office, so this position will require a lot from whoever gets it. I expect my assistant to be at my beck and call pretty much twenty-four hours a day. You'll have a BlackBerry and cell phone and I expect you to keep them on at all times." She's talking like I already have the job, while I try to keep my eyes straight ahead instead of on her ass as we walk down a long hallway, but it's hard not to stare. It's even harder not to picture myself on my knees, wrists bound behind my back, while my tongue plays between those pert cheeks.

Actually, I'd do anything she wants: massage her feet, get her coffee, spend hours under her desk tonguing her to orgasm. I'd even sit meekly, as I am now, while she flicks through papers on her desk. "I see here that you were the editor of your campus newspaper. Interesting. I'm curious how such a promising young man as yourself is now up for a position like this." She puts my resume down and leans across the desk, her ferocious gaze gobbling me up. Something in her brown eyes sears into me, and I think of a cat opening its jaw, teeth flashing. "It seems to me that you'd want to be the one giving orders, not taking them, and I'm not sure how you'd feel about working for me.

We're a big company but I run things with an iron fist. Employees are expected to go above and beyond, and this position calls for it more than any other."

"Well, I got into some trouble in school, slacking off a bit, if you must know," I say, my heart pounding. "I was spending so much time running the newspaper that I let my studies get away from me. But I've changed my ways and am now ready to take on real, adult responsibilities." I don't tell her that my male professors had failed to inspire the kind of diligence, not to mention lust, that she already had in me. There was no way I'd let someone like Ms. Davis down. "I'd be fully committed to making your day run smoothly." I don't add that I'd be fully committed to making her nights hum steadily along as well. I'm trying to quell my aching cock in my lap as I listen to her go through the duties that would be expected of me. It's much more than filing and answering phones. I'd be entrusted with an enormous amount of responsibility, would have to do errands for her at off hours, make phone calls, book trips, attend meetings, and make crucial decisions in her absence.

As she wraps up, I picture her sitting at her desk, while I stand behind her, massaging those majestic shoulders, helping to take away some of her cares. I tune back in to hear her saying, "I'll need some references from your old bosses, and I will confirm with you next week, but as long as you can prove yourself useful around here, you've got the job." She stands up and brusquely dismisses me, and I'm partly grateful because my arousal is too great to ignore. I'm tempted to use the bathroom in the building to jerk off, but I leave, walking by all those seemingly perfect girls. I feel their glares on my back as I wait for the elevator, then go to a nearby bookstore and relieve myself there, all the while thinking about being caught jerking off under my desk by Ms. Davis. I'm grateful that even though my grades weren't top notch, my senior advisor and journalism professor, who'd overseen the campus paper, had adored me.

When I get the congratulatory call from Ms. Davis a few days later, I'm ecstatic. "I'll see you first thing tomorrow, thank you so much, I truly appreciate this opportunity—"

She cuts me off. "Enough with the gushing, Brick. Just show up tomorrow and be ready to work." I do my best to get to sleep early, knowing I'll have to take the bus in for a few more weeks until I can find a nearby place of my own. I awake with the sun, my cock hard, fresh from a dream in which Ms. Davis takes her hair out of her bun and then lashes it across my face, then tickles my cock with her long tresses before instructing me how to wash, condition, and style it. I know none of the things I'm fantasizing about are in my job description, but there's something about this powerful woman that makes me feel like she might want to take things even further.

I arrive and do my best to put on a completely professional appearance. I'm thrown right into the thick of things from the first moment. Ms. Davis (whose first name is Vanessa, but I'm never to call her that) barely has time to introduce me to anyone, and I get lots of pitying looks from my new coworkers. "Hang in there," is their common refrain, and I surmise that my predecessor had only lasted a short while. Hints of her demise are everywhere, but I'm too frantic answering Ms. Davis's incessantly ringing phone, organizing the incoming mail, and trying to remember where things go and who's who that I don't have time to ponder the desk's previous occupant too much.

Finally, a day of sweating and nerves and nonstop running around (I ate a roast beef sandwich someone thrust on my desk at one point in about three bites) comes to an end. I'm afraid I'll get fired already for some imagined misdeed, but the office quiets and everyone else goes home, so I eventually do too. I'm hoping for a special message from Ms. Davis, but she seems intent on whatever she's doing in her office and I don't want to interrupt her. The rest of my first week follows pretty much the same routine, except that on Friday, just after six, I'm called into Ms. Davis's office. She summons me over the intercom, with the utmost formality, even though she could pretty much just yell from her office. I rise and walk slowly into her office, not wanting to let go of what promises to be a fabulous job.

"Sit down," she says, her voice severe. She looks me over, surveying every inch of my body until I want to shrink into the floor. Does she know about the lusty thoughts I've harbored? "I wanted to congratulate you on a successful first week. I know I threw a lot at you, and you handled it like a pro." My breath whooshes out of me with her praise. I'm not getting fired. Then her long nails tap sharply on her desk. "However, there are some additional duties of the job that I'm not quite sure you're capable of, so I called you in here to test them. These are duties of a more . . . *personal* nature," Ms. Davis says, her eyes drilling into me. I'm hard, and I wonder if she can tell. "Do you think you can handle these extracurricular tasks? Not every *man* is *up* for the job," she says, emphasizing my gender in a way that makes me squirm.

"Yes, Ms. Davis. I'm still available to you anytime you need me. For anything," I finish, hoping I don't sound too impertinent. But apparently, I don't, because then things take a turn for the surreal—and utterly arousing.

It's like she can see inside me with those penetrating gazes, because my new boss says, "Give me your tie, Matthew. I need it." This is the first time she's called me that, and I hope it means a shift in our relationship. Her voice is almost robotic, so stiff and formal, yet all the more seductive because of it. Part of me wants to be special to her, her boy toy, her trusted right-hand man, her plaything, but an even greater part of me wants to be a speck of dust, replaceable, inconsequential, someone for her to truly use, abuse, and discard. I detect glimmers that I am the former, but keep doubting them and assuming I'm the latter, and the mental seesaw has me permanently hard, wanting to please her and anger her all at once. When I don't move fast enough, she gets up, stands before me, towering over me really, and tugs on the tie, enough for it to choke me for a brief, beautiful moment. Then she turns, grabs a pair of scissors from her desk, and brusquely cuts it off me. "'For anything.' Those were your words, so I hope you'll remember them," she spits at me as she removes the tie from my neck. For some reason I still feel tight there, almost choked, yet I'm perfectly free.

Ms. Davis is still standing over me, perusing me, as if deciding whether to kick me out or continue her delicious torment. She drills that gaze into me for a moment, then moves to her office door, shuts it, and locks it. She returns, then runs the dull edge of the scissors against my neck, making me flinch. "You're pathetic, you know that?" she says. "Well, I guess you do," she murmurs almost to herself when my dick pops right up at her comment. She raises one leg enough to show me a glimpse of her pale thigh, then gently trails the sharp heel of her shoe along my cock. Not enough to hurt, barely enough to make contact, but more than enough to let me know that she's the boss of me in every way that counts.

"On the floor," she says, pointing, as if there's no need for using any extra words with an underling like me. I do her bidding, settling on the gray carpet. I'm lying faceup, practically inhaling tufts of carpet, dressed in a stiff, white shirt and perfect black pants, shoes shiny, while her dark green alligator heel holds me down in the middle of my chest. She's simply resting her foot there at the moment, not pressing hard, but my heart is pounding as if she were bearing all her weight on me. I can just about see up her skirt if I move my head to the side, but when I make an attempt, she's having none of that. She has taken my mutilated tie and is swinging it in the air like a victory lasso.

"You've been waiting for this since that first day, haven't you? I don't need to be a genius to see what it's doing to you," she says, referring to the monster erection I'm sporting. Her foot moves down, slowly but menacingly, to my cock, then she runs the edge of her shoe along my dick. I wonder if she'll kick me there, or on my balls; if she'll stand on top of me with all her weight; if she'll take off her shoe and shove her stocking-covered smelly toes into my mouth. She does none of these things, though I'd have acquiesced to any.

"Take it out," she says, kicking the air near my zipper, depriving me of that most desired contact. Still, the chance to show her what I'm packing, to maybe make her day with my dick is too precious to waste any more time. Under her watch, I reach over the shoe she's placed back on my chest and unzip my pants, fumbling to unearth my hardness. Then I lie back while my hard-on rises straight up into the air. As turned on as I am being almost naked beside her, I can't help but want her to touch it.

"Very good. Now, we're going to go over some rules of the office to make sure you've been paying attention. Good help is hard to find and I'd rather have a virile man like you than one of those pesky, peroxide blondes who keep applying. And if you tell anyone I said that, I'll make sure you're sorry," she says.

I swallow hard, worried now only about coming spontaneously. "Now, what's the password to my computer?" As she fires off this question, Ms. Davis removes her sleek black jacket. I can see her breasts through her blouse; she hasn't worn a bra today, but you'd only know that without the jacket.

"Bitchgoddess-oh-seven," I immediately reply.

"How do I like my coffee?"

These questions are easy, but the look on her face tells me my job depends on getting them right. "Black."

"What kind of thread count sheets must you request when I'm traveling for work?"

"Six hundred." My voice is getting more and more wobbly as she gets more and more naked. It's like I'm on a game show, and each question I get right grants me another body part unveiled. Soon her breasts are only separated from me by the air, and the sight of her pert, pink nipples is enough to make me ache.

"How often do I need you to water my plants?" Hmm . . . this is a trick question, because she told me to water them a minimum of twice a day, but preferably three. Two, or three? Will I look like I'm showing off if I say three? The last two days I've been so busy I've only done it twice, so I go with that.

"Wrong answer," she says, a cruel grin lighting up her face. "But you know what happens to boys who can't obey their bosses? They learn new ways to please them," she says. She steps over me so I can see her pussy. It's bare and pink and wet. I've only been with two other girls, and neither of them shaved, and both wanted to fuck with the lights out. Ms. Davis seems to want to view every inch of my aroused, terror-stricken body. Only the terror is quickly giving way to pleasure when I realize she is about to shut me up in the hottest way possible.

"Now, Matthew. This is really the only skill you need at this job. The girl who was here before you could barely find her own clit, let alone mine. She didn't know how to eat pussy, or to make my ass happy. She didn't know much of anything, but she did let me spank her sweet bottom, so I let her stay for a while. Before her was a football player type who got a bit too aggressive, thinking that we'd take turns being in charge. I want you to remember that I'm always in charge of you. I don't just need a secretary; I need a servant. A willing, devoted servant. You seem to fit the bill, but I want you to prove it," she continues, her voice commanding but not, surprisingly, cruel. Beneath her brusque words, I sense a tenderness, a capacity for giving that can only be revealed through this form of speaking. Not that I'm complaining; the way she's talking is only making me more aroused.

She surveys me one more time, and I must meet her approval because she gives me that same wicked, wonderful smile, then hikes up her skirt and lowers herself down so I'm enveloped by her pussy. It happens as if in slow motion, and soon we are no longer just secretary and boss, but owned and owner, man and mistress, servant and master. I relish not only the taste of her cunt as it meets my tongue, but also that she sees me as someone capable of absorbing her power and using my submission to strengthen her. Even though I'm young and perhaps idealistic, I know that she cannot seize power, cannot truly attain the levels of greatness she's capable of, in and out of the office, without an underling to support her. That is my job, and now, with my tongue, I do my best to excel at it. She makes it easy by pretty much shoving her sex into my mouth, by maneuvering all around, by using my face as her own personal Slip 'n Slide.

I moan against her cunt, feeling the vibrations reverberate from my lips to hers and back. I know I could get fired—hell, she could get fired—for doing this on company property, but I also have a feeling that anyone who tries to fire Ms. Davis would soon find himself in a similar position. Anyone would melt in front of her, and as she overtakes my mouth, I do feel as if I'm melting, into the ground, and into her. She's melting too, softening bit by bit as her grip on my ears loosens and her moans get softer. Instead of yelling directions, she's moaning, not words, just sounds. Ms. Davis is turning into Vanessa, turning from corporate to climactic, and all because of me!

I try to memorize the taste and feel of her pussy lips, so different from the tentative lapping I've done before. With her positive feedback spurring me on, I chance to raise my hands and slide them around her legs so I can play with those lips, stroke that clit. She lets me play with her, so that I'm feeling the wondrous sensual softness inside her. I was right—she does have a gentler side, and I'm touching it right now. Her face looks almost relaxed, younger, yet just as beautiful as before. She still controls me, which she proves by suddenly pressing my forehead to the floor with her palm and grinding away again. "Suck it!" she says, and I suck her clit, suck her lips, suck everything I can, wishing I had two or even three mouths to suck other parts of her as well.

Finally, after what feels like an hour but I later learn has only been fifteen minutes, she comes, her orgasm a rumbling, powerful wave crashing against my mouth, her body bouncing against me as she crests. She rises and looks remarkably composed for someone who's just had her pussy licked so intensely. I feel like we've just had sex on a fast-moving vehicle, or a comet. My heart is pounding and I'm glad I'm lying down. I'm so dizzy with desire for her, I almost ignore my cock. This craving, this need, goes deeper than my dick. But Ms. Davis hasn't forgotten it. She smiles down at me, then goes to her desk and returns with a small bottle. I don't know what's in it until she opens it and starts pouring the clear liquid directly onto my cock. It's cool and slippery and I moan. "Jerk yourself off. Give me a show. But don't come on my carpet," Ms. Davis instructs me. "Use this," she says, handing me a bunch of tissues.

I'd have thought it would be hard to masturbate in front of anyone else, let alone the woman of my dreams, who also happens to be my new boss, but it turns out to be surprisingly easy. I look up at her as she sits at her desk as if overseeing me. I don't worry about whether the style I use is what she wants, knowing she'll correct me if I'm doing anything wrong. Instead, I just focus on the extreme pleasure of being watched by her. In practically no time, I'm scrambling for the tissues as my orgasm bursts into them. She nods approvingly, though I'm suddenly shy. We've shared something so intimate, yet there is still a great distance between us. I remind myself we are not lovers, or even friends, but rather, still secretary and boss. For a moment, I'm wistful, and wish our positions were different so I could get even closer to her.

She walks over as I'm zipping my fly. "Very good, Matthew. I had a feeling about you when I saw you in the waiting room. Now, I have an early brunch tomorrow, but I'm going to need your assistance in the late afternoon. I have some . . . home office affairs to take care of. Filing, typing, foot massage, that type of thing. I'll expect you there at four." She doesn't ask if I'm free; she knows I'm the very opposite of free. I'm hers, pure and simple; even if she were to fire me, I'd do that kind of work for "free."

"Oh, and dress casual. Very casual, as in, no underwear. You won't be needing it." She dismisses me with another nod and I go the bathroom to reluctantly wash my face of her juices before walking back to my desk to shut off my computer and grab my coat. As I sign out, the security guard peers at me closely, as if he can see, or smell, or simply sense, who I am now. A secretary, but also a slave. A bottom through and through. A devotee. I give him a big, dazzling smile. I don't really care what anyone else calls me, as long as Ms. Davis calls me hers. And while I know that the formal holiday of Secretary's Day (now renamed Administrative Professionals Day) takes place in April,

I'm going to celebrate mine as of now, in June, because really, how lucky can a guy get? I've got a paying job and a boss who knows exactly how to whip me into shape, one who keeps me almost permanently hard, *and* wants me to "work" weekends. My Wall Street friends can eat their hearts out. I'll be too busy eating Ms. Davis to notice.

CAUGHT IN
THE ACT

S he didn't look like a vandal, or even particularly naughty, but it was Dylan's job as By the Book's manager to suss out any possibly illegal or damaging activity, anything that would interfere with the business, whether that meant kids with sticky fingers or adults trying to palm magnets up their sleeves or stick paperbacks in their purses.

But this woman, with her yellow flowered dress and literal flowers in her honey-blonde hair, her cheeks rosy and mouth glistening to match, wasn't trying to be surreptitious. She had a sharp-bladed knife and was slicing it evenly down the pages of a book, as if she owned it. Her hand was steady, practiced.

"Ma'am," he said, having been taught to always stick with that honorific, even if it offended some of the younger customers, "what exactly are you doing?" It was a ridiculous question, since what she was doing was perfectly obvious, but he asked anyway.

"I'm borrowing a story. I can't take this book home with me

and . . . I've read it five times, and simply need to have it." She said the words with such conviction, like this was a perfectly normal thing to do.

"You do understand that we can't sell this book you've now destroyed and we're going to need you to pay for it, right?"

"Why would I pay for a book that's missing pages?"

"That's exactly my point. Nobody will, so you've cost us the price of this book." He plucked it from her hand and read the title, his face heating up as he said the words aloud. "*Filthy Sluts and the Men Who Love Them.*"

"Is this one of your most popular titles?"

"I wouldn't know," he said, even though that wasn't exactly true. He didn't know how well every book in the store sold since he wasn't the owner, but he would have known if it was one of their most popular, because it would've been front and center in the main display, and if it were truly popular, would appear on their bestseller list, likely causing many outbursts and complaints. He'd never actually seen the book before, and despite stocking thousands of titles, he would have remembered the way the cover model was practically naked, her body only covered by the flimsiest of lingerie, the kind designed to reveal more than it concealed.

"Besides, that's irrelevant. It's our inventory, and you're stealing it. There's punishment that comes from stealing, young lady," he said, the words causing him to suddenly feel far older than twenty-eight. As his threat hovered in the air, he knew he was at a precipice. He could let her go, chuckle at the funny story—of course their budget included contingencies like shoplifting—or he could seize the opportunity before him, one he'd never thought would actually happen in real life.

"Is there?" she asked with a glint in her eye, her face filled with both defiance and desire, a look that told him she hadn't done this simply to take home a story, but for another reason entirely—to get caught. She'd been hoping for it, waiting to see what someone like him—Dylan, according to his name tag—would do. He knew in a flash she'd deliberately chosen this sleepy Wednesday when hardly anyone was in the store to partake of this crime.

That look on her face made him stand taller in a way no chiropractor with their notes about a string pulling on his head or the importance of good posture could ever do. Dylan had never felt so tall, so powerful, so dominant. He considered himself a goofy book nerd, but this woman with her utility knife and entitled air and hint of kinkiness was turning him into someone else, second by second, like a human morphing into his superhero self.

She stared at him with fire in her deep blue eyes, as if trying to assess him and tell him about herself in a few blinks of her eyes. The look was brief and blazing, and feelings he never expected to have at work washed over him as a plan formed in his mind. He would give her exactly what she deserved—and what he was sure she wanted.

"Yes, young lady," he continued, even though she was maybe five years younger than him at most. "Very severe punishment for doing what you're doing."

"What if I refuse?" she shot back, a carefully plucked eyebrow arching in a dare.

"Are you?" He wasn't backing down.

"I can't answer that until I know what the punishment is."

Now she was the one taunting him, and damn if his cock didn't leap at the tease, the promise, the temptation. "Get up," he said, all charm gone from his voice. He was half focused on her, half wondering who else was in the store. He could envision her so easily on her knees, that hair falling all around her face, hands shackled behind her back, while he slid his cock deep into her mouth.

She got to her feet, her sunny yellow heels another contrast to that blazing look on her face. *She should be in all black,* he thought, *a tough Goth girl looking for trouble.* But this woman with flowers in her hair may not have been Goth, but as she stood, sliding the blade back into its proper sheathed place, he felt the sparks igniting between them. He stepped closer to her; his body wasn't touching hers yet, but he was so close, he felt the heat radiating from her skin. He wanted to bite her shoulder, to sink his teeth into the freckle-dotted flesh being bared to him.

Instead, he leaned in so his lips were right next to her ear, so when he spoke, they couldn't help but brush against her skin. "To answer your question, if you refuse to pay for the book, I'm going to make you get on the microphone and read the entirety of"—he picked the pages she'd cut out off the floor—"'I Want to be Fucked so Hard I'm Sore.' to everyone in the store. If you felt okay about blatantly cutting it out of the book where anyone could come across you, you probably are a filthy slut who wants everyone to know it. I bet if I put my hand between your legs, you'd be a fucking sopping wet mess. If I shoved my fingers into your pussy they'd slide right in, wouldn't they?"

She didn't try to hide her whimper. "What's your name?" he growled, his cock pressing against his zipper.

"Janet."

"Such an innocent name for such a dirty girl, isn't it?" He wanted to fist his hand in that hair and tug hard, but he couldn't right here, and he needed to know for sure she wanted it. "Well, Janet, are you going to pay for the book, or are you going to take your punishment like the filthy slut you are? I have a few coworkers who would love to hear you read every last dirty word of this story to them."

While that was probably true, he was the only one working today, charged with closing up. The store's tracker had told him they were the only ones in the store; he'd locked the outside using their new virtual locking system, but he wasn't about to tell Janet that. Let her think she had an audience; she probably wanted one.

"Well . . ." she started, her voice wobbling just enough to let me know she wasn't as tough as her book excising would indicate, "while I do have the money to pay for the book, on principle, I'm going to take my punishment."

"Principle, huh?" Dylan made sure his words weren't just heard but felt against her ear; he was close enough that her shudder brought her shoulder in contact with his chest. The touch was like a shockwave, even through their clothes. For a moment, he imagined what she'd been planning to do with the story when she got home. Did she have the kind of vibrator she'd shove deep into her pussy? "So, for the sake of your principles, I'm also going to act out some of the things you read in that story, to help you deliver a strong performance. If you want me to stop, you can say X-acto. Like the knife."

"I don't think that's going to happen," she said, so quietly he almost thought he'd imagined it. Then he did what he'd been longing to do, sinking his fingers into her sleek, shiny hair, and tugging hard. With her head bent back, her neck titled up, her tits straining against the scoop neck dress, she almost made him forget they were in a bookstore, in his place of business. He wanted to lick and bite and seize her all over, especially when she let out a breathy sigh that made her breasts press even more tightly against the fabric.

"I don't think so either, not with a dirty slut like you." He might have thought saying the word "slut" over and over would make it lose its charm, but the opposite was happening. Those four little letters only made his cock harder, and he'd bet money she was getting wetter each time he said it too.

"Let's go into the back and put that mouth to good use." There were many other things he wanted to do with those glossy pink lips, but hearing her read the story, whatever it contained, was sure to make whatever came next even more exciting. He picked up the papers and indicated for Janet to walk in front of him so he could watch the swish of her flowy dress against her ass. It was such an incongruous combination, this daredevil of a woman in a dress that looked like it belonged to a woman frolicking in a field of dandelions. But instead, she was reading about filthy sluts. The combination of her innocent outfit and dirty mind made him want to grab her right there and pin her against a bookcase, to let his aching cock out and slide it home into what he was sure would be a very tight, hot pussy.

But he was also curious. Who were the filthy sluts in the book? And who were the men who loved them? Did they mean "love" as in "love" or "love" as in "love to watch be filthy?" And why had she chosen the story she'd chosen? His mind tumbled with possibilities and questions; yes, he was harder than he could ever remember being, but he was also deeply curious about this woman he'd never seen in the store before today. Did she make a practice of doing this? Did she have a collection of smutty pages at home she was looking to add to? Did she have any full books, bound the way they were intended to be?

Suddenly, Janet stopped short, and he almost knocked her over. He righted himself just as his body collided with hers, and now it was his turn to moan. "Why did you stop?" he asked, trying to be stern.

"I couldn't wait any longer to feel you bumping up against me," was her reply, followed by a trilling laugh as she wiggled her ass against his cock.

"You'll feel more than that very soon," he said as he pulled her hips back flush with his body. "Keep walking," he said as he reached around her and pinched a nipple, hard enough to make her yelp. Of course, feeling her beaded nub through the thin fabric of the dress and hearing the corresponding noise didn't make it any easier to keep walking and not throw her to the ground.

"You're just prolonging your punishment," Dylan told her. Did he imagine that she walked a little faster?

When they got to the employee room, she was still in front of him, and didn't step aside, so he had to press against her once again to put the key in the lock. "This way," he said with a hand on her shoulder, guiding her to the mic they used for storewide announcements.

He turned it on. "Check, one two, check." His loud words reverberated through the air. "It's on," he said, handing her the pages. "And so are you, filthy Janet." How were those two words even hotter than calling her a slut? Even if she'd been lying about her name, which he didn't think she was, pairing it with the word from the book's title that fit her perfectly ratcheted up his arousal.

She held the pages with their very neatly cut-through edge in her hand. He watched as she opened her mouth, but no sound came out. Her lips moved and seemed to start to form some words, but the mic only crackled with her breath. "If you don't read this, not only will you be disappointing me and my staff, who were very eager to hear what filthy sluts like to do, but you won't get to have any of this," he said into her ear, taking her hand and letting it rest on his erection. Her fingers immediately closed around the length, squeezing him.

"You want to get fucked, don't you, Janet? Hard and hot and fast, maybe while you suck on my fingers, or with my hand wrapped around your neck like this, don't you?" Dylan asked as he cupped his fingers around the curve of her sweet neck. Her hand wrapped itself even more firmly around his dick the moment he applied the lightest of pressure. He immediately took his hand off of her and extricated his cock from her hold.

"You won't get any of that, not a single touch, if you don't read those words. Plus, for disobeying, I won't even let you take that story home. I'll make you leave here with your pussy wet and aching and totally empty, with those hard, proud nipples not twisted or pinched or slapped or bitten."

She cleared her throat and immediately started reading. "I want to be fucked so hard I'm sore." Her voice was a little uncertain, the words barely above a whisper, but amplified by the mic. "I wake up every morning and my pussy feels completely empty and needy, like if I don't get fucked by a very big cock, I'll be miserable. Every day I go out looking for the biggest cock I can find."

As she found her reading rhythm, he lifted up that golden-yellow dress and smiled at her yellow lace panties, a scrap of a garment. Touching her between her legs, pressing the lace up against her wetness, practically had him coming in his pants. "I shower, get dressed, then go to try to seduce the first man I see. I don't care who he is—a stranger or a neighbor, young or old, any body type or race. I just want to know that he can fulfill that ache."

He teased her, keeping the little bit of lace a barrier between his fingers and what she really wanted, sliding it slowly up and down her wet slit, only lightly toying with her clit when he reached it. "This day, on my way to the newsstand, where I knew the owner, Stan, kept his own stash of dirty magazines in the back, I saw a man stroking his cock in the park. He was wearing a gray T-shirt and shorts, but he'd grabbed his cock and wasn't doing much to hide his jerking motions."

Dylan interrupted her, pushing aside the panties to shove

two fingers deep inside her as he did. "They're telling me they like your story. They're picturing every image. They can't wait to hear what the filthy slut does next." The truth was, his coworkers were English majors and literature snobs who probably wouldn't have wanted anything to do with such a pedestrian story, but they were the ones missing out. Janet could have simply said the word "cock" over and over again in her breathy voice and he would have been a goner.

She resumed the story while Dylan reached around her to stroke her clit with his other hand while his fingers pressed and curled and probed her depths. "I moved toward his cock as if drawn to it by a magnetic force tugging me closer. Here was my first cock of the day. I didn't care that we were in public where anyone might see us. That's how much of a slut I am."

Janet's body was responding to what she was reading just as surely as his was. The way she was tightening around him, making him have to work harder to press inside her as she squirmed and wiggled and soaked his fingers, told him the story she was reading aloud was at least partly her fantasy too, one she liked enough to need to own it so she could read it every day.

"I rushed toward him, running, not wanting him to finish without me. Even though my pussy was wet and throbbing, I sank to my knees. 'I want to help,' I said as I licked my way up his shaft, wanting to taste all of him. Being down on my knees felt so right, especially when he took his cock and offered it to me, as if he too knew I belonged there." The image of Janet on her knees was too much for Dylan. He kept stroking her with his fingers but had to take out his cock.

As he slid the zipper down, she gasped, but recovered, her lips bumping up against the mic as she continued the story. "'What a pretty slut,' he said as he grabbed me by the back of my head and guided my mouth into position. I didn't even have time to take a breath before he was pushing it into my mouth. It was a struggle to take it, but I liked the struggle. My pussy was fully engorged, slick as can be, as his large cock stretched my mouth open."

Part of Dylan wanted to stop her, to take the mic and bring it down to the floor along with them and have her suck his cock just like that, while broadcasting the sound to the empty store. But her voice was so full and rich and sensual, he didn't want her to stop this sexy soundtrack. He pushed her panties down her thighs, added a third finger, and fucked her hard with them, preparing her for his cock. She pushed back against him, keeping up the rhythm even as she resumed the fictional blowjob.

"I thought I might come before him; I was so overcome with desire. His hands roamed my face, stroking my cheeks and neck, sometimes giving one cheek a little slap that made me shiver. My mouth was as wet as my pussy, dripping with saliva, making it easy to maintain what I was doing and slowly swallow more and more of him. 'Take it all, you dirty come-guzzler,' he said, which only made me want to do exactly that. 'I bet you'd love to have a crowd of people cheering you on,' he said, which made me clamp down harder around his dick, even as my pussy clamped down on nothing, the ache inside me echoing outward. If this kept up, I was going to have to slam my fingers inside myself."

The story was totally over the top, but for Dylan and Janet, it was the perfect read, a surreal, sexy accompaniment as he rubbed the head of his cock against her warm, wet opening and then plunged deep inside. "Don't stop reading, Janet, or I'll take away my cock," Dylan impressed himself by saying, because she could start reciting the alphabet or making animal noises and there was no way he'd leave the nirvana of her clutching, skin-tight tunnel as it beckoned him farther inside. He slammed into her hard, knowing he wouldn't last long. He sniffed her hair, the scent of flowers and fruit filling him.

"I moaned against his cock to let him know that yes, I was so depraved I would gladly have welcomed a crowd. Every time he pinched my cheek or touched my neck or pulled my hair, I seemed to merge more tightly together with him, my mouth and his cock doing an intimate dance, one where each seemed made for the other. My throat relaxed, guiding him down deep until my lips were buried at the base. All the while, my pussy was tightening and releasing, engorged and deeply ready to be fucked hard."

At those words, Dylan began pounding even deeper into her, pulling her close with one hand on her hip, while the other pushed down her dress to get at her nipple again. He pinched it hard, twisting it until she made breathy little pants. He could practically feel the fiery ripple from her hard little nub straight to her pussy as it tightened around him with each pinch. He slowed down, not wanting to come just yet, even though a part of him wanted to release inside her right then and there.

"Just when I didn't think I could get any more turned on, he started fucking my mouth in earnest, as if what we'd just done was mere light foreplay. He'd pull me by the hair so my lips barely connected with the tip, then shove himself back in, hard. 'I have a dildo at home that a friend gave me as a joke. It's huge. I was sure it was too huge for any woman, but you, my sexy little slut, could probably take the whole thing in one go. Do you want me to take you home after you swallow all my come and have me tie you up so your arms and legs are wide open and all you can do is take this huge purple dong in that wet little pussy? Maybe I should gag that pretty mouth, but then I couldn't make you suck my cock again. So many possibilities for a girl who'll do anything. Is your pussy very wet right now?'"

At that, she paused and let out a barely-there "yes" as he continued to fuck her harder and harder, almost past the point of no return. "Tell them, Janet. Forget the story for a second. Tell everyone how wet your pussy is right now."

She cried out, the sound a garbled unleashing of her desire. "I'm so wet, so so wet, and Dylan is fucking me so hard but I want it even harder." He shifted his fingers to her clit as she told her imagined audience all about what he was doing to her. "I tore out the story because that's basically what I'm like. I want to be fucked every day, multiple times a day, the harder the better, and if I don't get that, I have to use my imagination."

Dylan was there, the sensation building up from his balls and about to overtake him. "I can only sleep well if my pussy is sore from being used like this. I try to hide it in how I dress, and sometimes try to tamp it down or take care of it myself, but it comes out. My biggest fantasy is to have one cock in my pussy and one in my mouth, both of them slamming into me at the same time, then overflowing with jizz that I can barely manage to swallow, but I do anyway." That was what did it—not her fictional tale, but the real Janet, the one who was baring a part of her sexual soul for total strangers. Dylan erupted inside her, the orgasm quaking his entire body, the strength of it shocking him. He pinched and played with her clit as he drove into her with a few more strokes. When he gave her three of his fingers, the ones that had been inside her, she sucked on them like she'd never tasted anything so delectable.

Her orgasm rippled through her, milking the last drops from his spent cock as she clutched the mic stand, needing to steady herself as her body quivered. Eventually, when her climax subsided, he pulled up his jeans, picked her up, and nestled her onto his lap. His cock was done for the moment, but there was so much more he wanted to do with her. "How does it end?" he asked. "The story," he added at her blank look.

"Not surprisingly, her pussy is very wet, and he fucks her on the park bench, and then later he takes her home and shares her with his friends."

"What made you want to take that particular story?" he asked, genuinely curious even though he figured the other stories in the book probably had a similar trajectory.

"I don't know. It just called out to me. It's so . . . dirty." Now, in the after times, Janet wasn't quite as bold; she could barely look at him.

"How do you feel now? Was that what you wanted?"

She looked up into his eyes, searching for the real question he was asking. "Yes, that was perfect. I don't know what I thought would happen, but this was beyond. Dylan, are there really other people here?"

He couldn't lie when she was being so polite. "No . . . but my coworkers really would find everything about you totally hot."

"Maybe next time they can listen . . . and watch." She smiled up at him, a mix of wicked and knowing and dirty and shyly nervous.

"There's a lot I'd like to try with you next time. If you're up for it. Oh, and here. You deserve this." He handed her the cut-out pages along with the rest of the book.

"Only if you sign it for me."

He grabbed a pen and scrawled the words quickly.

She looked at the page. *To my favorite filthy slut.* She'd chosen her location wisely. She flipped the pages, looking for even more inspiration, and shivered, knowing they weren't going to be leaving any time soon.

THE DEPTHS
OF DESPAIR

Evan is staring at me intently, waiting for the answer to his question. "What do you want?" he whispered directly into my ear. Such a short sentence for the very complex response it opens up in me. I want a hundred million things from him, but at this moment, I want something I'm not totally sure either of us can handle.

"I want you to make me cry," I tell him. I have to whisper it because the words, and the realization, are so intense I'm not sure I can own up to them. But it's true; every time I think about his hands crashing down on me, his words berating me, his power keeping me in my lowly place, things we've done hundreds of times but that I still clamor for, I realize I don't want something light and easy, something we can laugh about later. I don't even want compliments like, "God, you can take a lot." It's not a competition for me; I know what my body can do, but I want to see what we can do together, if we can take spanking somewhere it's never gone before, if we can make it propel us into a new place where we lose ourselves only to find people we've always wanted to be. I've wanted this forever, I realize, as I say the words, but had never felt close enough with a lover to go there before him. I want something altogether different from every other spanking I've ever gotten, the ones that were hot and kinky and nasty, but that shied away from even approaching the edge of oblivion. Only with Evan can I dare to approach that dividing line that could topple our over-the-knee pleasures forever, or consecrate spanking as the centerpiece of our relationship.

I've never had to use a safeword before, and most of the time, I've barely even had one I could use. I trust my lovers implicitly and have never felt the need for one. Buried within that trust, though, is a safety net I'm not sure I still want, a safety net that suddenly feels altogether too constricting. I've never liked the word "play" used to describe kink, or at least, my kink. There's nothing playful about it, even though I know all about safe, sane, and consensual, and that I can stop at any time. I can top from below like the best of them, but something in me has finally rebelled at this topsy-turvy state of masochistic affairs. I'm ready for the real thing, and am finally strong enough to take it, and Evan is just the man to grant me my wish.

If we were the marrying kind, I'd have a nice, shiny rock to flash around to all. We're not, so I don't expect that, but I married him in my heart a month after we met. He had his cock inside me, was fucking me doggie-style, and I moved, just slightly, almost imperceptibly. "Don't move, Denise. Don't ever move. Stay with me forever," he said. I could've dismissed it as pillow talk—most women would have—but somehow, I knew he meant it. We've had our ups and downs in the year we've been together, but I've always known that he was the one. Not The One, the mystical, magical, phantom lover meant to fulfill a woman's every need and fantasy before we can even think of them. Not that One, but this one, my special one, the one who makes my heart beat like we're on a crashing airplane, who makes me smile when he wakes me in the middle of the night with a particularly loud snore, then one whose eyes and cock compete for best feature. The one who's made me relearn what submission is all about.

Yet even after a year of me naked, over his knee, or up against the wall, or bent over holding my ankles, or any number of other positions we've tried to perfect our spanking regimen, we still haven't reached the heights, or depths, I know we could. I haven't cracked the surface of his sadism, haven't pushed him to bring out the truly mean top I know lurks inside, haven't let myself sink into the glory of sub space so fully I wonder if I'll ever come out. My fantasies have gotten more and more twisted, perverse, unreal. But I don't want an army of lovers or community-wide kink; I want Evan, just Evan. It's through no fault of his, or mine, that we haven't gone there, I've just always surrendered to the lure of his cock when the pressure seemed unbearable, right before I went over the edge I'm afraid I'll never return from. What if after this I want him to make me cry all the time? What if he takes that as a sign I need therapy? What if we become one of those couples where the man gets off on fucking his wife but not in the way that makes him rush home to her? What if he thinks I'm crying because I'm sad or in pain or don't love him anymore? I have no answers or crystal ball, only know that the tears are demanding an exit, and won't take no for an answer. They aren't tears of sadness, that much I know for sure; what these tears signify I don't yet know, but am convinced Evan can help me understand.

He grabs me by the scruff of my neck, and I whimper, just like I have before, but there's something different in his eyes.

They're feral, wild with a kind of desire I've never seen before, and that sight unleashes a wave of want inside me. My entire body goes tight, then limp. "Be careful what you wish for, Dee," he says. "Very, very careful." When I make a move to open my mouth, he shuts my lips, pressing them between his thumb and forefinger. "Don't speak until we're done. You'll know when we're done. You can make noise, scream all you want, but no talking, unless you need to safeword. Your safeword is 'emergency.' But I don't think you're going to come anywhere close to using it." He lets go of my lips, then just stands there staring at me. At an even six feet, he's got a good five inches on me so I'm looking at up him, my face just as serious as his.

Then in a flash, he's grabbed me and moved us over so he can slam me against the wall. This is no gentle crash of which I'm just as complicit; *he* slams *me*, and it hurts, but I like the pain. A lot. My face smashes into the familiar white space, his hand against the side of my head. I've been up against countless walls since I met him, but never so close, where it's like I'm inhaling the paint. I've murmured, prayed even, into wood and brick and paint. But now my lips aren't so much touching the wall as merged with it. My body goes on red alert as he smears me into the wall. My pussy is pounding, demanding attention in much the same way my heart is thudding. "Stay there, whore." He knows that word sets me off, but this time, his voice is gruffer; it's not a playful term of endearment, and I almost feel like one. I wonder what I'd do if I really were a whore with a client who wanted to treat me like this. I focus on the plaster against my skin, on his hand that has just stabbed me in the lower back. Okay, not stabbed, but the pressure there is exquisite, his palm digging into the spot where my back curves, his thumb resting against my anus.

Then his hand booms down against my right butt cheek. I'd

thought I couldn't sink further into the wall, but I'd been wrong, because somehow, I become one with it. It hurts, and not in the way my ass does. My facial pain isn't quite the sweet, stinging, arousing pain that spanking brings, but this pain still manages to feel good in its own way, reminding me what I'm capable of in the name of getting off. I know my face will be red later, probably my breasts too. His hand keeps coming down against me, spanking me furiously in a way that surely has to singe his palm as much as it does my bottom. Then his teeth are sinking into the back of my neck and his four fingers are turning the backs of my thighs red. "Denise, now's as good a time as any to tell you. It's over." He's spanking me hard the whole time he speaks, and the smacks are so loud I almost can't make out what he's saying. "I didn't know how to break it to you, but I'm moving out. I've found my own place, over on Larch. I've got two more weeks here, and I'll try to be as discreet as I can. I was waiting for the right time to tell you, but now's as good as any, wouldn't you say?" He's talking like we're having some kind of adult conversation, meanwhile my entire stomach has dropped, yet my pussy is still on fire.

So is my ass, where he's still spanking me. I've had my hands up above me on the wall, but they start to drop. All I want now is to curl into a ball, wrapped around myself. *Fuck spanking*, I think, about to whisper, "emergency," when he presses his entire body against mine, lifting my hands back above me and pressing his palms to the backs of my hands, hard. "Keep those there, Dee. I said two more weeks, and don't think I'm not gonna get the most pussy out of you as I can before then. I don't want to forget this ass," he says as he pinches the skin there.

I'm not crying; I'm numb inside. Did I bring this on? This wasn't what I wanted. I keep my hands above me just to spite him. Now I won't cry, just to show him. "Stay right fucking there, whore," he says, and despite myself, I feel a shudder. He knows why it triggers me so—I used to be one, at least the worst kind of one, one who gave it away to anyone who so much as looked my way, succumbing to the word I'd been called since sprouting 38Ds senior year of high school—yet it also thrills a deep, secret place inside me. I was a slut who was so far gone she thought of herself as a whore, and even got off on the *blasé* way I could pick a guy up, bring him home, and chuck him out the door. But that nameless blur of men and cocks were nothing compared to the power I tapped into with Evan. Even the good guys, the ones trained in the art of BDSM, who worshipped my ass as much as they punished it, couldn't come close to what we have. Had. I don't know anymore. His hands are everywhere at once, firing off blows that make my whole body light up in recognition of my place, my role in this apocalyptic scene. I briefly wonder if he'll offer me money that I have to take from him with my teeth, as one guy did when I did a brief stint stripping. Yet even with his horrific words ringing in my ear, the image makes me wet. I picture him shoving dollar bills into my cunt, into my mouth, gluing them to my body, marking me as a whore once and for all.

My mind goes a little quieter as he slips the blindfold over my eyes. "Get over here," he says, grabbing me by my nipple, pinching it as he pulls me across the room. The point where our bodies touch stings, but a soothing, familiar heat travels lower. *I've asked for this, I want this, we'll deal with the aftermath later,* I think, as I feel him bend me over the spanking bench we bought in our first heady, kinky weeks together. *Who will spank me on it when he leaves?* I wonder as he settles me over it so my ass is perfectly poised. I expect the spanking to start up again immediately, and perhaps because of that, it doesn't. I can't see, but I can hear him moving around, the flick of a lighter, the

sharp inhale of a cigarette. I don't approve, but gave up lectur-
ing him long ago.

"You'll be rid of this smell soon enough," he says, as if reading my mind. He blows hot smoke against my ass, and I tremble.
I'm waiting, patiently, if you ask me, but he just strokes my ass
cheeks with the tips of his fingers, tickling me more than anything else. "I'll miss this ass, Denise. I hope you believe me. It
just has to be this way."

"Is it Monique?" I ask, before I can stop myself.

"Does that fucking matter, Denise?" he snarls, this time
pounding me so hard my stomach feels like it's colliding against
the seat of the bench, even though they're already connected.
He's smoking and spanking, somehow, as if he has all the time
in the world, as if he isn't providing not just the tears I asked for,
but countless more as well.

"Yes. No. I don't know," I sob, wanting to rewind to the
start of this scene. I try to let my mind go black, especially when
he moves around to kiss me hard, his breath smoky. He pulls
back and I see him draw the cigarette right under my lips, close
enough that I can feel the orange flame, before he moves aside
and puts it out right on our bedside table. This is a mean side
of him I've never seen before, something beyond sadistic, like
he wants to hurt me all the way through, not just make my ass
quake and smolder.

"Well, it's none of your business. Not anymore," he says,
and turns his back to me. He hasn't shackled me, yet I couldn't
move even if I wanted to. The bench is my savior, my companion, my safety net. I keep thinking he's going to bust out some
exquisite new toy, a wooden panel, a ruler, a cane. He likes
to make me scream and flinch, to mark me, render me as his
fully and completely. He likes that I'm into spanking, but always
finds ways to make me feel like an amateur spankee who hasn't

quite reached the levels of masochism his latest toy warrants. But this time, he goes back to that trusty favorite: his hand. He has ways of curving that body part that turn it into the sickest instrument around.

"Don't say a word, Denise. For once, just keep your fucking mouth shut." He sounds like someone else entirely; he's put on an accent to go with his words, Queens blue collar instead of his usual clipped, cultured, Westchester doctor voice. Yes, he loves playing doctor with me, another thing that'll have to end now, I suppose. "Good. I'm going to spank you until you're all cried out, and I'll be the judge of that."

Strangely, even though he starts with hardly any warmup, just raises his hand like a whip and strikes me smartly across my cheeks, I can't cry just yet. I clamp my eyes shut, breathe through my nose, and focus on the pain. This I can process, this I can deal with, this I think I want. My pussy is getting wet and yet somehow, I hardly feel it. "This not hard enough for you?" he asks, then digs his short but strong nails into my ass after one particularly rough blow.

This goes on for thirty-seven minutes. I know because he tells me; he's been looking at the clock, must want to get this over with already. I wonder why he doesn't just use a paddle or something already when I feel his hand hit me and then a burning sensation. He's added something to his palm that makes it sting like hell. Next, he shoves what I'm sure is our metal dildo into my cunt. He plunges it in without any hesitation, then goes right on with the searing smacks that really feel like he's added chili pepper or something to his hand. It burns, and hurts, but I still open for him to fuck me with the toy, or rather, my pussy does. My head is still locked on what he's just revealed.

When an hour has passed and only one lone tear has dribbled down my cheek, he stands me up and then has me kneel before him. He takes off the blindfold. I want to look into his eyes, but I don't. I stare down at the ground, hardly knowing who he is anymore. Then he strikes me across the face. This isn't a loving tap or even a sexual smack. He hits me, just once, across my right cheek. He's a lefty, so it stings real good. "I got her a spanking machine. The one you always wanted. It's spanking her right now, warming up her ass just for me." He reaches for my nipple again, twisting it until I cry out. I wonder why he's telling me these things, why he's being so mean. I wonder if I'll have to move to avoid seeing the two of them around.

I picture her, then, her ass, a good one-third the size of mine, raised up on that sweet machine while it pummels her over and over and over again. Evan and I had gotten off watching women being spanked by those machines, and I'd been angling for one for months. Monique's new in town, was, I thought, a new friend. He's known her less than two months, and already she's usurped my place. That's when the tears start, first a few on one side and a few on the other, weak little rivulets of salt water. That's when Evan takes me across his lap, my favorite. He used to do it before bed sometimes, telling me he loved me while using the meanest wooden paddle we owned. Now he does it and I just let the tears fall onto the ground. At first, I put my arm in my mouth to stifle my sobs, but then I just let loose. His smacks are no harder than before, but they feel harder, somehow. We both lose track of time as the spanking seems to go on forever, my cries only ending when he shoves four fat fingers into my pussy and smacks my ass some more. Finally, I'm all done. I've come in a quick, almost rebellious burst. I don't want to give him that satisfaction, but I can't resist his touch. I look up at him through the haze of tears, searching his eyes for an answer as my throbbing ass welcomes the cool air from the window.

* * *

When it's over, I try to sneak off to the bathroom, my face streaked with tears, my body seeming to sag under its own weight. I want to be alone, to curl up in the bath and merge into the bubbles. But he grabs me again, roughly, hugging me so tightly that at first I don't realize he has tears in his eyes too, tears that are slowly sliding down his face. "What are you crying about?" I ask bitterly, selfishly liking the comfort of his solid strength.

"Dee, my sweet Dee. I'm not going anywhere. I'm yours. Forever, remember? But you wanted me to make you cry, and I knew I had to go far, far down to somewhere foreign and scary to really make you scared. You're a tough woman to crack, even though you don't always realize it."

I stare at him in disbelief, wondering whether he's an evil genius or a truly sick bastard. I guess part of why I love him is that I'll never truly have the answer to that, I just have to keep lowering myself to the depths of despair, and seeing if I make it through.

YOUR HAND
ON MY NECK

Your hand on my neck is all it takes to make tears race to my eyes, to put my body on red alert, to let me know that I'm about to go insane. It's that simple . . . yet of course, your fingers going for the jugular will always be more complex than I can ever truly describe. It's the fastest way to get my attention, to snap me out of whatever place my mind has wandered, back to where it should be: on you. Forget about when you raise your hand to spank me or reach for my nipples to pinch them or even when you grab my arm to shackle my wrist to your bedposts, all of which you know I adore; your hand on my neck is what makes me unbearably, almost impossibly, wet.

Is it because you were my first? Is it because I trust you more? Or is it because those tears that rush forth, the gasps that claw their way to the surface, the panic that bubbles just below the surface, speak to me in a language deeper than words ever could?

Sometimes, because you know me so well, because you know what it does to me, you do it while we're sitting across from each other at a restaurant. To an outsider, it probably looks like a light caress, like your hand could just as easily be stroking my arm, your thumb caressing my inner wrist, or smoothing my hair, or tracing my lips. And you could be doing any of those things, but you're not: You're wrapping yourself from thumb to forefinger around the expanse of my neck, pressing just enough to make my lips go slack, my breath get short. You're telling me so much without saying a word, and my first instinct is to do what I do in bed: bend my head back, elongate my neck, shut my eyes, give more of myself to you.

But we're in public, so I wait, and soon the moment passes. A couple can hold hands, under or even above the table, or play footsie, with no problem, but the intimacy of choking is probably pushing the envelope, even in Manhattan. Still, I think about it, even while waiting for my burger and fries, about how it feels when you press harder, when my throat constricts and the gasps become sobs and I want to thrash and struggle so I can feel you clamp down harder.

That's what happens when we're at home, alone. We'll be making out, giggling, me lying next to you, rubbing the wiry, warm fur on your chest. One minute I'm kissing whatever part of your skin is closest, and the next you've flipped me over. Any clothes I might've been wearing disappear real fast. Your fingers are hard, strong, insistent, all ten finding my most vulnerable places and staking their claim. Actually, that may not be totally true. Five slam down against my neck, and I arch it and my back up to meet you, while other fingers slam hard inside me. Usually, I like to talk, but I have nothing to say now, even if I could make more than strangled noises.

I want many things at once, but I know you have only so

many hands, so many ways to torture me, so I have to wait and see which of your methods you'll choose today. I've never told you this, but no one else has ever made me want them to squeeze me right there so powerfully. I won't lie: I've been choked before. I've had a hand over my mouth, had my head shoved into a pillow, been muffled and gagged by other men. But no one has ever made me want it like this. I wonder sometimes if there's some secret button inside me, invisible to everyone but you, that you know to press, to lean on, that makes me so wild, because I swear that when you put your hand there, when your eyes go from easy to a little angry, when your voice goes gruff and deep and a little mean, when your hand becomes, for these sweet moments, the sexiest of weapons, I would do anything for you.

Maybe I don't have to tell you, maybe you can see it in my eyes, because without my having to ask, you climb on top of me, keeping your hand firm so all I can really move is the rest of me, from my neck down, yet those parts don't matter as much. It's all in my head, literally, all the blood and passion and lust and masochism and need. That, plus my oral fixation, means that when you wrap your legs on either side of my face and present your cock to me, I open as wide as I possibly can. Your balls hit my chin and your half-hard cock slides against my tongue, and I shift what little I can to make my mouth as wet and tight as possible for you. Your hand tightens on my neck while your other one grabs the back of my head and lifts it up to meet you, positions me where you need me to be.

There's really no other way to say what we're doing: you're fucking my face, my mouth, slamming into me over and over. You tilt my head so the tip presses against my cheek and I drool and struggle to keep up. You briefly let up on my neck and I breathe in deep, wish for a smack across the cheek, a hard, stinging one, but I don't get it. That's the kind of request I find hard to make, because to ask for it is to admit to a level of perversity from which there's no return, though perhaps that's a silly distinction because here you are choking me with such precision, then molding my mouth to your cock. My pussy almost hurts, I'm so turned on, but I don't want you to fuck me, not with your dick, not now, because that would take away from what you're going to give me very soon: your come all over my face.

You know I want that, know I love when you beat your dick against me, shove your balls in my mouth, but you make me wait, perhaps because you know how bad I need it. You tease me, the insides of my mouth your personal sex toy as you rub the head there, denying me all of you all the way down. Your hand cups my neck while you rub your cock up and down my face, in my mouth, wherever you want. "Do you want my come, you little whore?" you ask as you jerk yourself off above me, your hand doing the job I should, rightfully, be doing. If my arms weren't bound above my head, I'd be reaching down and touching my clit, maybe slapping myself lightly there, pushing my fingers inside, anything for relief from the intensity that's overtaken me down there. Instead, I just press my legs tightly together, squeeze my inner muscles, try to inch closer before I feel that first hot drop hit me. I open wide and you slide inside, practically melting into me, your fingers seeking out my hard nipple and twisting it around as you explode. You manage to pull out before it's all gone, to moisturize me with a cream so rich Lancôme could never hope to compete.

I only think about it later, after we're done, when your come is drying on my skin, how much I loved you choking me, not being able to breathe in the usual way, only moving the parts of me you wanted me to.

Last week, you gave me a special gift: two hands there, each taking half, the pressure greater than one alone could handle.

Your dick got even harder as you slammed into me, your weight shifting into your arms, making it hard for me to swallow. The shallow sound of my breath was loud in my ears as I willed you to twist a little. I longed for clothespins, imagined them standing upright on my nipples. You pulled one hand away to slap my clit, and I turned my head to the side, beckoning to the sheet, asking it for something I couldn't ask of you. You knew, though, and tightening your grip on my neck, you slapped my cheek, the sting ringing in my ear. Slapping my face requires much more precision than spanking my ass. A stray slap down there can be corrected easily; a misplaced stroke can stop everything up above. Maybe because you've hit my sweet spot countless times, you know where on my face I crave it most, that fleshy apple bulge of my cheekbone, the part that makes me flinch, my teeth clamped. I look up at you through filmy eyes; I can't look too directly because that would be too much, for both of us. There has to be a veil for me to let you do this. It's why you'd stroke my neck across the table at a restaurant, or even lightly pinch my cheek, but would never in a million years slap me like this. Even a tap on the ass can be tolerated in public, but not this. This is more depraved somehow, and we both know it. My lips start to tremble and you lift your hand from my neck to cover them. You wind up covering part of my nose, too, and I force the panic to wind its way back down my throat before you slap my cheek again. Your dick is still inside me, but I wouldn't say you're fucking me with it, more like holding me in place, making sure I know you could fuck me at any time.

You switch hands and smack my right cheek, and I make sure my eyes are adamantly shut so I don't see the blows coming, don't know what's going to happen, because that would ruin it a little bit for me. I feel you pull out and fear it's over, fear you've tired of me, are bored by what's increasingly becoming less of a game and more of a need. But instead, your hand lingers on my face, seeing how much of it you can cover. I arch up against you, my back curving, straining to be covered by you. You give me what I want, pinching my nose, just for a minute, but long enough to make my insides seize up. You let go but then your face is right next to mine, the stubble I adore so much brushing against my cheek. I think you're going to whisper something to me, but instead you bite me there, the fleshy part of my lower jaw. Not hard, but I'm sure it'll leave an imprint. My clit is aching, but I can't think about that too much because you grab my hands in yours and then tickle me under my arms, which is uncomfortable yet arousing, a potent combination. That's followed by a sharp slap across my face, first one, then the other cheek. I want to ask you to do it harder, but I just think it, wondering if you'd be insulted were I to make such a request.

You take my silence for disinterest and do, indeed, slap me harder. Maybe it's my imagination but you jab your cock into me when you do it. I've only slapped someone's face in real anger, not like this, so I don't know what it's like, but I hope it makes you hard, I hope hurting me gets you off the way lying beneath you does to me. I don't want to ask because as much as I may imagine what you're feeling, I'd prefer you to show me with your body rather than your words.

You pull out and then shove your fingers into me, hard, claiming me, before finding something better to do. You turn me over and shove my face into the pillow. I breathe into it as you hold me down. This is more impersonal than when you choke me, and I'm not sure which I like better. You can't slap my face or spit in it or see it like this, but you can make sure I know my breathing—or not—is up to you. You can let go and know I'll stay there, still, waiting for you to lift my head. You can attach the brand-new spreader bar, the one you told me about in great detail but have thus far withheld, to my ankles. I never used to think not moving my legs was such a big deal; my wrists, yes—they're as sensitive as my neck, and even the lightest of scarves gives me goose bumps. But like this, facedown, like I could be any girl, any body, my wetness right there for you to see, or stuff, or slap, I get it. I get what it means to let you have me on your terms.

I get that you know how good it's going to feel when you once again force your cock inside me, because I'm so tight. I get that it's not really about my neck at all, not even about my pussy. It's about not having a say, having to wait for every breath. It's about going to that place where nothing else matters except where you'll touch me next, if you'll touch me next. It's about going to a place where I have no control—of my movements, my thoughts, my tears. Those start to soak the pillow, and you lift my face to look at me, keeping me twisted there when I try to burrow back in. You don't rush to untie me, thankfully, but stroke my cheek with your thumb, then move it down, pressing into my neck, grabbing my nipple. You get up, and I sink back against the bed, before lifting myself up for the collar, the one that's a little wide, that you buckle almost but not quite too tight.

Then something new is inside me, something piercing, cold, hard. Metal, I think. I shudder at the weight of it, and the realization that you want to come in my mouth, that this is just a way to butter me up, to make me frantic before I get filled up. You massage the entrance to my sex, the sleek lips that are now swollen and tender, working the toy deeper inside. In truth, I don't know if I like it, because you're teasing me with it, edging it just far enough but not letting me wiggle back against it. I get used to this flirtation, and just when I do, you shove it all the way inside me. I feel like I have to pee, and twist from side to side. "Take it," you say, your voice deep, hard, unyielding.

I do, at first, for you, because I don't want to fail here. Then I take it for me, for the precipice of pleasure you make me teeter on. I take it for all the reasons I'm scared, for all the ways this shakes me to my core. I take it because I like the tears, like the pain; take it because, for whatever twisted, crazy reasons, my body responds. My pussy and brain stop battling and simply agree to let you go there, go to that place that seems almost impossible to take, yet like some drawn-out video game, the reward is yet to come. Your hand goes tight around my neck, you must be leaning your weight there, even as the metal drills into me. Your spit lands on my face, first next to my lips, then on them. You lean down and bite me, not my neck or my nipple, but my breast, a place you say with your teeth is more for you than me.

Yet somehow, every inch of my body, because it's yours, responds to you. Each breath that tries to escape and doesn't boomerangs back in arousal, doubling, tripling, multiplying my excitement to infinity. Part of me doesn't want to come, just wants to see how much fuel you can add to my fire, how much you can make me want the pain, the torment. I flash on an image of you dragging me down into the hotel pool, then pulling me up but covering my lips with yours. I think of the many ways you've tested me. You tell me to open my eyes and even though I don't really want to, I do. I'm afraid of what I'll see, because it's much easier to face the ways our kinks intertwine when I don't have to do so literally. Seeing your hand coming toward my face, after you've placed my hand on the toy and insisted that I slam it deep, is more intense than the ensuing slap could ever be. You've told me you want to set up a mirror so I can watch you strangle me, watch myself almost go limp, and I've resisted.

The toy is no longer so cold, and I know I'm on the verge. You take it out and soon replace it with something even bigger, something my body responds to by clenching shut. "I can't," I say softly, sure that it's true, but you let up on me and take the time to slather me with lube.

"You can and you will," you say, and I try to relax as best I can, even though every instinct in me is telling me what you're attempting is impossible. I can take your hands wrapped around my throat, crave it even, but this toy is twice the size of your cock, or feels that way, anyway. You've told me before that you think about a man with a giant dick fucking me while you hold me down, pinning me there, forcing me to shut up if I scream by making me suck you. I think about that as the toy slowly sinks inside. It gets about halfway, which already feels bigger than having a fist inside me. I take slow, measured breaths, a sign of my freedom, before your hand clamps down, twisting my head sideways, covering my nose, like you don't want to look at me. I know you do, you just want to see me raw, messy, tear-streaked, and sweaty, my face covered in come. You want to see me help-less without you.

I turn over at your command and press my head into the sheets, smell the detergent more than the sex in the air. You spank me while you hold the dildo there, pushing it in when I try to squeeze it out. I don't cry, not out loud, anyway. I don't think about coming even when I do, even when I gush. I think about you, about how you look at me before, during, and after. I think about how you take me to the brink, and sometimes I don't want to come back. I think about you tightening the collar as far as it will go. I think about how lucky I am that we aren't doing any of this for each other, at least, not just for each other, but for ourselves. I'd hate being the recipient of a pity choke, a mercy slap, a charity face-fuck.

You don't hold me gently when we're done, at least, not yet. Later, when we sleep, you'll be greedy, grabbing my leg to drape it over you, my arm to stick to yours. Now, you push me onto my back again and put your hand there. I'm sore and tired and spent; wasted, really, but still, that's once again all it takes, your hand on my neck, like it belongs there.

STANDING
ROOM ONLY

E ver since George died eight months ago, I haven't wanted
to go to the swinging parties we frequented for over three
decades together. He was the one who introduced me to the
lifestyle. I entered it as a curious, innocent twenty-two-year-
old, who'd never even dated more than one person at a time,
let alone tumbled around in a bed with five other people at
an orgy.

We somehow found a balance between our loving, private
life as a family of four and being GeorgeandSally, a pair always
spoken of together among a group who became like a second
family. I know swingers have a certain reputation among the
general public as basically being all about sex, and some certainly are, but for us, it was as much about community as coming. We spent hundreds of Saturday nights getting naked in
every way with about a dozen other couples just like us—normal, everyday couples who wanted to find a way to spice up
their sex lives.

When George didn't wake up that morning, I was heartbroken at the loss of such a wonderful man, the love of my life, and for what I knew this would mean for my social life, my private life with him. It's not that my swinger friends didn't reach out; they all attended George's funeral, and no one outside of our world knew where we'd really met. They all had seamless cover stories and offered genuine comfort. They sent flowers and dropped off meals and called and emailed. My mailbox was filled with cards from many whose last names I was finding out for the first time.

But once my most acute grief passed after a few months, once I started feeling those sensual stirrings and taking out my favorite vibrator again, I realized that I couldn't go back to those parties. As fun as they were, the lifestyle was part of what I did with George. I couldn't envision myself going without crying, without feeling his loss more than anything I might gain. We're such a close-knit group, with new couples only joining every year or two, that I would stand out, a third wheel among pair upon pair.

I didn't want to try to recreate what we'd done together; I wanted to blaze a new trail. I didn't come out and say this at my grief support group, but I must have given away some hint of my desires, because after a meeting last month, one of the guys, Eric, who's about a decade younger than me, took me aside and asked me if I wanted to go for coffee. I usually headed straight to my car and beelined for home, burrowing under my covers as I let all the feelings that surfaced in the meeting well up, overflow, and suffuse my body, or taking a long walk on the beach, letting the sound of the waves clear my mind until it was blessedly empty.

But this afternoon, I was ready to talk—about me, not just my grief. Tucked into a corner of the busy coffeeshop, Eric told

me about SRO. Most people thought it meant Standing Room
Only, but the quarterly event actually stood for Sensual Release
Opportunity. It was a party, an "elevated orgy," as Eric put it,
especially for people forty and over, though they could bring
guests who were eighteen and up. The vibe was all about being
slow and deliberate, not about simply scoring, though if that's
what you were after, there were ways to do it.

Eric showed me a few of the officially approved photos—
cameras and phones weren't allowed for attendees, and everyone photographed by the event photographer gave their permission. The room looked dark and enticing, with disco balls and
colored lights flashing. I could almost feel the movement of all
those bodies pressed in tight together, moving to the beat of a
DJ tucked away in a booth.

I stared at the mostly naked bodies—SRO was clothing optional, and most opted for their birthday suits, finding
clothing antithetical to their purpose there. Some, however,
were dressed in everything from lingerie to latex. I saw men in
body-hugging short-shorts that showcased their firm asses, big
women in cutout bras, some wearing nipple clamps and glitter
and nothing else.

The best part was that these all looked like people I might see
around town, not models out partying in between other stops
in their glamorous lives. They looked like people I might want
to talk to if I ran into them at the library or walking our dogs,
which is exactly what I craved. I wouldn't know what to do with
myself if an impossibly gorgeous younger man started chatting
me up, or if a bouncy, flexible, youthful couple wanted me to
show them what sex with an older woman was like. It would be
too much, especially since I didn't have George around to relay
the news to.

George was always my first confidante whenever anyone

flirted with me when I was out alone. I'd rush home, eager to share every breathy detail, which George lapped up. Sometimes I got the impression he wanted me to do more than flirt, to say yes to whatever they were offering and fill him in on the details later, but we were partners in all things, including sexual exploration. When he was alive, I didn't want to do more than flirt. It was enough to feel the weight of a man's gaze dropping far below where was polite when I wore a low-cut blouse as he held the door for me, or cherish the heat crawling up my back when a waiter brushed against it as he helped me to my seat. We had our swinger parties for when we wanted to get truly wild.

George always told me how beautiful I was, and he never stopped, even as I got older and my body started changing in ways that made me feel farther and farther apart from myself. Whereas I'd sometimes run my hands along my legs, over my hips and waist, or even cup my tits and try to reclaim that juicy side of me, George never struggled with desire—for his own passions or for me. If I wanted to wash my hair, I had to get into the shower while he was still asleep, or else he'd pounce on me.

So now what I craved most was somewhere I could be the new me, a mix of the old Sally who'd once let near-strangers pour a whole bottle of chocolate sauce all over her chest and suck it off at an agonizingly slow pace, the one who'd been the first to pose for our group's nude calendar, who encouraged the crowd rather than hovered at the edge of it, and the new me, who felt like I didn't quite belong anywhere except my own bed.

"Look, Sally, there's no pressure—from me or anyone else. We don't recruit; in fact, we've had to tamp down our admissions lately because we've been absolutely at capacity. We like a snug fit, but we want people to have room to move around. Unlike actual sex clubs, we don't have room for any mattresses or couches or other furniture. It's literally standing room only, but people find ways to get busy, to enjoy the space for what it can offer—anonymity, if you desire, and passion, however you define that."

I looked deeply into his brown eyes, trying to sense if there was anything he wasn't telling me. "And you're sure nothing is expected of me even if I show up there and take my clothes off?"

"Sal, you could walk in stark naked and there still wouldn't be any requirements or expectations. You'd get plenty of admiring looks—those are encouraged—but I promise on behalf of my gender that's as far as it goes unless you want it to go deeper. Men can be gross, there's no question about that, but I've never seen such a respectful and welcoming environment. The organizers want everyone to go home feeling like they've just visited a magical space where their every wish can be fulfilled. Well, almost every."

For the first time since George's death, I felt a pure spark of longing, one that pierced through my entire body, pooling deep within me and making my sex physically ache in a way it hadn't since longer than I could remember. Suddenly I was ravenous for what Eric was offering, for the chance to shed being half of GeorgeandSally and discover who I was separate from the pair I'd imagined growing old together.

"Okay. I'll be there on Saturday."

"We could go together. If you want," he said in a rush. I looked at Eric with his thick black stubble, long, floppy hair, deep tan, and kind eyes. "No pressure. Just so you have someone familiar. But if you want to be totally free and unencumbered, that's fine too."

"Can I think about that offer?"

"Sure. Call me tomorrow," he said, and took my phone and put his number in. I hadn't had any interest in connecting with support group members outside of our meetings. At first it was too raw, and by the time I got somewhat of a handle on my grief, I was trying to keep a lid on it, to not let it overtake all hours of the day. I know that's not really how emotions work, but that's how I had to do it, to set it aside so I could work and see friends and enjoy myself without feeling like I was betraying his memory with every laugh or smile. I wanted to compartmentalize the group, not have my phone blow up with people just as needy and lost as I was.

We said goodbye, and I drove home in a daze. I looked up the site for SRO again, zooming in on some of the people, picturing myself among them, slithering along as sleek, sweaty bodies pressed themselves against me, as I got lost in the crush. I put my phone down, closed my eyes, and took out my Magic Wand massager. I'd gone through many over the years, but it had been my go-to sex toy since before I'd met George. He'd teased me about it at first, asking if I needed something that "big and loud," but the first time I let him watch me use it, he understood, and had used it on me plenty of times, sometimes in front of our swinger friends.

Now, though, it was just me and my favorite toy, the power of it vibrating against my clit and along my wetness, opening my mind as well as activating a yearning I hadn't known I wanted. Just as George had introduced me to swinging, I'd assumed that if we were ever going to try something else new and different, he would initiate it. I'm not a timid person by any means, but I preferred those roles, preferred him to take the lead because he'd never steered me wrong.

He did the same for planning our vacations and selecting restaurants. He just had a knack for reading me like one of his beloved mysteries that I always found scattered around the house wherever he'd put them down. He had an intuitive sense about what I'd like and what I wouldn't. I didn't think SRO would've been his type of scene—he didn't love big crowds or super loud music—but I knew he would've encouraged me to go if he'd known I was interested. He would've waited for me in the car, eager to hear all about it.

But I didn't want to think about the old me; I wanted to focus on the new me. I decided to use a different name when I was there, a name I'd never been associated with before, one that would help me arm myself emotionally if I slipped too far back into Sally. I chose Esme; there'd been a student in one of my college classes named Esme who was so glamorous, whether she was wearing makeup or not, with her blonde hair teased up high, eyeliner perfectly done, lips a bold, don't-mess-with-me-unless-you-can-take-it red. She'd told me her name meant "Loved" and she wanted to get married as soon as possible. She was a glorious mix of contradictions, tough but sweet, ballsy yet romantic.

We'd lost touch after the class ended, but I'd never forgotten the way all eyes would turn to her when she walked into a room. I didn't want that much attention on me then, but I liked the idea of it. Once I met George, it was his attention I wanted most, his eyes gazing up from my feet on up over a tight red dress that clung to me from my ankles to my neck as he did the first night we met at a fundraising dinner.

"Esme," I said aloud as I stared at myself in the mirror; my short brown hair had grown enough that the curls were visible, the same curls George used to—no, I wasn't going there. I shook my head and told myself, "George didn't know Esme. You don't know her either, but it's time to get to know her."

I went through everything in my closet, down to the last blouse and ancient jeans, to find the perfect outfit in case I wanted to keep my clothes on. A clingy black skirt made of a shimmery fabric I've always considered one of my sexiest. It makes my ass look amazing but doesn't feel tight, like it could be perfect for the beach or a fancy dinner. I added a black lace push-up bra and my favorite black tank top, figuring in that environment, less would be more.

I put on the outfit and fiddled around with my makeup, trying to channel the real Esme, but also be myself. With my tousled brown curls, I thought a maroon lipstick and complementing eye shadow would look best. I wear so little makeup on a regular basis I had to go on YouTube, painstakingly practicing with my rarely used eyeshadow palette and liquid eyeliner. George had liked me bare-faced, and over the years, I'd started to believe that's what I liked too.

But the new me—Esme—staring back at me when I was done was the kind of woman even I, who consider myself about seventy-five percent straight, would look at. I wasn't trying to hide my age, but I still wanted to put my best foot forward, even though in the dark, I wasn't sure who'd actually notice the details of my makeup.

But this new look wasn't just for them—whoever *they* were, and it wasn't for Eric, though the way he'd reached out to me and his big, muscular arms did get me a little hot. Being Esme was for me, a gift to myself after two-thirds of a year of emotional darkness. I was ready to emerge and see what I was capable of as a sexual woman without a partner.

I texted Eric to ask if he could pick me up. *I'd be happy to. Can't wait to see you in a new setting.*

Same, I replied.

On Saturday, I took extra time getting ready, recreating my earlier look, but skipping panties, and checking in with myself. I knew I could back out if it got to be too much, too heavy, too real. But all I felt was eagerness; the idea of slithering between all those bodies, without the need for polite conversation or getting to know anything about them beyond how their body felt against mine was intoxicating. I'd never done that before, not even before George. I'd always dated, going through the courtship rituals I thought were proper. Now, I was ready to say, fuck "proper." I wanted to abandon myself and give my body over to something bigger and grander than what I was used to. I slipped my bare feet into black platform shoes I'd dug out of the back of my closet, grateful for the extra height.

Eric arrived right on time, a total gentleman. Usually, he wore a T-shirt and jeans to our meetings, but tonight he was dressed in black shorts and a black shirt that made me want to touch it. "Hello, Sally," he said with a twinkle in his eye, like he were picking me up for a regular date.

A tingle I hadn't felt in longer than I could recall started at the top of my head, warming my face and working its way down my body, making my heart pound. His lips looked different tonight, even though I'd seen them so often over the past eight months. I'd never given them another thought, but now I wanted to know what they'd feel like against my lips. I could have found out easily enough—he wore his longing in the depths of his eyes—but I didn't want that, not yet. Tonight, I wanted anonymity, escape, ecstasy.

"Actually . . . could you call me Esme? I'm trying that name on for tonight, to help me get in the spirit."

"Of course. It's my honor, Esme." Hearing the sensual name from Eric's lips made me tingle even more. It was amazing what those two little syllables could convey, especially the way he said them, soft and firm, full of promise. I let him help me on with a thin shawl, his fingers sending electric pulses along my skin when they briefly brushed against it. I willed myself to hold on to that sensation, to stay open and willing, to not be held hostage by my past, but welcoming of the future.

"I'm so glad you're joining us. I think you're going to have an amazing time."

"I hope so," I replied.

We were silent in the car, each lost in our own thoughts. Mine stayed firmly in those possibilities, as I pictured what might happen, all those bodies, all those hands, all those lips. It had been a long time since I was that fresh-faced newbie at the swingers' parties—complete with jokes about "fresh meat." I ran my hands along my arms, then looked at myself in the mirror of the window shade. I smiled at the soft wrinkles around my eyes, the makeup that this time had come out perfectly, accenting my face but not trying to hide my age. I may have had a new name and a sexy outfit, but I was still open about who I really was, and all that my years on this earth had taught me.

We arrived on a nondescript street, and stepped toward a building that looked like it could've been a factory or an office. A small sign said "SRO" above the door, but you'd have to know it was there to take it in. "Hey, Eric," said the man at the door, a beefy guy with a kind smile. "Who've you got with you?"

"This is Esme," he said. "It's her first time."

"Welcome, Esme. I'm Troy. Let me know if you need anything, and you can always come outside and take a break."

"Thanks, Troy," I said, letting out a breath I hadn't realized I'd been holding.

"Ready, Esme?" Eric asked.

I smiled, genuinely sure of my answer. "As ready as I'll ever be."

He opened the door, and as nondescript as the outside had been, the inside was the opposite. The walls seemed to vibrate with noise, a pulsing but not too loud beat, while disco balls and strobe lights flashed all around. There were maybe a hundred or so people there, dancing and kissing, sliding and writhing, as if all were one giant mass of humanity.

"More people will probably arrive soon," said Eric. "I'll go get us some water, okay?"

I nodded, and watched him disappear into the crowd. I was hovering on the side, observing everyone, when a woman about my age sidled over. "Want to dance?" she asked. Her bronzed skin had a sheen to it, like she'd been dancing up a storm. She wore a skimpy red baby doll nightie that clung to her, showing me she didn't have on a bra or panties. Her smile was friendly, not demanding, simply offering.

"Sure," I said, taking her hand, figuring Eric would come find me. I wiggled along with her through the crowd until we were surrounded by other bodies. The songs morphed from one to another, most without lyrics, as I let myself get lost in the crush. At first, I danced near the woman and her friends, none of whom, thankfully, tried to introduce themselves. We didn't need words to do that; we had our bodies.

A few songs in, I looked up to see Eric offering me a bottle of water. I took it but instead of drinking from it, I poured some down the front of my top, smiling as the icy water worked its way down my front, cooling me off even as I was heating up inside.

I gave Eric a thumbs-up and returned to dancing, sometimes moving closer toward the woman and her intimate circle of friends, sometimes dancing apart from them. There was one man in the group, who looked to be in his mid-sixties, a strong, thickly-built, teddy bear type, who kept making eye contact with me. He was wearing only a pair of bike shorts, and was clearly sporting a hard-on. My gaze kept traveling toward him, and every time, I looked down, as if to make sure his erection was still there.

I wanted it, wanted him. I'd never done anything this brazen before. I'd looked at plenty of men, sure, but I'd never touched a man whose name I didn't know, one I'd probably never see again. Our swinger parties always involved some kind of get-ting-to-know-each-other icebreaker before we got so intimate. But my mouth and pussy were telling me I didn't need to know his name to want him, or to act on that want.

I moved closer to him, which involved brushing past sev-eral others; the room was indeed living up to its standing room only alter ego, as more people had joined. Eric had told me the organizers kept careful track of the maximum number of people allowed, and often had to turn people away when they hit capac-ity. When I was standing right in front of the man, I reached up and stroked his cheek, gazing into his eyes, while others shim-mied around us, some of them also locked in tight embraces. I glanced back and saw Eric give me a smile and a nod.

I let the rest of the room fade from my mind to focus on the man who was my object of desire—for the moment, anyway. The beat of the music was pounding through me, as if I were dancing even while standing still. "Hi," I mouthed.

"Hi," he mouthed back, and then I stopped talking, shut my eyes, and put my arms around him. It was a hug and an invita-tion as he put his arms around me, his hands massaging my ass through the skirt.

We stood like that, swaying silently, content in the motion and the feel of each other's bodies. I closed my eyes and leaned in close, nuzzling against him as if he were someone I actually knew and trusted. Maybe because I did know and trust Eric, a part of me felt the same for this man whose cock was pressing against me, not insistently, but patiently, as if to let me know he would wait for me until—if or when—I was ready.

I turned around, pressing my ass against him, watching all the naked and clothed people, some of whom were outright fucking on the dance floor, others who were getting handsy, others who were simply in group grope sessions. The sight of all those bodies, where the tall, thin, "perfect" form was rare, was beautiful. This wasn't a place to see and be seen, although plenty of ogling was going on; this was a space to truly engage in the titular sensual release, whatever form that took. One woman was even doing a handstand, looking totally content.

I lifted up my skirt, suddenly eager to show off my ass for this patiently waiting man. He cupped my cheeks, massaging them as I raised my hands above my head, giving in to the music, to the newfound freedom I'd acquired. I would never have asked for this freedom, but now that it was mine, I wanted to savor it. I reached behind me and pressed the man's fingers along my slit, showing him how I liked to be touched. I caught Eric's eye and smiled, tilting my head just enough to beckon him over.

He walked slowly, as if afraid I'd change my mind, but I kept eye contact on him as I sank back against the man's wide, probing fingers, welcoming him into my pussy. He let me be the tour guide to my innermost terrain, sinking back until his digits were fully inside my tight channel, then sliding back up. It takes me longer now to get aroused, and often I need lube for sex, but at this pace, I was able to catch up slowly.

Eric was approaching, his eyes roaming from my head on down. I lifted the tank top over my head and tossed it into the crowd, where a tall, skinny man caught it and shimmied into it. I leaned back, pressing my head into the man's shoulder and thrusting my breasts forward. The stranger kissed the back of my neck, then licked it as I waited for Eric to touch me. I'd thought I wanted total anonymity tonight, but this was close enough. I didn't peg Eric for one to kiss and tell.

When Eric was right in front of me, I slid down the man's body, dropping as low as I could, then rising to press myself against Eric, then back against the man. Eric pressed tight up against me, his belt buckle against my lower belly, pushing me right up against the stranger. When Eric leaned down and sucked on one of my nipples, keeping the lace bra in place so it added more friction, my knees almost buckled, but the stranger had placed his hands on my hips, pulling me tight against his erection.

"Yes," I whispered into the air, the sound lost amidst the music, but loud in my mind. I was agreeing to so much with that one breathy syllable.

The stranger's hands dug into my hips, pressing hard, and suddenly I knew I wanted him, right there, like this. I reached, my hand jammed between my bare ass and his jeans, reaching for his zipper and pulling it down. I popped the button and reached in for a smooth, hard, thick cock. He pushed his pants down, kicking them off, while I kept my firm grasp on his dick as Eric continued to feast on my nipples.

In some ways, it was unusual for us not to be talking, for me not to hear any words of encouragement, but in place of words, I was listening with my body. I noticed every tightening or loosening of the stranger's grip on me, how his cock was pulsing with heat and power in my hand, how Eric's tongue and teeth were working together to torment my nipples into hard peaks.

I reached into my tiniest purse and pulled out a small bottle of lube, handing it to the stranger. He understood my message, opening it and slicking up his cock, then gliding his sleek fingers between my legs. This time, they entered quickly, deeply, with more urgency than before. I was more than ready, pushing back against him, revved up from the way Eric was still going at my nipples like he simply couldn't get enough.

When the stranger took the lead, pressing and twisting those fingers, expertly curling them and coaxing my G-spot out to play, I melted, going limp as the two men took charge. I alternated between closing my eyes and opening them to stare back and those who were watching us.

"Ready?" I heard in my ear as the stranger pulled his fingers out and then immediately placed them before my lips.

"Yes," I called back to him as I took those fingers into my mouth while his cock pressed against my wetness, then pushed inside. It had been so long since a human, not a toy, had entered me like this. Everything about tonight felt new, even though I'd been getting fucked for decades. I'd enjoyed many cocks, but never like this. I tugged on Eric's floppy waves of hair, pushing the stranger's fingers out of my mouth so Eric's tongue could find its way inside.

As the stranger developed a rhythm, the three of us fused our bodies, all of us pressed closely together, a small part of a larger force overtaking the room, where around me I saw all manner of pairings as the lights bounced around. I separated from Eric, then reached for his pants, suddenly wanting more than just kisses from him. There was no pressure from Eric, or anyone else there; all the pressure was bursting through my body, bubbling up from deep inside, from a well of lust that had had its lid on for far too long.

Now that I'd started to unleash it, my desire couldn't be tamed, it just wanted more and more and more. Eric helped me get his pants off, and then held his cock out to me, an offering, a summons, a plea. The stranger let out a feral grunt as I bent over, allowing his cock to enter me even more deeply. That small but intense shift had me eager to take Eric all the way down my throat, to have these two men in every sense of the word.

I reached for Eric's hips, pulling him closer, sucking him deep. I wasn't exactly standing, and we may have been taking up a bit more space than everyone else, but nobody seemed to mind. From the corners of my eyes, I could tell we had an audience, and knowing people were watching me take on two men in such a flagrant way only spurred me on. I found a rhythm that worked for all of us, as Eric pushed into me, pressing me back that much farther against the stranger. We didn't need words to share our needs, just body language, as I swallowed and sucked, tightened and released.

The room's lights dimmed to almost full darkness, so I closed my eyes and stroked my clit, fully in my body. There was no room for grief, only glee as I became one with the two men, a trio of seekers, all after the same explosive thrills. The more I played with my clit, the closer I got to mine, and when Eric dug his nails into the back of my neck, the pain triggered an orgasm unlike any I'd ever experienced. I shuddered around the stranger's cock, which made him pump that much harder, while I tightened my mouth just as I was squeezing the stranger with my pussy. I rode out my climax and waited for them to join me. It wasn't long before Eric in turn gifted me with his own explosion, and the stranger followed suit. I swallowed what I could, wiping the rest off with my arm.

When the stranger slid out of me, I leaned back against him, wanting more contact, some kind of closure. Eric smashed himself against us and we stood together, the stranger leaning against the wall, the two of us atop him. I'd come there seeking a sexual rebirth, an entryway to my new future. As I watched the room sparkle with light as more people pressed onto the floor, their sweaty, sleek bodies adding to the room's heat, I knew I wasn't done. There was more I needed from this room, and I wasn't going to leave until I'd gotten it.

ABOUT THE AUTHOR

Rachel Kramer Bussel (rachelkramerbussel.com) is a New Jersey-based author, editor, blogger, and writing instructor. She has edited over seventy books of erotica, including *Crowded House: Threesome and Group Sex Erotica; It Takes Two; Coming Soon: Women's Orgasm Erotica; Dirty Dates: Erotic Fantasies for Couples; Come Again: Sex Toy Erotica; The Big Book of Orgasms*, Volumes 1 and 2; *The Big Book of Submission*, Volumes 1 and 2; *Lust in Latex; Anything for You; Baby Got Back: Anal Erotica; Suite Encounters; Gotta Have It; Women in Lust; Surrender; Orgasmic; Fast Girls; Going Down; Tasting Him; Tasting Her; Crossdressing; Cheeky Spanking Stories; Bottoms Up; Spanked: Red-Cheeked Erotica; Please, Sir; Please, Ma'am; He's on Top; She's on Top; Best Bondage Erotica of the Year*, Volumes 1 and 2; and *Best Women's Erotica of the Year*, Volumes 1–9. Her anthologies have won eight IPPY (Independent Publisher) Awards, and *The Big Book of Submission*, Volume 2, *Dirty Dates*, and *Surrender* won the

National Leather Association Samois Anthology Award. She is the recipient of the 2021 National Leather Association John Preston Short Fiction Award.

Rachel has written for *AVN, Bust, Cosmopolitan, Curve,* The Daily Beast, Elle.com, Forbes.com, Fortune.com, *Glamour,* The Goods, Gothamist, *Harper's Bazaar,* Huffington Post, *Inked, InStyle, Marie Claire, MEL, Men's Health, Newsday, New York Post, New York Observer, The New York Times, O: The Oprah Magazine, Penthouse, The Philadelphia Inquirer,* Refinery29, *Rolling Stone,* The Root, Salon, *San Francisco Chronicle, Self,* Slate, Time.com, *Time Out New York, The Village Voice* and *Zink,* among others. She has appeared on *CBS Sunday Morning, The Gayle King Show, The Martha Stewart Show, The Berman and Berman Show, NY1,* and Showtime's *Family Business.* She hosted the popular In the Flesh Erotic Reading Series, featuring readers from Susie Bright to Zane, speaks at conferences, and does readings and teaches erotic writing workshops around the world and online. She consults about erotica and sex-related nonfiction at eroticawriting101. com. Subscribe to her newsletter at rachelkramerbussel.substack.com and follow her @raquelita on X and @rachelkramerbussel on Instagram.